*Un*raveling

Sudnya Shroff

Dear Pramila,

Enjoy!

Much love,
Sudnya

9-29-2012

Unraveling
Copyright © 2012 by Sudnya Shroff
Book design by Sudnya Shroff
Cover design by Jing Wu
Cover image by Shruti Moghe, Shruti Moghe Photography
Author photograph by Divya Jakatdar

First hardcover edition: September 2012
Hardcover ISBN-13: 978-0-9857318-0-9
ISBN-10: 098573180X

Printed in India by Pragati Offset Pvt. Ltd., Hyderabad

For Akhil, For Divya, For Kapil

*H*ad to go crazy to love you
Had to go down to the pit
Had to do time in the tower
Begging my crazy to quit

Had to go crazy to love you
Had to let everything fall
Had to be people I hated
Had to be no one at all

Sometimes I'd head for the highway
I'm old(er) and the mirrors don't lie
But crazy has places to hide in
That are deeper than any good-bye...

— Leonard Cohen

Prologue

This is the story of Shalini Mistry Kamdar, who bid her family good-bye on that Friday morning in November 2008, as her ride to the airport waited outside; who planted a kiss on her husband Amit's lips; hugged her son Aarush tight and smothered his face with kisses; and then left. As she did every three months. To visit her aging father, Narsidas Mistry, in India, usually for a period of ten days, and always returning with Aarush's favorite Chitale's *bakharwadis* and her comforting, bubbly laugh.

Only this time, she did not come back.

Aarush

One

The birds chirped in glee, welcoming the early morning dew. The light from the rising sun streamed in through the slits of the wooden shutters of his bedroom, marking the night's conclusion and gently announcing the beginning of a new day. Aarush squinted one eye open, rolled over and tried to bury himself back into lazy slumber, a heaviness that refused to release its hold on his growing teenage body. The neighbor's dog barked as the newspaper delivery car drove past the front door and pitched a plastic-wrapped paper covered with more advertisements than news articles. For a moment Aarush felt a sense of peace and quiet. He leapt out of bed, even before the thought had had a chance to complete itself, pulled on his track pants and sprinted down to haul out the garbage and recycling bins.

It was a clear spring Tuesday morning in April of 2009. The trucks would rumble their way down the street any minute. Two Tuesdays in a row Aarush had missed taking them out in time. Both mornings he had rushed as the sound of those groaning monsters awakened him, only to be rewarded with the frustrating sight of their retreating back ends and loud, clanging sounds that prevented the truck drivers from hearing his calls to stop. Both mornings, he had also needed to load the trash bags into the back of his olive green '97 Honda Accord, and drag them to a nearby apartment complex where he could take care of business. Aarush was determined not to repeat the same failure thrice, as his effort not to repeat it twice had already failed miserably. He was relieved when his body set off its internal alarm, taking pity on an overworked teen-age brain, and enabled the perfect execution of this weekly task, however close a call it might have been.

Aarush took a few deep breaths and gingerly walked back over the sandy front yard in his bare feet, taking a short cut into the house through the side door of his father's office. Automatically, he glanced at the couch, though he knew his father wasn't there. Traveling for work. What he had always done, ever since Aarush could remember. He had merely increased the frequency and lengths of these trips since his wife's departure, as though staying at home only summoned painful memories. Anything, any excuse to escape from it. Like his father, Aarush struggled. He understood him, empathized with him. He even envied him.

His father's loss was his loss as well. His mother had been in his life almost as long as she had been in his father's. He could probably say in all certainty that, as a percentage of time spent across each of their life-times, she had spent twice as much time being his mom than she had play-ing Dad's wife. They both struggled with her loss, not unlike lost puppies, walking around the house in a daze, begging her irritated voice to call out for one of them to pick up the trail of dirty laundry, envisioning the clouds of soap suds on loose hair strands as she washed the dishes at the kitchen sink, and yet at other times, willing her to walk in through the garage door, wondering aloud if it would ever strike the men in her life to get off the couches and help her unload groceries at the sound of the garage door rolling up. Most of all, Aarush envied his father, the ready escape he had from the pain. As though the universe were trying somehow to make up for the cruel discrepancy created by the disastrous turn of events in their personal life, on the professional front, his father was being showered with awards and recognition from all over the world. His groundbreaking research in probability theory, a branch of mathematics concerned with the analysis of random phenomena, was finally gaining attention from colleagues and critics alike. Under the current woeful economic conditions, the success of his invaluable models in predicting the volatile stock markets had made Amit's expertise highly sought after. As a result, he was being invited as a guest lecturer by universities and as a consultant by financial institutions across all continents. His work and the consequent travel gave him the opportunity to get out of the place that used to be their comfort zone, their safe place. Not anymore.

Aarush dusted the sand from the soles of his feet on the office floor carpet as he pulled the door shut behind him. He walked across to the whiteboard, his father's favorite wall accessory (*Dad would have one on every vertical surface if he had a choice*, Aarush thought), and glanced down the list of things his father had bulleted for him. Aarush needed to check with the gardener about fixing a broken sprinkler head that was bleeding water and rotting the lawn in one corner, while the opposite end of the yard was as dry as the Sahara desert, with every plant that had previously thrived, dry and wasted as if it had been afflicted by the worst drought in years. The gardener usually arrived just before eight — perfect timing. Aarush could direct him to the problem areas and still be able to drive himself to school, get a decent parking spot, and get to his algebra class that started at 8:35. Aarush made a mental note that he could postpone washing the cars until the next morning. That left him only one more thing to be completed before his father returned early afternoon the next day — pick up the package he had ordered from Amazon.com that was being held at the post office, because there was no one to take delivery. Aarush wanted to make sure he picked it up without drawing his father's attention to it. So he would *have* to do it today, or risk the post-man leaving another reminder with the new mail, which might find its way into his father's hands.

Aarush checked his phone for text messages. One from Sam, his friend since freshman year in high school, informing him that he would see him directly at lunch after morning classes, code indicating not to try and reach him until lunch, that he would be skipping classes and Aarush shouldn't worry about him. Which also gave Aarush the idea that, in all likelihood, Sam had planned a rendezvous with his girlfriend to celebrate her birthday. Which was exactly the thought that Aarush didn't need. Because that made room for Lara to find her way straight into his noisy mind, adding to the existing turmoil.

Oh, Lara, I have been such a jerk, he thought.

It had been a long, turbulent few months in their otherwise stable relationship, which was definitely teetering at the moment.

Because of me, of course, he thought.

But then, Aarush had been through a hell of a year. He could find any number of reasons to justify his less-than-stellar behavior. He knew he was being unfair to Lara, taking her with him on one emotional roller coaster after another, only without really giving her any heads-up or recovery time.

Aarush tried to shake off his guilt about how he was handling their relationship. But guilt there was. And self-sympathy. And pain.

12

Anger too, serious anger. What was he angry about? Circumstances, maybe. Destiny, perhaps. His mother, definitely.

And yet, if it hadn't been for his mother, Aarush would have never met Lara. They were related by blood, after all.

Aarush hurried into the kitchen and grabbed the last spotted banana from the fruit basket that lay brooding in the center of the island. As he hungrily gobbled the mushy fruit, he picked up a clean towel from the laundry room and started the shower.

Who doesn't love long, hot, never-ending showers…

●●●●

Aunt Kathy lived two streets north of where the Kamdars lived. His mother and Aunt Kathy met when Aarush started kindergarten at their neighborhood school. If Aunt Kathy had been of Indian heritage, Aarush would have addressed her as Kathy *maasi*, a natural way to describe his mother's sister if she had had one. At Aunt Kathy's fortieth birthday party, his mother toasted her glass:

"To Kathy, my dearest friend and sister by choice, I sincerely hope in our next lives we meet at birth and not have to wait thirty years…"

Aunt Kathy had one daughter, Sophie, a curly-haired redhead, with blue eyes full of mischief, gregarious with the kindest heart. Even at the age of five, it wasn't out of character for Sophie to notice the child whose mother had forgotten to pack a snack, and be the one to share hers. Or much later, in junior year, when she noticed that Aarush stopped hanging out for lunch with the group, she would track him down in the library just to spend time with him. Aarush could see through all of her excuses, ranging from need-your-help-with-this-third-order-differential-problem to hey-Aarush-can-you-help-me-with-my-college-essay. That Sophie and Aarush were of opposite sexes never seemed to get in the way of either their mothers' or their own friendships.

Over the years, his mom and Aunt Kathy shared almost everything — clothes, shoes, toys, carpools, books, recipes, diets, walks, secrets, promises, laughter, tears, beginnings, endings — not the least of which was the religious dedication with which they approached the planning and the meticulous implementation of the details surrounding their annual retreat to Arizona. Which they then made fun for Sophie and Aarush by arranging play dates with each other every day while they were gone. That it satisfied the cost-saving requirement of hiring a single babysitter to take care of the two of them was a bonus that cared to please only the two mothers. And it suited them that Sophie and Aarush remained comfortable with each other even as they went through the years from elementary to high school that included all the not-so-fun boys' and girls' stuff as well. Later, when the children were old enough not to need an adult to bring them home from school, Sophie and Aarush would walk home, his backpack hanging off one shoulder, while she pulled her neon blue Zuca behind her.

"Emily emailed an 'I love you' e-card to Ishaan; Roger's dad bought him a new iPod; and we are going to Singapore this Thanksgiving!!" Sophie gushed as they turned around the corner of Rosita and Campbell. She had won their customary thumb-wrestle toss to go first.

"True, true, false," Aarush guessed.

It was a game they had played since their days in kindergarten when the facts were more trivial. They'd throw out three "facts" and let the other guess which were true, which were false.

"No-o," she said, delighted that he had got them all wrong, "False, false, true!"

"No, you are not going to Singapore!"

"It's your turn, Aarush, c'mon, tell me," she prodded.

"I want to know all about Singapore. When and how did that get decided? Didn't you say your dad hated travel?"

He couldn't think of anything exciting that had happened all day, or all week for that matter. How was he supposed to come up with three?

"No, Aarush, please, please, please. I will tell you all about Singapore, and I have an idea how you can come with us too," she bribed.

"Ryan is going to private school next year; Mr. Rodriguez found a box of condoms in the boys' locker room; my painting sold on craigslist for forty-five dollars," Aarush blurted in a single breath, his curiosity piqued by her bribe. He wanted her to quickly guess and move on to more important things, exciting possibilities, like Singapore. And how he might go too.

"Condoms, OMG!!! True, true, true," she squealed with an increasing crescendo.

"Oh Soph, true, false, true. I made up the condoms bit." Aarush couldn't help smiling. Sophie was so predictable. Anything to do with boys, sex, romance, and she wanted it to be true.

That was November, 2004 when they were both twelve, when Sophie's bright idea worked. Not only did Aarush join them on their trip to Singapore, his mother came too. The deal was, Sophie's father's work required him to have meetings with his Asian clients. Singapore, with its central location, made strategic sense to locate for the two weeks he needed to spend there. Sophie's father fundamentally abhorred the idea of any separation from his family. He had convinced his company to pay for a two-bedroom apartment suite instead of a hotel room that cost the same. Sophie had also brought to her mother's attention the fact that her father would not only be busy all day, but that he may need to make overnight trips to Malaysia and Indonesia during that period.

Wouldn't it then be a good idea to invite Aunt Shalini and Aarush to join them for at least part of the trip?

They waited with bated breaths, keeping their fingers and toes

15

crossed, vowing not to chew gum until their travel plans were set in stone and there was not even a remote possibility of jinxing this carefully manipulated adventure. It took their mothers two entire days and many frustrating calls to airlines before they were able to work out the logistics around frequent flier miles, airline tickets, and Aarush's mother's idea to combine a visit to her father — *Nana* as Aarush called him — for a week after.

"It would be a shame not to! Did you know that Singapore is only five hours from Bombay?" she had rationalized.

••••

The water had run cold. Aarush had been in the shower for almost twenty minutes. He adjusted the hot water faucet, gradually turning it clockwise every few minutes, to ensure the continuation of the long hot shower. But like everything else, all good things came to an end.

Aarush dried himself and pulled on his favorite jeans, the same pair that he had worn all week. He layered himself with a long sleeved thermal, a soft cotton T-shirt, one of those freebies his father got at a marketing conference, and a Cal sweatshirt — his father's from his college days. As Aarush glanced in the bathroom mirror, armed with his toothbrush, he realized he had worn his sweatshirt inside out. He laid the toothbrush on the counter's edge, using one hand to hold his inner layers down, and the other to wiggle out of his sweatshirt. In trying to correct his clothing mistake, he accidentally jerked the toothbrush off the counter, the toothpaste flying and landing in a blob partly on the floor, and partly on the shower door. In attempting to clean up the mess with some toilet paper, he pulled too much off the roller. He smeared the toothpaste that had found its way onto the glass shower door, made a second attempt to clean it using more of the same toilet paper, this time wetting it under the faucet. Maybe it was too wet, because it only left more residue on the glass, and pieces of soggy toilet paper everywhere. Irritation built inside him. He tried to calm himself, breathing deeply, each breath a four-count inhale followed by a four-count exhale. That was how his mother had described a long breath. He could almost hear her whisper those words in his ear — or so he imagined. All of a sudden, he found himself in a heap on the floor, in a fetal position, his chest tight, a deep piercing pain cutting through his heart, as he realized anew that she was gone. Sobbing uncontrollably he gave himself over to the grief.

Aarush had finally discovered that allowing himself to cry actually helped. Eventually, he would experience a combination of fatigue and respite, emotionally semi-dry, like hand-wrung clothes ready to be line-dried.

After what seemed like a long time, Aarush gathered himself together. He left the mess he had created in the bathroom for Maria, the housekeeper, to take care of. She would come the next morning.

It was almost eight o'clock, Jose would be here any minute.

He had better not miss Jose or else there would be even more plants in distress.

••••

The Parking Gods are happy with me, Aarush thought as a car pulled out perfectly in time for him to pull in, and right outside his math classroom. A little stroke of good luck, enough to put a skip in his walk. That and the sense of accomplishment he felt for having been able to explain to Jose, with his limited Spanish skills, the sprinkler crisis in their garden. It came to Aarush in a flash that today was as good a day as any to have a meaningful conversation with Lara. He owed her that much.

It wasn't that he missed her terribly. It wasn't even that he couldn't wait to see her. Maybe he did, a little.

••••

It had only been one week since their argument, if you could even call it an argument. Lara's definition of an argument would include two people, actively in conversation, stating their points, most likely differing in their opinions on the topic at hand. And theirs had gone something like this:

"Aar, why didn't you show up for the movie last night?"

"Mmm...I got busy," he replied timidly.

"Busy with what?" She wouldn't let it go at that. Aarush should have known better.

"You know...applications..." he mumbled.

"Which we have been working on together all year?! Really? Or are there colleges that you plan to apply to without telling me?"

Silence. He had nothing to offer.

"Don't you have anything to say?" she pleaded.

More silence.

What Aarush almost said, but bit his tongue, was that he didn't feel like hanging out with a bunch of excited, happy, crazy, funny seventeen-year-olds, even though he was one of them. That right now they all annoyed him.

What he could have said, to salvage the situation, was that he was sorry, he should have called and cancelled instead of simply not showing up.

What he really wanted to say was that he was sad, very sad and would rather be with her, just her and him, so he could talk to her and feel better like he always did.

But what did he do? He said nothing.

There had only been one active participant in the conversation.

Could he really blame her for stomping off in frustration, her smoothie unfinished on the table?

And the entire conversation had taken place after she had waited patiently for Aarush that morning outside his painting class, so he really couldn't have missed her. Neither Lara nor Aarush were the kind who made scenes or behaved irrationally. They both knew each other's schedules. Now they had enough time to talk over a smoothie, so they walked to Jamba Juice, only two blocks from school. He offered to pay for her smoothie, a desperate attempt at redemption. She wouldn't let him. He should have known better than to expect to be let off so easily. He had been ignoring her emails and text messages. Truly, he wasn't avoiding her, he was just too ashamed of his inability to handle his emotions or communicate. He felt seriously inadequate, convinced that she was better off with him out of her life, even while he desperately wanted her to stay in his. Especially now that he had a new plan bubbling away in his head. He was reminded of the package that needed picking up from the post office.

••••

Aarush fished out his phone as he walked to algebra class, texting Lara before he could overanalyze, rethink, or change his mind. He asked her if she would come over to his house after school. He knew she'd be in her Advanced Spanish class, and would not look at her phone until at least after 10:00. His phone said that it was 8:30 and he had five whole minutes to settle himself in class.

••••

Aarush was in the backyard, hand-watering the parched side

of the garden, when he heard somebody at the garden gate. He twisted around, still trying to keep the water directed on the plants. Only a few more areas left to water. But, alas, it was just his imagination, a wicked squirrel, toying with his mind, teasing him with boundless scampering and making sounds that did no more than offer a forlorn heart some false hope.

Aarush finished school at 4:00, checking his cell phone dozens of times. No text from Lara. In not replying at all, at least she hadn't flatly refused to see him.

He had confidence in several of her qualities. Though she had every justification for being mad, Lara was too polite to ignore him, as he had done her. She would be courteous enough to let him know that she couldn't make it. Unlike Aarush, who had simply not shown up when a bunch of friends decided to go to the movies together. At the time, he had rationalized that she wasn't really alone, so why bother? Besides, it was easier to avoid questions when he didn't have the answers himself. She would have also made an effort to come up with an ironclad excuse, whereas he had none to offer. Thoughts of her having finally given up on him tormented him. Well, it was about time. She had been devoted to their relationship even when he seemed distracted. She had been persistent in keeping the communication going when he had succumbed to silence. He had been unpredictable, moody and difficult. Now add unreliable and undependable to that list. How he wished she'd call or text. How he longed to see her walk through that gate. How he begged the universe to make her appear!

As Aarush was thinking these distressing thoughts, his left brain (responsible for logical and sequential reasoning, he had been told) decided to switch gears and start working. It struck him as a distinct possibility that she might not have got his message. And he had built an entire narrative around her not showing up, based on an assumption that was quite possibly flawed.

Very scientific, he thought as his heart glowed with hope. Why hadn't he thought of that before? He felt an urgent need to find her. He had wasted two precious and anguished hours waiting. Finishing the by-now futile plant revival efforts, he rushed to his car. As carefully as his guarded yet optimistic impatience would allow, he backed out and drove the three winding miles to Lara's house up in the hills, trying to manage his expectations. Random thoughts with varying possibilities raced through his mind as he tried to keep his eyes on the road.

Maybe her phone had run out of charge...she might have forgotten to carry it with her.

Immediately, though, he ruled out these two possibilities. She had had enough time to get home and take care of both.

Maybe she had dropped and broken her phone. Or someone may have stolen it and she could not receive the one crucial text he needed her to see that day.

Under these vital circumstances he was willing to believe even far-fetched ideas. Either way, Aarush had what he needed. A reasonable pretext to set aside his stubborn ego and do the right thing, what he should have done in the first place.

Aarush rang the doorbell and waited impatiently. He didn't hear any movement inside the house.

That's really strange, he thought.

Again, he rang the bell, his heart sinking.

●●●●

He parked himself at her doorstep, trying to imagine places that she might be.

Doing homework at Sophie's? Or out to dinner with her father? She had said he was going to be in town this week. Or maybe she was inside, and just didn't want to see him…

He decided to wait until she returned. She would have to come home for the night. And so Aarush clung to that thought.

His growling stomach seemed to drown the sounds of the evening crickets, irritating him with their apparent joyful state. Aarush pictured the perfect evening with Lara, sitting around their kitchen table, talking through their issues, having a meal of some sort. Sitting on her doorstep losing inspiration, and starving for comfort of any kind, did not in any way fit his plan.

After what seemed an eternity, and just as Aarush was preparing to surrender to practical sensibilities, he heard tires on gravel. Bounding toward the driveway, his eyes automatically scanned Aunt Kathy's white Toyota Highlander, looking furtively for his person of interest. Sophie was in the front passenger seat and Lara sat in the back. He was sure the joy and relief emblazoned across his face must have been obvious.

Within moments, the car stopped, and there was a flurry of activity followed by a barrage of instructions. Lara's golden retriever, Penny, lay prostrate and sedated beside Lara.

"Oh, Aarush, am I glad to see you! I could use a pair of strong hands," Aunt Kathy called out. "Please help Lara carry Penny in through her back door."

"What happened?" Aarush asked, his eyes on Lara.

He opened the door to Lara's side and she stepped down, a blanket in her hand.

"Penny swallowed some poisonous mushrooms in the backyard and started vomiting this morning. I called Sophie because I had no idea what to do." Lara held his gaze. She looked exhausted. How he longed to hug her, hold her close and tell her everything was going to be okay.

"My mom had the day off work and happened to be at home when Lara called." Sophie said, filling in.

"Thank God for that! Poor Penny, she needed a thorough flushing of her abdomen," Aunt Kathy added, as she returned to the car, having unlocked the back door and left it ajar.

"If we had been even fifteen minutes later, Penny would have been in serious trouble," Lara whispered. There were tears in her voice.

He picked up Penny in his arms, her dead weight making the transfer from the SUV's higher-than-normal backseat to the house a test of his biceps and triceps burn tolerance. Lara hastened into the house and spread the blanket close to the kitchen heat vent, Penny's customary spot. Aarush lay Penny on her right side with her face tucked between her front paws. As he instinctively reached to scratch Penny behind her exposed ear, her favorite place, Lara reached out simultaneously and their fingers brushed. They both froze, but not for long. They looked at each other, and all it took was that moment of knowing. He felt certain in his heart that everything was okay, that she had forgiven him. That she had not given up on him.

"Lara, why don't you go take a shower and try to relax?" Aunt Kathy suggested. "You've had a long day. The worst is behind us, really. The sedation will continue to work wonders. And, Aarush, I'm sure you'll find pizza or something in the freezer. Amy Jo's good about that. Why don't you make a meal for the two of you?" Then, looking at Soph, she added, "If we leave right away, we can still make it to the soccer team parent meeting."

Obviously, Kathy had assumed that Lara and Aarush had dinner plans together.

"Sure. I can do that." He couldn't have been happier.

"You two will be okay?" Aunt Kathy asked one more time.

In unison Lara and Aarush nodded and watched Aunt Kathy and Sophie walk out the back door.

Then they both stood in the kitchen as if someone had turned them to stone. From the sound of the tires on the gravel, braking and reversing, then changing gears, Aarush could picture Aunt Kathy maneuvering the Highlander down the driveway. Within moments the car was sounding far away.

"Aar..."

"Lara..."

"I'm sorry," he offered weakly.

"No. I'm sorry," she said.

"Why are you sorry?"

"That you didn't come sooner." She smiled through her fatigue.

Aarush took three long steps, not difficult in view of his six-foot length, and scooped her into his arms. He held her close, felt her tiny body soften as she let go of the tension. They stood there, holding each other, for a long time. He kissed the top of her head and couldn't bring himself to let her go.

"I'm so, so sorry," he whispered, once more into her ear, his arms wrapped around her petite frame. With a tight squeeze she forgave him.

"Where's your mom?" he asked, still holding her.

"She's had her phone turned off all day. She's assisting Dr. Dubois in some long surgery. She told me she'd be unreachable until at least 10:00 tonight but that she'd check in with me from time to time." Lara's mother was an ophthalmologist and specialized in ocular surgery. Her parents weren't divorced but didn't live together either, her father visiting them every so often. He had a job somewhere in the Midwest. Lara didn't talk much about him.

"She called when she was on a break and knows what happened. We were at Adobe Animal Hospital at the time. She talked to Auntie Kathy," Lara continued.

Reluctantly, Aarush released her. "Go," he urged, "A nice hot shower will make you feel better. I'll find something for us in your freezer." Gently, he prodded her in the direction of her bedroom.

By the time she returned to the kitchen, Aarush had preheated the oven to 400°F and placed a Trader Joe's pizza on the top rack. He set the timer on the microwave for 20 minutes and set two plates, side by side, on the narrow countertop. She emerged a new person, with color in her cheeks and a towel tied into a turban around her wet hair.

She sat herself down on one of the bar stools and claimed the corresponding dinner plate. Aarush sat beside her. She reached out and took both his hands, one in each of hers. Then she lifted each hand, and lightly pressed them to her lips. They both smiled. Aarush freed his right hand and tucked a loose strand of her wet brown hair back into the purple Turkish towel turban.

"Feeling better?" he asked, reclaiming her hand.

"Uh-huh," she said, "especially now that you are here."

He turned his palms around and gave hers a quick squeeze, characteristically at a loss for words.

"Aar, if you don't tell me what's on your mind or what's worrying you, I can't guess what's going on in there. You know that, don't you?"

Should he tell her? He had picked up his package from the post office on the way back from school. At least that much had gone according to plan. He had not planned for what came next.

●●●●

Lara and Aarush had spent all year preparing applications for college. Sophie was an accomplished soccer player and had registered during the summer with the National Collegiate Athletic Association (NCAA) Initial Clearing House. She had known all along that soccer was her ticket to college admission and had worked hard through high school with that goal in mind. Last summer, the summer before senior year, their mothers took them to visit most of the UCs. They made mini vacations together while exploring campuses in L.A., Santa Barbara, Santa Cruz, Berkeley and Davis, all packed into Aunt Kathy's SUV. UC Berkeley had recognized

Sophie's talent and recruited her even before winter holidays. Her parents were proud and relieved; Sophie was ecstatic. Lara and Aarush, on the other hand, were following the more traditional and tortuous college admissions path. Lara's meticulous nature and planning skills had come in very handy.

She had converted her room into their very own college application office. There was a blackboard on one wall where she maintained a laundry list of all the things they had to do in the very near future, this week, for instance. As they added to their list of colleges, Lara marked and kept track of their application deadlines on a calendar she had hung on one side of the blackboard. They had taken their AP tests last May and had done decently well. They had registered and taken their SATs in late fall. They had worked on their essays, written their applications, carefully printed and collated all the appropriate paperwork for each college, licking and gluing envelopes when needed, and responsibly distributing recommendation letter requests with stamped and addressed envelopes to favored teachers. Only because his father had insisted, Aarush had even applied to Stanford, the only private school on his list. Stanford rules stated that, if one applied via "early decisions" and was accepted, the applicant *must* accept the admission offer. One would think an early acceptance would ensure relief. Not for Aarush, however. He secretly hoped to move farther away from home and fervently prayed for an unfavorable outcome.

"Aarush," she took a deep breath before she asked, "can I ask you something? Are you trying to hide something from me? Is there something you should be telling me?"

How did she know? She had just offered him the perfect opening. Then why was he so torn?

Tormented between confiding in her and protecting her from what he knew would only cause heartache, he agonized over the contents of the Amazon package, over what he had originally dismissed as a farfetched thought now shaping into a concrete plan, his conflicted decision around it all and how it was going to affect them. Affect more than just the two of them.

••••

Shalini

Two

She gazed out the oval porthole window of the economy cabin as Korean Airlines flight KE23 sat patiently on the runway, waiting for its turn to take off. Every time Shalini took a long overseas flight, especially one where she was flying by herself, she went through extreme moments of reflection and rumination. There was something about being in a giant bird overseeing the magnificent spread of the earth beneath that sent her soul overflowing with gratitude, and threw her into deep throes of concentrated meditation.

As she stared out the window, the aircraft still on the runway and cars gliding past atypically on an otherwise chock-a-block Highway 101, her thoughts returned to the morning. The picture of Amit and Aarush together at the breakfast table was still fresh in her mind. Amit was reading the newspaper and eating breakfast, looking up every now and then to engage in the conversation, a limited sprinkling of monosyllables not unlike the thinly distributed raisins in his cereal.

"Mom, will you go with Nana to Dwarika this time too?" Aarush was always curious about the compulsive rituals Shalini shared with her father.

"Yes, Rushu. And I will order the same veg club sandwich and cream of tomato soup." She had smiled as she rinsed the last few utensils from the sink and loaded the dishwasher.

"I've always wondered why you didn't go out and eat Indian food when you were young?"

"We called that *food*, sweetheart." Shalini's expectant eyes instinctively darted in the direction of Amit. She saw him grin, not so much for the humor, as for the effort. Shalini was not known for possessing this particular talent. Any attempt made at wittiness, even a failed one required acknowledgement. And applause.

"Well, Nani prepared such wonderful traditional food at home. Going out meant eating pizzas, burgers, soups and sandwiches. That was the real treat for us."

"Like we eat sushi when we go out," Aarush said.

"Yes, Rushi. Now I go back to Dwarika because of nostalgia. It brings back fond memories, for both Nana and me. It's not just about the food, either. It's about people we have grown up with. Like the manager, Mukesh, who welcomes us every time with warm recognition; or the waiter, Raju, who knows our order without us telling him anything. Dwarika was our equivalent of California Pizza Kitchen, you see."

Shalini's mother cherished the nights they went to Dwarika as much as the rest of the family did, only for different reasons. She got a day off from planning and preparing dinner.

"Will you also walk up to Hanuman Tekdi?"

"Yes dear, but I'll do that early in the morning with Shireenmaasi."

Shireen was Shalini's childhood neighbor, her very first friend, still unmarried and living next door to her parents to this day. Hanuman Tekdi was a steep hill, a mile behind her parents' home in Pune, the small town where Shalini had grown up. At the top of the hill stood a small temple that celebrated Hanuman, the Hindu deity belonging to the ape-like race of forest dwellers, a central character in the Hindu epic *The Ramayana*. It took twenty minutes to climb the steep slope, seek blessings from Hanuman, and then fifteen minutes to climb back down. Add the mile to and from the house and the expedition took under an hour. Just one more ritual that Shalini had religiously looked forward to and practiced every trip. This ritual, though, was one that she had shared with her mother.

Narsidas Mistry was the oldest of four siblings. Right out of high school, he joined his father, to help start an automobile parts manufacturing plant, becoming a major provider of motorcycle seats to Bajaj Auto Ltd., India's leading two-wheeler manufacturer located on the outskirts of Pune. Their business thrived with the growth of Bajaj's market. Shalini remembered only a life of privilege. Not ostentatious by any standards, but comfortable and without want. Business and politics, became entwined as they did worldwide, and it was impossible to grow without the two worlds intersecting. Over time, Narsidas built a wide network of connections. In the later part of his life, not having had the opportunity to go to college, he dedicated his free time and fortune toward building educational institutions in Pune. As a result, people from all parts of his life, industrialists and politicians, neighbors and distant relatives, came knocking at his door for help with college admissions for their children. Since neither Shalini nor Amit had showed any interest in taking over his business, he eventually ended up selling it to his nephews. Now he focused all his time and energy serving on boards of various schools and colleges, enjoying mentoring the new generation of administrators in their vision to increase affordable learning opportunities for Pune's youth.

It had been three years since Mother lost her battle with cancer. After her passing, Shalini made a promise to herself to visit her father every three months. It seemed so unfair to uproot him from his familiar surroundings and bring him to live with her. Besides, he enjoyed good health even at seventy-five, and it was obvious that he lived a full life.

Since Mother's death, Shireen had taken her place in this morning ritual, accompanying Shalini to Hanuman Tekdi, helping alleviate the pain of her loss, as they reminisced and trudged along, one step at a time.

"What else, Mom? You said you'd also do one new thing with Nana every time you visited, right?" Aarush always held Shalini to every word she uttered.

Shalini must have said in passing something to that effect after her last trip. It was a good idea but a hard one to implement. Father was not adventurous about food. So that ruled out trying new restaurants and new cuisines which would have been fun for a foodie like her. And easy, too, considering new joints around town were propagating like rabbits. She would have to think of something else.

"I think I'll take Nana to the movies this time. A Hindi Bollywood film is not really his thing. I keep taking him to his favorite Marathi plays and Hindustani classical music concerts. But maybe some English movie at E-Square?" Shalini said, coming back to his question. E-Square was the most happening place in Pune at the moment. A multi-theater cinema, or a multiplex as it was called, was a novel concept. And especially for her father.

Just then, the bell rang.

"The cab's here, Mom."

Shalini started the dishwasher, then kissed Amit mechanically, more out of a need to display normalcy than anything else and mostly for Aarush's benefit. Wrapping her arms around Aarush, she kissed his cheeks, forehead, chin and nose. They had an agreement that no matter how old he got Shalini would retain the exclusive privilege to kiss him as much she wanted so long as they were not in public.

Her suitcase and handbag stationed at the front door, Shalini took a deep breath, glanced around, making a quick mental check to ensure everything was in order, and as she always did, bid a silent good-bye to the house.

She could hear the engine in the belly of the monstrous plane, a groan that rapidly became a deafening rumble as it rolled down the runway and within no time soared, a majestic eagle ready to stake its claim in the skies. She found herself nodding off, her head resting against the seat back, as the plane continued its ascent. She remembered the anxiety that used to overwhelm her every time she took a flight alone, a fear of dying in a plane crash that intensified more than ever after Amit and she had been blessed with Aarush. A common maternal fear, she was told. Interestingly, Shalini noted today, somewhere along the way she had left behind that feeling of dread. As her ears popped from the change in air pressure, she couldn't help noticing how much more relaxed she felt in her seat. Her body glided even as she dozed, each individual cell levitating upward and forward in perfect harmony, like birds flying in a perfectly synchronized formation. It wasn't long before the airplane circled around the bay and over the bridges connecting the peninsula to the East Bay. As she gazed out her window, it struck Shalini for the first time that the Bay Bridge, the San Mateo Bridge and the Dumbarton Bridge looked like parallel strands of pearls wrapped around a plunging neckline. She felt the excitement of inspiration bubble in the pit of her stomach. She knew the image would be the subject of her next painting. *How have I not noticed this before?* she wondered.

"That's so you, Shalini!" Marzia would have laughed had Shalini spoken aloud her last thought as she used to when they were in college. "You notice something ordinary in our everyday routine. Then you are filled with wonder as if you are seeing that mundane thing for the first time, ever. Then you use it as your motivation to create some *Bhagwan-jaane* (God knows!) crazy, ridiculous, fantastical work of art!!" Marzia repeated this with flourish every time she got a chance and to anyone who

32

would listen. That was so Marzia! Marzia Batliwala. Shalini's Kathy in India. Her biggest fan, friend and philosopher, all in one.

••••

Shalini finished her twelfth standard state board exams in the science stream at the renowned Fergusson College in Pune. She was eligible to get into any of the pure or applied science undergraduate degree programs in the University of Pune. But from the bottom of her heart she knew that she did not want to continue in that direction. She was also certain that if she followed that much-beaten path it would lead to only one of two possibilities. Either she would end up being a doctor or an engineer. At the time, doctors and engineers were being produced in India in the hundreds of thousands, productivity rates that would easily put to shame even those boasted by car manufacturers of the likes of Toyota, GM etc. All Shalini wanted to do was to paint.

Why she didn't want to pursue that which was coveted by everybody else, was a question that plagued her parents, especially her mother. Shalini had no good reason to justify her choice. She dreamed of art school. Her fingers itched to play with brushes and color. Her hands yearned to feel and shape clay and stone.

The last two years in Fergusson College had been torturous, to say the least. To please her mother, Shalini had agreed to give science a shot.

"Shalini *beta*, you are in the top twenty-five on the admissions list at College of Engineering, Pune. My dream has come true!" Shalini had never seen her mother happier than the day the results had been announced. She had surpassed all expectations, her own included.

"Lata was telling me that you should enroll for GRE and TOEFL test prep classes in your first year in college itself."

Latamaasi was their next-door neighbor whose son had just finished his final year in electrical engineering. He had received news of having been accepted at Iowa State University, and Latamaasi couldn't stop talking about it. Mother, having never had the opportunity to attend college, was determined that her daughter pursue graduate studies abroad, preferably in the United States and in the science stream — no questions asked.

"I have even made photocopies of the list of the top fifty universities that you should apply to."

Toward this end, Mother completed her research, dreaming that her daughter would one day become famous for some scientific innovation that would contribute to the betterment of the world.

When Shalini finally gathered enough courage to bring up the topic of what she truly desired, all hell broke loose.

"What do you mean you don't want to study engineering?" Shalini had suggested that she move to Bombay to join the prestigious Sir JJ School of Art.

"Shanti, Shanti. Can you please calm down? Let's give Shalini time to think over her decision." This was the only ray of hope her father had offered that day.

He turned his gaze from Mother to Shalini.

"I hope you are giving this some serious thought, Shalini. This is not the time to be frivolous or indulge in passing fancies."

Both Shalini's parents encouraged progressive thinking and financial independence, but they differed significantly in their approach and outlook as to achieving those goals. Mother thought Shalini was being flippant with her desire to throw away a perfectly sensible opportunity in the most prestigious Engineering College while choosing a path she was convinced would lead to a dead end.

"Why can't you do all that painting-*vainting* as a hobby, on the side? Narsi, put some sense in Shalini's head, please," she implored.

After several days of raised voices (actually, only *one* raised voice,

34

Mother's), shedding of tears (Mother and Shalini) and skillful balancing of wills (Father), Mother caved in with great reluctance.

"You can still change your mind, *beta*, you know that, don't you? Next year, if for any reason you realize that you have made the wrong choice, Pappa and I would never be angry. I know they would let you enroll in the engineering program. So what if you lose a year?" she offered, stubbornly clinging on to that last strand of hope.

Shalini hugged her father with unbridled joy. He was the only one who understood how unhappy she had been, who had been aware of her restlessness and had recognized her longing, her yearning to pursue her passion. He gave Shalini the best gift of all — blessings to follow her dream.

How Shalini wished to prove her mother wrong! To show her that her misgivings were unfounded. To validate her father's faith in her and make him proud.

Why do I feel that I have failed them both? she thought with anguish.

●●●●

"Would you like something to drink?"

The hair on her neck stood up as an intense shudder travelled down her spine. Her chest tightened with pain. The image of a newborn baby, wrapped in a receiving blanket, flashed across her mind's eye.

"Would you like something to drink, ma'am?" The voice repeated.

She could see the baby as it was taken away. She could feel her body turn heavy and immobile. Her heart felt as if it had been stabbed by a hundred daggers.

"I have Coke, Sprite, orange, apple and tomato juice. Red and white wine as well," the stewardess pressed, as Shalini continued to stare blankly at the pretty face, the perfect skin.

"Tomato juice, please," she finally muttered. The heat of intense guilt rose up her neck and colored her face. *The same color as the tomato juice*, Shalini thought, staring into the plastic cup as she tried to shake off, one more time, that last image.

••••

Shalini moved to Bombay with much trepidation, and enrolled in the bachelor's program in fine arts at Sir JJ School of Art. Her father accompanied her, helping to find paying guest accommodations with a family whose reference he got from a friend of a friend of a friend. They boarded a Colaba-bound BEST bus after de-training at the Victoria Terminus Train Station where Deccan Queen, the dutiful prestigious train of the Indian Railways, commenced and terminated its daily Bombay-Pune round trip. At the President Hotel bus stop in Cuffe Parade, they got off the red double-decker. A gentle breeze bearing a strong scent of drying fish welcomed them as they made their way along the sidewalk next to fisherman's colony in Colaba, located almost at the southern-most tip of Bombay. They continued several blocks, asking pedestrians and taxi drivers for help locating the address scribbled on a piece of paper. After going in circles a few times, they finally reached their destination, an old, dilapidated bungalow aptly called Joona Bangla. Her first memory of the place included peering through the broken and rusted bars of a tired iron gate, making a feeble, but dignified attempt at guarding the decrepit and rundown building.

"Wow, wouldn't this make a great location to shoot a horror film? It has the perfect makings of a haunted house!" Shalini exclaimed as her father tried to open the gate.

A monstrously large and dignified mansion, draped in peeling plaster with mold and moss embellishing its exterior, desperately begging for a fresh coat of paint, it stood in all its magnificence, stubborn and unwilling to renounce its former splendor. This was a rare sight in Bombay, where skyrocketing land costs and uncontrollable housing demand had resulted in vertical skyscrapers replacing most bungalows. It took Shalini not more than that instant, however, to fall in love with the place, the telltale signs of lost grandeur conjuring up fantastic stories in her young romantic mind.

Marzia answered the door.

"Ammijaan, somebody is at the door for you."

Marzia looked at Shalini with a big smile, and Shalini could not resist liking her instantly. Ammijaan and Marzia had been expecting them, as they had called ahead.

"*Salaam bhaiji,*" greeted Ammijaan, using the flap of her burqa, or as Marzia would later correct Shalini, the *pardi* of her *rida,* to wipe the sweat from her brow.

In no time Shalini learned that the *rida*, worn by Marzia's Bori community women, distinguished itself from other forms of veil by being colorful and often decorated with patterns and lace.

The *rida's* difference from the traditional black burqa, however, is significant beyond how it looks, in that it doesn't call for covering of women's faces like the traditional veil. It has a flap called the *pardi* that usually hangs on the back like the hood of a jacket, but is not used to conceal the face.

"*Namaste behenji*, I am Shalini's father, Narsi Mistry. We come from Pune. Mr. Imtiaz Bohra gave me your address and phone number. He said you were looking for a girl PG. And that your daughter has just enrolled in JJ School. Shalini has admission there as well. Do you have an opening?"

Paying guests were colloquially referred to as PGs.

"*Inshallah*, you couldn't have come at a better time. Here, come on in. Why don't you sit down." She beckoned them to an old, worn-out velvet couch that sat alone in a large living room with one old television set directly across from it and a small wooden end table next to one of the armrests.

"Marziajaan, can you please get some water for the guests?"

They sat down, and before long Marzia and Shalini were having their own conversation, Marzia excited to have company and more than happy to show Shalini, a newcomer, around Bombay.

"We'll take the bus together to JJ everyday. I'll take you to my favorite food places. The *pav bhaji* from the street hawker near Eros theatre is the best. Croissant has the only salads worth consuming. It's too bad you eat only vegetarian food, otherwise I know just the right place for the best prawns in town!"

Marzia talked non-stop. She was a hopeless food enthusiast. Her sincerity and affection were so infectious, Shalini couldn't help but reciprocate. Unknown to them at the time, it was the beginning of the most beautiful friendship.

Much later, Ammijaan would confide, it was the return of pure happiness to Marzia's face, long gone since her father's death, and in so far as Shalini's residency, the immediate chemistry that sealed the deal for her.

Marzia's father had died in a car crash on the treacherous Bombay-Bangalore highway when she was twelve years of age. Marzia's father's untimely death, unplanned finances and Ammijaan's (as Shalini took to calling her) gullible nature almost brought them to the streets as deceptive male relatives hoodwinked them of their inheritance. Ammijaan's brother stepped in just in time, contacted a lawyer friend, a certain Mr. Bohra, and helped his sister keep the house.

Ammijaan, a proud woman, refused to become a burden on her brother's family, her only surviving relatives. With a roof over her head, and Allah by her side, she started generating an income by means of what she knew best. Cooking. She started providing lunch and dinner *tiffins* to struggling artists and students who flooded their neighborhood due to its proximity to art school. It didn't take her long to realize that this was not enough to sustain them, however frugally they lived. She began to consider renting rooms in order to supplement their income. It was then that she solicited advice from the same Mr. Bohra, who happened to mention it to a cousin in Pune, who in turn had passed on this information through another friend to Shalini's father. Since they were two women living alone, Ammijaan was naturally only comfortable considering women paying guests. She was not concerned so much for her own safety as with the safety of her young, coming-of-age daughter. Address in hand, Shalini's father boarded the Deccan Queen to Bombay, reassured by the knowledge that his daughter would be in good hands if this housing situation worked out. And it did.

As was expected, the Batliwala ladies lived month to month and could never quite keep up with maintenance on the bungalow beyond what was absolutely necessary. Shalini couldn't have been happier. How could she ever have conceived the many ideas that she did, or receive inspiration for the many assignments that she undertook had the structures of Joona Bangla *not* been falling apart?

••••

Her body was shaking uncontrollably. Her face was wet with tears as she hiccuped and sobbed, sobbed and hiccuped. Her father's stoical face cast downward, his eyes never leaving the baby. The cold stone walls of the building closed in on her like a tomb. Her breathing was shallow, her lungs hurt as if she were drowning in her own tears. If only she *could* have drowned. If only something could take away the pain.

The veins in Shalini's temple began to throb, her heart to palpitate. She felt darkness descend on her like a stormy cloud, bringing with it impending gloom. Immediately, she made a conscious effort to practice *pranayama* techniques of meditation, a tool that helped her manage her panic attacks better than any medication prescribed to her over the last two decades — deep, slow, belly breaths, each inhale at least four to six counts long, followed by a long, four- to six-count exhale.

Shalini could hear Aarush scold her. "Ma, you need to practice what you teach me!"

Practicing was much harder when she was alone. And she had at least ten more hours before they would land in Seoul. Shalini felt the panic. Panic brought by her own demons who would not let her find peace, however hard she tried. Wasn't time supposed to heal? How much longer would this take? Surely seventeen years was long enough.

Shalini felt the pressure gradually build up in her bladder from that morning's multiple cups of tea and now, the tomato juice. Her anxiety attack only made it worse. It was always accompanied by severe claustrophobia. She suddenly felt excessively confined, pressed into her corner window seat. She excused herself, put to use her childhood skill with hurdles, and hopped over the knees of neighboring passengers as she wiggled out of her seat to the aisle, her handbag in tow. She wove her way to the far back of the plane, first to the restroom to relieve herself, and then to the stewardesses' station for a glass of water. She fumbled in her handbag, found an Ambien and swallowed it with a gulp of water. It wouldn't take long to fall asleep.

I'd choose the dread of dying in a plane crash, anytime, over the demons that follies of my youth have left me to live with, she thought. *Without a doubt, no questions asked*...were her last thoughts before passing out.

••••

"HI SHALINI!" Marzia cried from behind the stainless steel railing separating the families waiting to receive arriving travelers. Any of the bystanders would have assumed from her exuberant enthusiasm that Marzia was seeing Shalini after at least a decade, not three months! Her eighteen-year-old son, Murtaza, stood shyly behind her, most of his handsome face hiding behind a neatly trimmed beard and mustache.

"How are you?" Marzia gave her a long tight hug. "When will I stop missing you?"

"Never. Ever."

She asked Shalini the same question, without fail, every time she came to receive her. And Shalini replied with the same two words. It had become their special routine. Every time they exchanged this scripted dialogue, it boosted their belief in the one thing that they hoped neither time nor distance would ever change — their unconditional love for each other and the deep connection they shared.

Once they crossed across the arrival zone of the Chhatrapati Shivaji International Airport, as the Bombay airport was now known, and walked to the short-term parking area to their car, Murtaza loaded Shalini's lone bag into the trunk of their white Maruti Zen.

"How was your flight? You must be so tired. Your eyes still have those dark circles under them. When are you going to learn to take it easy, Shalini? You promised me you'd come back looking better. Are you okay?" Marzia still talked just as much, bless her heart.

Shalini tried to keep her eyes focused outside the back window of the racing car. The roads were empty. After all, it was 3:30 a.m., the ideal time to be driving in Bombay and the only weird time that international inbound flights from the U.S. seemed to land. Nobody in the airline scheduling department seemed to be at all concerned about the families who had to stay awake, only to drive across town to receive their loved ones.

Shalini squinted her tired eyes and concentrated on the illusion of a long, never-ending, continuous neon light that the racing street lamps created.

"How has it been between you and Amit? Is it getting better?" Marzia persevered, her question lined with concern.

Shalini pretended not to hear what Marzia asked. But her silence and her pretenses were both unsuccessful in putting an end to Marzia's line of questioning.

"Marzipan, later...please?" Shalini said finally, raising her eyebrows, her index finger on her lips, shushing and signaling her hesitation to discuss anything around Murtaza.

The ensuing silence surely had at least a little to do with sleep-deprived brain cells that left Marzia's unable to immediately maneuver the conversation in a different direction. Neither the silence nor the hypnotic effect produced by the blurring street lamps, however, provided any hindrance to Shalini's racing thoughts. Marzia's question had nudged her precariously balanced mind, rudely spinning it out of its orbit and awakening tremendous distress.

What is better?

"Shalini, are you ready? We are late. Why aren't you ready?" Amit asked urgently as he entered through the garage door.

"Late? For what?" Shalini was in her overalls, lounging in their hammock tied between two hundred-year-old oak trees outside their living room. Shalini's favorite place. She was taking a break while her painting lay drying in the sun.

"I have to speak to the math grad students at Santa Clara University. They are awarding me an honorary doctorate today. I texted you a few hours ago," he said impatiently.

"I haven't checked my phone since morning. I have been working on..."

"Whatever. You need to get ready. We'll be late if we don't leave in two minutes."

"I can't possibly get ready that fast. Look at me." There was paint in her hair, on her arms, her face — everywhere.

"What's the use of a phone if you don't even check my messages..."

"I have been painting for the last five hours. And you know I don't carry the phone on me like an extension of my body. Besides, isn't it a bit last minute to tell me?" Shalini felt her irritation grow.

"I texted two hours ago! Two hours is enough time for a woman to get ready." Amit was furious.

"First of all, don't talk in that condescending manner. Secondly, I didn't mean enough time so I can get ready. I need advance notice so I can plan my day accordingly. My work needs planning too."

"It's a painting, for heaven's sake. You can come back and complete it anytime."

"What do you mean, anytime? I can't get inspiration back. The mood, the setting. When will you understand that I can't turn these unquantifiables on and off like a switch?"

"You have just wasted precious time arguing when what you should be doing is getting dressed so we can leave."

"Leave? I'm not going anywhere."

Amit stared at Shalini, shell-shocked and speechless.

When he eventually said something at all, the word emerged as a whisper. "What?"

"You heard right. This is no way to talk to me. Or ask me to join you. I can skip one engagement. And I *am* going to. I guarantee, I won't be missed."

"Tell me you're kidding, Shalini?"

"No Amit, I'm not. In fact, I have never been more serious."

Red-faced and fuming, Amit departed.

Amit was having a great year, one award ceremony after another, felicitations and guest appearances everywhere. Shalini was proud of his accomplishments. She knew enough to recognize that being a tenured professor with enormous research grants at a prestigious university like Cal was no small accomplishment. He was just starting to receive the recognition he had yearned and toiled for over many years. She saw him at his most passionate in the world of academia. His world. Probably his *only* world, so far as she knew.

Why does he do that to me? When will he understand that I can't be his accessory? That it's my turn to do something for myself? To enjoy a sense of fulfillment, the completeness, the exhilaration of belonging and contributing to our species as he does? I am standing up for what I want, what I believe in, expressing my needs, both to serve my desires as well as to prioritize my life in order to serve them. Which means bringing Amit's attention to the injustices of his expectations of me.

Is this really better?

For me in my personal growth…probably.

For us? I don't know. I'm sure Amit doesn't think so.

"Murtaza, why don't you tell Shalini aunty about your award at the music festival? Do you know, Shals, A.R. Rahman was the chief guest and he said Murtaza has a really bright future in playback singing. He is going to be our next Sonu Nigam…"

Mercifully, Marzia's voice brought Shalini back from the memory, the outburst with Amit just two days ago.

"Oh, Mummy, stop…you are too much…" Murtaza blushed, embarrassed by his mother's gushing.

"Congratulations, Murtaza! This is amazing news. What was this festival all about?" Shalini hoped her enthusiasm sounded sincere. She really was excited for Murtaza. She just didn't trust her emotional poise. She wanted to talk to Marzia and knew it wouldn't be long before she would get back to the subject of her marriage to Amit. But she just needed time to gather her thoughts.

••••

What is it that changes love?

She could still remember, as clear as day, the first time she ran into Amit.

It was early December 1991. Shalini was at Jazz by the Bay, a restaurant along Marine Drive that showcased some of the best jazz in Bombay.

As the management added other genres of music to their repertoire, they renamed it to Not Just Jazz by the Bay. Shalini loved the place, the music, the crowd and the ambience. A certain signature kind of people hung out there, smoking with abandon and drinking without hint of inhibition. Shalini was certain that a few in that crowd were definitely high on dope or doing drugs. All she needed for a high, though, was to simply hang out there and for a time vicariously experience freedom. Freedom from her rigid and conservative upbringing that labeled everything at this place wrong. Even if it meant only for a few hours. She felt free of restraint, a crazy feeling bordering on recklessness.

She had been in this state, dancing on the floor when she noticed Marzia walk in with somebody. Two things had surprised her then — the sight of Marzia at Not Just Jazz by the Bay, knowing she had a toddler at home, and the most unlikely character with her. Shalini should have suspected foul play instantly, but she was too distracted by the oddness of the situation. Even without Marzia, Shalini wouldn't have missed Amit. She *couldn't* have. He was so obviously out of place, it was almost painful to watch. For one thing, he wore a dress shirt with a tie, he was clean-shaven, with neatly combed hair parted to the side. For all anybody knew, he could have been a character out of a period movie. His awkwardness in an environment obviously alien to him, left Shalini feeling sorry for him. Inexplicably, it elicited a protective maternal instinct. She couldn't explain, even to herself, a draw toward someone who was so unequivocally a mismatch. His shy eyes, lowered to the floor, as Marzia tried to introduce them over the loud music, remained her most endearing memory of that night. Shalini barely heard what Marzia said, and Marzia for one was relieved that her friend didn't. Before Shalini knew it, Marzia had left them under some pretext, just as abruptly as she had appeared, and Shalini found herself responsible for entertaining this duck out of water.

One thing led to another and Shalini realized she had agreed to see him again the next day. As she learned more about him, she felt in awe not so much of his achievements, which she saved for her mother, but for his humility in spite of them. She saw a gentle and sincere person hiding behind a painfully introverted exterior. What started as a friendship grew into a deep caring. But what Shalini couldn't persuade herself to do was to fall in love. It was nothing like the ideal imaginary relationship she had dreamed of, and Amit was not the partner she'd pictured. But, then again, she couldn't pinpoint anything wrong with him, either. Not just Amit, but the entire family seemed a perfect match. Cultured, educated, only son, living abroad. An accomplished scientist with a great salary. And Amit had grown to love her, or so he told her on their last evening out.

What more could she ask for?

And Mother was ecstatic. In her wildest dreams Shalini wouldn't have imagined that it was even remotely possible for her to be with some-one that would have made Mother happy. Lately, she had lost trust in her own judgment.

After more than three years in Bombay, she was no longer the confident Shalini who had disembarked the Deccan Queen with her fa-ther in June 1988. Her short bob replaced two long braids, jeans and T-shirt the traditional *salwar kameez*. Mostly, though, she was no longer the girl who stepped off the train onto Platform 8 three years earlier, her face aglow with promise. Promise that had been deeply rooted in her unques-tioned belief that the world was hers to conquer and she would do it on her own terms.

••••

She would find out much later that this was not a chance encoun-ter but one that had been strategically orchestrated with Marzia after much pleading from Mother.

"Shanti, Shalini is so young. She is just twenty years old. Why don't you let her be?" Father had objected.

"Narsi, I was only eighteen when you agreed to marry me. Since when do you find twenty young? Besides, if we start looking for a boy now, we might find someone for Shalini in the next who knows how many years? Boys from the U.S. are so choosy these days. Shalini is adamant about not discussing what she'd like in a life partner. She doesn't understand that life is not all about love and fresh air! It's all your fault, Narsi. You have spoilt her and made her get carried away with her idealistic whims rooted in unreality."

Father's seeming indifference and lack of cooperation aggravated Mother no end. To add to that, Marzia seemed to change the topic of conversation every time Mother enquired about Shalini's likes and dislikes. Marzia's behavior totally foxed Mother. After all, Marzia had been married for two years already, to Saleem Batliwala, a distant cousin who shared their same last name. They were betrothed and wedded in Marzia's first year at JJ, and they even had a one-year-old. So what if Saleem was in Dubai while she finished college? Sacrifices were part and parcel of life and if made early, guaranteed good things in the future, Mother believed.

"Ask Ammijaan. Maybe she'll be able to put some sense into your naïve romantic head."

Mother counted on Ammijaan to take over when she failed to penetrate Shalini's stubborn armor. Ammijaan had become Shalini's surrogate mother and had Mother's sometimes envious, but mostly unconditional, blessings to be. All year, Mother had been sending her résumés of eligible bachelors. Shalini was in her final year at JJ. Since she had not lived up to Mother's expectations by becoming a famous scientist in the United States, Mother busied herself by investing her energy and hopes into what she thought was the next best thing for her daughter. Marry a famous scientist in the United States. Shalini had been totally uncooperative and impossible to persuade, so Mother had solicited Marzia's help in setting her up with these "suitable boys."

"I have a really good feeling about this boy Amit, Marzia. He is the first boy who has specifically mentioned on his résumé that he is not interested in an engineer/doctor girl…" This piece of information caught Marzia's attention.

"The only way I can get Shals to meet anybody is if you let me do it my way, Shantimaasi." Marzia had finally succumbed to Mother's relentless pleadings and emotional blackmail.

"Please ask what's-his-name…"

"His name is Amit. Amit Kamdar."

"Yes, yes…Amit, if he's interested, that he'll need to come to Bombay to meet Shalini." Marzia knew she was pushing it. This was so not a done thing.

"But…but, *beta*, how can I make such a request?"

"Maasi, that's the only way I can set up a meeting, can't you see?" Marzia implored, knowing she had only a few ways to pull this off.

••••

"You'll learn to love him." Father had kissed Shalini on her forehead when she had announced her decision to marry Amit. And she had learned to love him.

••••

They had reached Marzia's house, the penthouse of a ten-story building that had replaced Joona Bangla.

While Murtaza lugged Shalini's heavy bags to the guest room, she followed Marzia to the kitchen for a glass of water. Before Marzia could ask her again, Shalini retrieved a novel from her handbag, *The Dive From Clausen's Pier* by Ann Packer, and handed it to her friend. Marzia's eyes scanned the open page where Shalini had marked this paragraph. When

Shalini had first read it, it had eerily described exactly how she felt about her relationship with Amit. She had been unable to read beyond that point.

> How is it that I can trace a line through fifteen years from one happy day to another but can't locate with any accuracy at all what happened to me next? A slow draining away of my feelings for him, a trickle I hardly noticed at first until the level was so low it was all I could notice, until what remained was dark and murky and it seemed that in no time at all I'd be bone-dry...

What is it that changes love?
"I'm tired. Awfully tired," Shalini sighed.

••••

$\mathcal{A}$arush

Three

His room was uncharacteristically in a mess. He had opened the Amazon package, the box with its packaging strewn across the floor. There were five books in total, three relating to grief and loss, and the other two travel guides for India.

Lara's question of last evening was weighing him down. How was he going to explain to her what he planned to do? What had started as the seed of an idea had grown into a fully formed plan.

"Are you trying to hide something from me? Is there something you should be telling me?" The question kept looping in his mind as he tried to come up with the gentlest way to break his news. Because there was no good way. Aarush and Lara had spent their last two years strategically planning college applications with hopes of getting into the same university. Now he had to tell her that he was going to abandon that effort, ditch her and embark on something entirely different.

After his mother had died last November, Aarush latched onto Lara as his emotional anchor. His father was dealing with his own grief. And all the time Aarush felt the need to show a strong front so as not to be an additional burden. But he was breaking inside. On the outside he put up a reasonably good show. He was able to function on autopilot by staying emotionally numb. Inside he felt dark and depressed. He was having dreams in which his mother was alive, and vibrant and cheerful. He wanted those dreams to go on and found it enormously difficult, if not impossible, to get himself out of bed. That she had died in India, and that her body was never found, worsened the pain. He didn't know about his father, but not seeing her physically dead left him hoping she might just be alive. Hope and thoughts that drove Aarush crazy.

"Why didn't you listen to Dad?" Aarush clenched his fists and bit his lips to stop the flood of tears threatening to undo him. He felt his grief turn to intense anger as it always did.

"Amit, I need to extend my stay in India. I'll only be here three more days." Aarush still remembered her voice on the speaker phone the last time Amit and he talked to her.

"What is so important, Shalini, that you can't address it the next time you go?" Aarush could clearly hear the exasperation in his father's voice. Amit wasn't a man who reacted well to change. He liked sticking to plans. Changes made him nervous. Besides, without his wife he really was a fish out of water.

"Amit, I'll explain it all to you when I get back but I need to take care of something really important that has come up. My father needs me to take care of some property issues, and the earliest the lawyer is willing to see me is on the twenty-sixth of this month. If I extend my trip by a few days, I should be able to take care of it."

"I guess then you have already decided. What can I say?" Amit had threw his hands up in resignation, a frown clearly revealing his displeasure.

Usually, Aarush thought his father was too demanding of his mother, and so his sympathies were always with her. He had even tried to lighten their mood by saying, "Dad, it's only a week. We'll be fine. Mom, don't worry."

But this time, he wished he had supported his father and pressed his mother to take her scheduled flight. Why hadn't she listened to him? If she hadn't extended her stay, she would be safe and sound at home. And their home would have remained their joyful, safe haven. How this thought drove Aarush to bitter anger!

As soon as they received news of her death, Amit and Aarush had taken the next flight out to Bombay. The two weeks there passed in a daze. Nana's face was unbearable. Amit looked helpless; usually for organizing activities in India, it was Shalini who ran things. Amit was devastated but forced to take charge. Mostly, this time in India was all about the rituals and ceremonies surrounding the last rites.

"I know it sounds strange, but had anybody asked me before Mom died if I would ever perform all those rituals, I would have adamantly refused," Aarush mentioned to Lara when he returned, and continued,

"But I have to confess that, had it not been for those rituals, Dad and I might never have had been able to get through those days. I don't understand why Nana escaped to Bombay that week. I think it would have helped him to stay back. The hundreds of relatives and visitors that came to express their condolences helped us stay as sane as we possibly could by never leaving us any time to think."

Lara ran her hand through his hair. They were taking a break from a bike ride, sitting in an opening off highway 35, having completed almost twenty miles, before turning around.

"How were your mother's friends? They must have been beside

themselves, huh, bug?" she asked.

"Shireenmaasi took over the kitchen in Nana's house and Marzia-maasi answered phone calls for us from well wishers. They kept themselves sane by staying busy," Aarush explained.

At the end of the Hindu thirteenth-day rituals, they returned home. Nana adamantly refused to come back with them. Shalini's death had orphaned all three of them. None knew how to help themselves, let alone another.

Kathy set Aarush up with a grief counselor as soon as he landed. She and Amy Jo took turns preparing meals. Maria started working longer hours. Sophie and Lara helped Aarush keep up with his schoolwork. Lara took over his college applications at that point. Most of December and January was a blur. The only news he remembered from that period was Sophie's sports scholarship at UC Berkeley.

Aarush met the grief counselor every week for the first three months, only because Kathy physically picked him up and drove him to the counselor's office. And Aarush was too polite to refuse. Just as he was thinking that this was a complete waste of time, the counselor said something that made him rethink.

"Aarush, you have to think of a way to find closure. There are several ways to do it. One way might mean writing a letter to your mother with things that might have been left unsaid. Another way would be, especially since you have this embedded in the Hindu tradition, through traditional ceremonial practices that achieve the same end result. Then in situations like yours, some of my patients have said that what helped them was actually going to the place where their loved one died, especially when it happens so far away. It might even help to spend some time there and talk to people who were in her life in the days before her tragic death. Give this some thought, Aarush." Then she had suggested a few books for him to read.

For several reasons, what Dr. Lawson suggested clicked for Aarush. He had always had a strong desire to go back and explore the country where he was born. For the first time in a long time, his dreams changed. Instead of not wanting to get out of bed, he couldn't wait for the sounds of birds tweeting first thing in the morning. Because every day brought him closer to the end of senior year. He saw himself going back to Bombay and reliving more than just the last days of his mother's life. Aarush started making plans.

That day, as soon as Kathy dropped him home from his appointment with Dr. Lawson, he went online and ordered books she had recommended as well as travel guides to India. Aarush didn't know how exactly he was going to pull off his plan, but he was going to be eighteen pretty soon. He had faith it would somehow work out.

When Nana called the following Saturday, as he did every week, Aarush said, "Nana, I haven't talked to Dad yet, but I have a question for you. What do you think about me coming to stay with you for a short time?"

"You know I'd be thrilled to pieces, Rushu. Were you thinking of coming during your summer break, June, July?"

"June, yes. Actually, I was thinking a little more long-term than just for the summer break. Maybe more like a year." Aarush had looked around the room then, making sure that his father wasn't within earshot. He still hadn't broached the topic. He wasn't ready. He wanted to figure out a fool-proof plan first. Over the years, Shalini and Aarush had figured out *how* to present what they wanted, in order to guarantee Amit's approval. Research, research and more research. Think logically — extremely difficult for right-brained people like Shalini and Aarush. Somehow, they had trained themselves with years of practice.

Now Aarush was more concerned about Lara. How would she react? Would this devastate her? Lara and he had hoped to get into the same college, or at least colleges close enough so that they would be able to see each other often. How was he ever going to explain this radical new plan to her?

They met when she was a junior; drawn to each other because of what they shared as well as what they complemented in each other. They attended the same high school, but she was one year older. Until then, they had not crossed paths. Had it not been for what happened on that fateful day in the year 2007, they may never have met.

It was a bleak February day in 2007, Aarush's sophomore year. Lara and her mother, Aunty Amy Jo, were on their way to Northstar Ski Resort in Lake Tahoe to meet with another family for a ski weekend. It was an unusually cold day, the road sheeted with ice. Their car skidded at one of the treacherously twisting bends in the Sierras, not thirty minutes from their destination. The car collided with the side of the mountain and then flipped. Aunt Amy Jo fractured her right arm and hip, but Lara wasn't so lucky. Her head bumped the side window and she ended up hemorrhaging, in addition to sustaining a broken femur, a broken nose and missing teeth.

Fortunately, the police and paramedics arrived in time to get them out of the car and administer emergency treatment. Lara needed to be airlifted to Oakland Children's hospital; she was losing blood rapidly. Her larger issue was discovered when she reached the hospital and nurses ran a quick test to determine her blood group for transfusion from the blood bank. She was found to have one of the rarest blood groups in the world — known as the Bombay Blood Group.

Individuals with this blood type can receive blood only from someone with the identical blood type or risk a serious immune reaction, usually fatal. This blood group, also known as the hh antigen or Bombay phenotype blood is so rare that it is found in only four persons out of a million in the general population. For some reason, this occurrence is one per ten thousand in Bombay. (The name given to this blood type originates in this statistic.) Luckily for Lara, not only was Shalini one of those ten thousand people, but she also happened to be on Aunty Amy Jo's email list.

Shalini had been a regular visitor to Dr. Amy Jo Vintner's office, because Aarush had suffered from vision-related issues since childhood. Blood banks almost never stock the Bombay blood type because it is so rare. Both Amit and Aarush were aware of Shalini's rare blood type and often teased her about being truly one of a kind.

"Oh my God! Amit, we need to go right now to Oakland." His mother had shrieked, her eyes glued to her cell phone screen. Amit looked up from the computer. Aarush was startled. Shalini was given to shrieking but it was usually in delight. This one bore an ominous tone.

"What happened?" Amit asked. Shalini was still staring at the phone screen, scrolling down and reading aloud the email.

"Dr. Vintner and her daughter have been in a serious accident. The daughter is very critical and in the ICU at Children's Hospital in Oakland. This email sent out by her assistant is asking for anybody that has the Bombay Phenotype Blood Group to please respond and come ASAP. Oh-my-God, Amit, let's go."

Aarush had never seen his father respond so fast to any request his mother made. Before he knew it, all three of them were racing up to Oakland.

●●●●

Lara's first few weeks had been touch and go, requiring surgeries to reduce pressure of the skull on her swollen brain as well as blood transfusions. Shalini had stayed at the hospital, on call throughout most of that time. It was not surprising then that his mother and Lara developed a uniquely strong bond during that period. Aarush was definitely caught off guard when he found himself falling in love with Lara, infinitely strong as she lay there, uncomplaining in her hospital bed, clearly suffering. What had been even more miraculous to him was that Lara fell in love with him too.

Her recovery was slow. Two months in the hospital, the first in the ICU, the doctors struggling to reduce brain swelling. Once that had subsided and she was out of immediate danger, they performed reconstructive surgery on her nose and mouth, accompanied by agonizing dental work. It was almost May by the time she came home from the hospital. Then there were several months of home recovery.

Almost every day Aarush visited her. He would go to the library and check out her favorite books. He loved reading aloud to her. Once, a few days after she had come home, he remembered having a sore throat, and it struck him that reading aloud may not be fun for either of them. He brought a movie instead. She had directed him to her pantry where he finally found, after much sleuthing, packets of microwaveable popcorn. He carried her from their downstairs guest bedroom, which had become her room while she recovered, to the family room to give her a change of scene. As the corn popped, a staccato drumbeat to the uniform hum of the rotating microwave turntable, wafts of the salty buttery treat escaped from the kitchen to the family room. He was happy.

"Aarush, I'm so sorry. Can I bother you with one more request?"

He never could, and never had been able to make Lara understand, that no request from her could ever be bothersome.

For one thing, she hardly ever made any demands. In fact, for someone as thoughtful and non-demanding as Lara, the entire post-accident experience of being bedridden and dependent on others for all her needs, had been a test not just of patience but of her will as well.

His affection quadrupled when occasion after occasion and under the worst of pressure, she exhibited what Aarush loved most about her — her grace.

"I know, I know. I won't say sorry again," she said when she recognized the expression on his face. "Would you mind bringing my red wool blanket? It's upstairs on the top shelf in my closet."

And so upstairs he bounded where he found the blanket without difficulty and returned in a jiffy.

He spread the blanket over her, fetched popcorn and cans of Coke, then made himself comfortable in her mother's rocking chair, diagonally across from the wall-mounted, sixty-inch, flat-screen TV. Lara was propped with cushions on the couch directly across from the TV, cozy and comfortable under her red blanket.

"I should ask Dad to buy one of these for Mom this Christmas." A total electronic gadget fan, the flat-screen had seduced Aarush instantly.

"What? The rocking chair?" Lara gazed at him quizzically.

"Well, that's not exactly what *I* was thinking, but now that you say it, Mom would much rather have this rocking chair than that TV." Lara found this so funny, she laughed aloud.

They watched *The Matrix* that night. Or at least attempted to. Thirty minutes into the movie, Lara beckoned Aarush to come and sit beside her on the couch.

"It's a much better view from here. And you wont have to crane your neck."

Aarush was more than willing to get out of the rocking chair, not his favorite piece of furniture. He moved the glass center table to within a comfortable distance and carefully arranged Lara's legs on it. Then he plopped himself next to her, instinctively stretching his right arm along the back of the couch. She pulled him closer, unfolding and spreading the red blanket over both of them.

"Here, get under the blanket," she said. "See how good it feels." She tugged on his T-shirt sleeve.

Aarush may have thought he looked cool on the outside, but his heart picked up pace the moment she had asked him to join her on the couch. He felt an irresistible urge to hold her, to run his hands through her short brown hair, just growing back on her shaven head, to take her hands in his, to touch her face and trace the scar that ran like a train track over her right ear. To kiss her lips.

They paid no further attention to Keanu Reeves through the remainder of the film. Their muscles tensing in anticipation, their hearts beating wildly in their chests, their hands instinctively found each other's under the blanket. And without warning, just like that, so did their lips.

It was an evening Aarush would never forget and not just because it was the first time he had kissed a girl, a girl as beautiful as Lara. But because Aunty Amy Jo had walked in through the garage door at that single inopportune moment.

They wondered, both Lara and Aarush, how long Aunt Amy Jo had needed to wait, uncomfortably no doubt, before they even realized her presence in the room.

"Uh-huh..." When they didn't hear her clear her throat, she had finally dropped her handbag on the tile floor to get their attention.

They jumped out of their skins, in a daze, unable to perform even the simple task of untangling themselves.

"Mama...?" Lara looked up sheepishly, her face red.

"Hi, Aunty Amy Jo." Aarush blushed, mortified.

"Hi kids." Aunty Amy Jo was obviously trying to keep a straight face, bit her lower lip to suppress a smile and pretended to get busy in the kitchen.

Lara and Aarush looked at each other and burst out laughing in part to overcome their embarrassment, but mostly from sheer lack of any other tool to expend the burst of energy that their intimacy had fomented inside them. Energy that represented a new phase in their budding love. Aarush leaned down and brushed his lips lightly on the scar over Lara's right ear, squeezed her hand, and asked for her permission, with a quick chin lift toward the door, to leave. She frowned in mock sadness, then followed it with a flashing smile. Reluctantly she let go, their fingers lightly tracing over each other as she slid her hand out of his, sending a tremor down Aarush's spine.

"Bye, Aunty Amy Jo," Aarush called out as he let himself out the front door as fast as possible, maneuvering his way so that he wouldn't have to face her.

Aarush leapt as high and as far as he could from Lara's porch, over four steps, screaming noiselessly at the top of his lungs with joy. He hopped along random flats of bluestone, the stepping stones forming a pathway that meandered through the Japanese landscaping of Lara's front yard, to his bicycle, which stood leaning against the gate. With his helmet secured to his head, he biked the three miles to his house, unable to wipe the stupid grin off his face, try as he might.

Over the next few months, their friendship deepened from a caring to love.

Surely what he felt for Lara was love. It has to be love.

He had never before felt such a feeling, so splendid...

They talked a lot. They walked a lot, Aarush pushing Lara's wheelchair initially. They laughed a lot. They bared their hearts. They let each other reveal vulnerabilities. So when Lara expressed concern about the angry looking and permanent scar on her cheek and scalp, he'd kiss it and tell her, "That's my favorite feature, Lara. Otherwise you'd be just like any other girl."

Or when she worried about never being able to play a sport again because the accident had reduced her right leg an inch, he'd reassure her, "We'll swim together. And I'll teach you how." Swimming was his sport. His mother described him as a fish in water. He was determined to share this passion with the newest and deepest love in his life.

Lara couldn't attend school for the rest of that year. In fact, she repeated her junior year, which is how they both ended up in the same graduating class of 2009.

So something good had come out of her terrible accident.

●●●●

But overnight Aarush's world turned upside down. Their roles now reversed, Lara became his rock. His intention had been never to desert Lara. But he was no good around her, let alone for her, until he could put to rest the tumultuous, oppressive mayhem in his head.

●●●●

"Aarush." A knock on the door startled him from deep slumber. "Aarush, are you there?"

Dad, he thought.

He jumped out of bed and threw his blanket over the mess on his desk, not wanting his father to see what he was up to.

Aarush had fallen asleep. It was late evening; the sun had dropped below the treetops. He didn't have classes that day and had spent most of his time exploring and researching his plan. After accounting for the time difference between California and India, he had made a call to Marzia-maasi that morning. She was going to forward some information he had enquired about by email.

Aarush opened the door. The bright lights from the hallway blinded him momentarily, and he squinted through sleepy eyes. "Hi Dad," he murmured as he stepped out. "How was your trip?" Aarush closed the door behind him and made as if to walk downstairs with his father.

"Are you feeling all right?" Amit wore a look of concern. "I have never seen you sleep at this time of the evening."

"I'm good. I stayed up all night for an assignment that was due this morning," Aarush lied with a straight face. *A white lie*, he thought guiltily.

"Are you hungry? Was wondering if you'd like to go out, catch up over dinner?"

Amit had just returned from an overseas trip to Indonesia, and it was probably breakfast time as far as his stomach was concerned.

"Let's go. I'm famished. I could definitely eat some food." Aarush heard his stomach complain. It occurred to him that he had skipped lunch, too preoccupied with strategizing and worrying.

"Let me wash up and find fresh clothes. I'll only be a few minutes."

"Sounds like a plan. I'll freshen up too."

As he brushed his teeth, Aarush tried to construct the best way to broach the subject consuming him. He pulled on his jeans and a light sweater all the while formalizing the approach he would take. He went out into the hallway and took the stairs in his usual signature way, skipping every other step until there were two steps left at the very bottom, where he'd jump over both as far as he could, directly to the landing. Even at seventeen, some habits died hard.

Amit was already at the garage door.

"I can drive if you're tired?" Aarush asked, making his bid to drive his father's BMW.

"Sure, sonny boy, you know how much I love to be chauffeur driven," Amit said with a wink.

They headed to the Los Altos Grill, their favorite steak restaurant downtown, and easily found seating for two.

Amit scanned the choices on the menu. "Do you know what you want?"

"Yes. The usual." Aarush didn't need to look at the menu. He knew exactly what he liked and didn't see any reason to try something new. Just like his father. It used to drive Shalini nuts.

They placed their orders, the two of them quiet. Not awkwardly so, but awfully silent, Aarush's nervous energy expressed by the uneasy jiggling of his leg under the table. He gathered his courage and finally took the plunge.

"Dad, I want to ask you something. Actually ask you for permission to do something that I really want to do."

"Sure, Aarush. What is it?"

"I hope you understand where I'm coming from and aren't too disappointed. I don't want you to get too worried or anything like that." That only inspired a frown and Aarush knew instantly he should have opened his case differently. The harm was already done.

"What is it? Are you in some sort of trouble?"

"No, no. It's nothing like that." Aarush realized his father was probably fantasizing driving tickets, bad grades or something to that effect, and he was obviously relieved.

"Dr. Lawson said that in order for me to really get myself out of the rut, I should try some way to get closure." Amit resisted the idea of counseling and was not a big fan of psychiatrists. But he wasn't left with much of a say when Kathy announced that she had already signed Aarush up with one. That she was giving Aarush no choice. And that Shalini would have wanted him to. And Amit knew without doubt that Kathy was absolutely right.

"It's a good idea for all of us to find a way to experience closure. I agree with her. But haven't we already done that? What about all the final rites and rituals that we performed in Pune?"

Lucky Dad, Aarush thought enviously. *He has been able to get there sooner than I have.*

"I want to take a break before college for a year and go stay with Nana instead. And I know what your next question will be. I won't be fooling around but will make good use of my time. I've offered to volunteer at the Mahila Seva Gram orphanage. I'll teach the kids English. Nani used to, and since she passed away, Mom said there was a big hole in that area at the Seva Gram."

In this way, one word by careful word, Aarush finally divulged what he had been agonizing over during the last two weeks.

Amit was silent. He wasn't one to get excited or upset, or at least not one to react without really digesting the information. Aarush had rehearsed well for the barrage of questions that would follow.

"Have you...?" Pause.

"You must..." Another Pause.

"Hmmmm."

He had never seen his father speechless. Even more surprising was the fact that there was no sign of the usual round of rapid-fire questioning. Weird as it seemed, Aarush was actually disappointed by this fact. He had labored over the many possibilities and had come well prepared. He couldn't help but think that his strategy of playing the Seva Gram volunteer card was what had left his father speechless.

"Well," Amit finally said, taking a deep breath, "what if your Stanford admission comes through?"

"I thought about that. I will probably hear from some of the UCs soon too. I talked to my school counselor who told me that sometimes, under special circumstances, you can put in a request, and colleges are often willing to defer admission up to a year."

"Let me sleep on it. We'll have to talk to Nana too, though I can't see him being anything but happy." This was his father's way of saying yes.

Aarush's body finally relaxed, sheer relief. He had crossed his first hurdle.

"Dad, I asked him already. I'm sorry I didn't talk to you first. I wanted to make sure it was even possible before I got you all worried about it. I wanted to make sure the English tutor spot was still available at the Mahila Seva Gram."

Amit raised his eyebrows, apparently surprised by his son's take-charge attitude.

"That's fine, Aarush." He paused before adding, "Can I tell you how proud I am of you, son?" A smile replaced the lines that grief and worry had engraved in his father's face over the last few months.

••••

Aarush climbed up the stairs to his bedroom, feeling significantly better as he expected to. And lighter. He had just overcome a major obstacle. Not only had Amit not shown any serious resistance to his plans, it seemed he might even have his support. It was only after Aarush closed the door behind him and his eyes registered Lara's picture that any trace of relief about his father fled, replaced by a roiling in his gut.

While he had thought of his father as parental hurdle, Lara was the real stumbling block.

While he had been hoping his dad would let him go, Aarush worried that Lara might *want* to let him go.

And while he had expected Amit to put up a resistance, he was hoping Lara *would* do just that.

If she did, he would crumble. Cave in and change his plans.

But he knew Lara too well. She would rather crumble, collapse or cave in to her own sadness than stop Aarush from doing what he needed to do or felt compelled to do. So he was tormented, conflicted, guilty.

How he wished he had the confidence to believe and to reassure Lara that something good would come of this too.

••••

$\mathcal{S}$halini

Four

"It's ten years today since Ammijaan passed away," Shalini stated somberly. She had chosen her dates for the trip to India with the intention of spending this day with Marzia. Ammijaan had passed away peacefully in her sleep on November 16, 1998. Murtaza had been eight years old.

"I wish she had lived to see the completion of the construction of this building," Marzia sighed. She was standing at the gas range making *adrak* chai, or ginger tea.

Shalini jogged Marzia's memory, while she sat at the kitchen table, turning pages of *The Times of India.* "Remember, she was thrilled when Saleem brokered this deal with the builder to take over Joona Bangla as is, build this multi-storey building and guarantee her this four-thousand-square-foot penthouse."

"And the *suttarfeni* she distributed to celebrate?" Marzia smiled with fond memories. *Suttarfeni* was Ammijaan's favorite *mithai*, a lightly sweetened dessert made with very fine long fried noodles, white in color, resembling locks of an old woman's hair.

"Let's go get some from Bikaner Mithaiwala today. I haven't eaten it in years. In fact, since that day." Shalini felt a pang of intense craving for Ammijaan, more than for the *suttarfeni*.

"A meaningful way to celebrate Ammi's death anniversary," Marzia agreed.

"Oof! There I go again." The tea boiled over the edges of the saucepan, a predictable occurrence once Marzia and Shalini became engrossed in their conversations.

Marzia poured the tea into two teacups, first straining it through fine steel-mesh to separate the tea leaves. The rising steam brought wafts of cardamom and ginger fragrance that instantly opened up Shalini's blocked sinuses. "Mars, will you come to Pune with me tomorrow?" she asked. "Ouch!" Shalini had scalded her tongue again. The tea was steaming hot. After the very first sip she set the cup back on the table. She had never been able to drink at the temperature everybody around seemed to with ease.

"Sure, I'll go with you. Haven't met Uncle in a while. Anything going on?" Marzia was always quick to sense something was not quite right.

"I don't know. Something Pappa said last trip."

"What did he say?"

"Remember, I bought him a Nokia phone last time I was here? You know how he hates changing devices. But the one he had been carrying around looked more like a cordless."

"How can I forget? He complained endlessly about it," Marzia chuckled.

"I told him I'd make the transition easier for him. That I'd transfer

67

his contact list from the old phone."

"Good thinking. Although, wouldn't it have been better for him to do it himself? Isn't Uncle notorious for reading instruction manuals, fine print included?"

"I saw Ram's phone number listed on his old phone."

"What?" Instantly Marzia's brows furrowed.

"I know. That's exactly how I reacted."

"Maybe it was some other Ram."

"It said Ram Rugge. How many Ram Rugges have you heard of?" She could hear the irritation in her own voice.

"Did you ask him why?"

"Of course I did," Shalini said impatiently.

"Sorry, I didn't mean to upset…"

"No. I'm sorry, Mars." Shalini had every reason to feel exasperated, but it had nothing to do with Marzia.

"Maybe it was just a carryover from the previous phone."

"Marzia, there were no cell phones in 1991. There is no reason for Pappa to have his number."

"So what did he say when you asked him about it?"

"He looked surprised, for sure. But you know Pappa. He said nothing. Just mumbled something about having met him by chance and how they had exchanged numbers."

"Did you tell Uncle your happenstance meeting with Ram in Singapore?"

"No, I didn't. I couldn't. I didn't think it was necessary."

Shalini hadn't even told Marzia everything that had happened in Singapore, though it tore her up, withholding anything from Marzia or Kathy. But she just couldn't bring herself to share this. This was a deeply internal struggle. And Shalini was convinced that in sharing her turmoil with anybody, even Marzia, she might somehow wrong Ram.

And haven't I done enough of that already? she thought.

"So what's going to be different this time? Do you think he's going to tell you anything more about Ram?"

"I don't. It's not about that. I want to talk to him about Amit and me. How we've grown apart. And how I can't make it work anymore. My demons are getting the better of me, and I need to address them first. And I am not sure how Pappa is going to hold up. I need your moral support."

••••

It was almost four years ago over the Thanksgiving week in 2004 that Kathy and Shalini had made the Singapore trip with the kids. It felt so much longer...

In the picture of Aarush and Sophie she still carried in her wallet, the one they took after having breakfast with the Orangutans at the Singapore Zoo, the two of them looked so much younger. Aarush, thirteen at the time, hadn't yet shown signs of facial hair. A late bloomer, he stood a whole head shorter than Sophie. Who would have guessed that in less than two years, he'd be six feet tall and need to shave not once, but sometimes times twice a day?

Kathy's friendship and close association with Shalini assured one thing — Aarush and Sophie grew up like siblings. And like siblings, they couldn't have been more different. Not just physically, but also in temperament and interests. A fiery redhead, Sophie was bold, headstrong and obstinate. Aarush was painfully shy with an even disposition. Not one to throw tantrums, he stretched himself thin, trying to please the world. Where Aarush was academically inclined, Sophie was a natural athlete and had an inherent disinclination to schoolwork. She waited till the last minute, a perfect procrastinator. A constant source of friction between them, Kathy butted heads with Sophie over her incurable dallying.

"Why don't I have Aarush ask Sophie to do homework together?

Maybe that will help her stay on track," Shalini suggested when she realized it was driving Kathy over the edge.

"That would be a lifesaver. And it will definitely be more effective coming directly from Aarush," Kathy agreed. She let out a deep loud sigh and continued, "I've tried bribing her, encouraging her, even threatening to take away privileges, like sleepovers, movie nights with friends. I've cut her allowance. Once I even threatened to put an end to soccer. Nothing has worked. If Soph doesn't get more Bs than Cs on her report card, even a sports scholarship won't be enough to get her admission into college."

The study-buddy plan not only helped Kathy out of her predicament, it also ended up helping Aarush. Socially awkward and lacking confidence, Aarush had not made friends easily. His struggles in previous years with hearing difficulties and eyesight issues had turned him inward. It worried Shalini.

So it started with Aarush lending Sophie a hand with her homework. Sophie was so pleased with her improved grades that she couldn't stop showing off her best friend. Soon enough, word spread through school, and kids who otherwise would not have crossed paths with Aarush started asking for help with schoolwork. His gentle nature and his natural teaching prowess quickly resulted in friends. No wonder Aarush's confidence blossomed as did his friendship with Sophie.

So it came as no surprise to anybody that Sophie conspired to include Aarush in the Singapore scheme, such was the level of their comfort with each other.

Sophie put her brilliant negotiation skills to work in November 2004 when David, Kathy's husband, had to make a two-week overseas trip during Thanksgiving. Once she had her mother's okay, Sophie coaxed Aarush and Shalini (neither of whom really needed any coaxing) to join them for the week. Shalini liked the fact that Singapore was close to India, and she could combine a quick trip to her parents as well.

"Mom, I'd love to visit Nana-Nani. But I'll miss school if we go to India after Singapore. I'm not sure Principal Julian will be happy about that." Not one to miss school, Aarush sounded worried. And the school had been clamping down on extended vacations, so Shalini knew his concern was not without basis.

"Aarush, you can come back with Kathy and Sophie at the end of the week in time for school. Dad will be home by then."

"Great. That should work, Mom. I'm so excited." He wore the happiest smile that day. Aarush loved travel, one of her endowments.

••••

Kathy, Sophie, Aarush and Shalini landed at the Changi International Airport at 1:00 a.m. Sunday morning and took a cab to Frasier Suites, where David had rented a three-bedroom apartment suite for two weeks. He had already been in Singapore for a week when they arrived. The location of the suites could not have been more perfect. It was only a few blocks from the busy Orange Road Shopping District. In fact, every place was within a thirty-minute cab ride. All four of them welcomed the hot Singapore weather when they first landed. After all, they had just left behind the beginnings of a very chilly and cold fall in the San Francisco Bay Area. It didn't take more than one afternoon, though, for the tropical heat to take its toll. Not used to the humidity, Kathy and Sophie found the afternoons especially unbearable. At least Aarush and Shalini had experience with their regular visits to the Indian subcontinent. Kathy and Shalini compiled a list of places they planned to take the kids — the Singapore Eye, the Zoo, the Botanic Gardens, the Science Center with its water park and the Sentosa Island with all its various theme parks and attractions. Once they figured out that the afternoon blistering heat would be the perfect time to hang out at the pool or go to the water park at the Science center, they worked all the other plans around that fundamental requirement.

David offered to stay home with the kids a couple of nights that week, so that the ladies could go out and explore Singapore's varied food heaven. Kathy had researched the food scene in Singapore, specifically, the famed Singapore Food Festival that was held annually during the month of July. The food festival wonderfully profiled Singapore's diverse offerings of local and international food, as was evident from all their travel guides.

"Singapore, my dear Shalini, is unquestionably, the food capital of Asia." Kathy was single-minded in her focus, ensuring an unforgettable gastronomic experience wherever they went. "How can we ever truly understand the heritage and culture of a people without exploring and experiencing what defines us as human beings? Food, I say, is the essence of travel," she'd said with a certain fanfare.

Was it any wonder that Shalini's two best friends were so similar?

"This guide says we get the best chilli and black pepper crab at this seafood restaurant located near the Tennis Center. It's not far. Let's go, Shalini."

"What about me, Kathy? I don't eat crab," Shalini cried, though she really didn't mind. There was always something meatless to be found for a veggie like her.

"The seafood restaurant comes first along our route. I promise we'll head next to Casuarina Curry. The travel guide promises it to be a vegetarian's paradise. They serve the best *roti pratas* in town and are known for their signature super-fluffy bread. Apparently some trademark intricate folding and tucking of their dough. Yum-my."

"Sounds terrific. What should we wear?" Shalini asked as she went out to the balcony to get a feel for the temperature.

"I say, let's go strapless," Kathy laughed, following Shalini.

"In that case, I'll need to go shopping." Shalini hadn't brought anything exciting with her. The thought of going out, just the two of them, sparked in Shalini a desire to dress up.

"Good idea. Singapore malls and stores stay open late." They looked at each other in delight.

"It's 5:00 p.m. Let's head to Orchard Road. We can each get new outfits and then head out on our food rampage." Kathy had turned around decisively and was halfway back across the air-conditioned living room, calling, "David, Daaavid," even before the plan had time to register in Shalini's brain. Having made up her mind to fit in all that they had just talked about, Kathy felt the necessity to leave that instant. "Can you please take care of dinner for the kids?" Kathy knocked on the bathroom door.

"Sure, honey. No worries. What's the hurry?" David emerged from the bathroom, towel in hand, face still dripping, interrupted by his better half's urgent knocking.

"Sudden, evolving and mushrooming plans, dear." Kathy kissed his cheek and grimaced almost simultaneously, not expecting the wetness. "Pun intended," she added with a wink.

They grabbed their handbags, slipped into their sandals as they blew good-bye kisses to Aarush and Sophie, who, engrossed in playing Pacman on David's laptop, didn't so much as give their mothers a fleeting glance.

Shalini and Kathy took a taxi to Tangs, a large and popular department store, on Orchard Road. It took them no more than ten minutes to whisk a dozen outfits off the racks and head to the dressing room. Kathy and Shalini wore the same size outfits, but for reasons that were apparent only to them (they called them their fruit problem — one was an "apple" and the other was a "pear"), what looked great on one didn't flatter the other. But then, wasn't there a silver lining to every situation? They never had to sacrifice an outfit just so the other could have it.

Needless to say, they emerged from the dressing room and the department store in new strapless dresses, shopping bags stuffed with their old clothes. As they stepped out, a sprightly breeze greeted them, their spirits flitting in concert with the rippling hemlines of their new outfits.

Dressed in their newest fineries, Shalini and Kathy settled themselves at a corner table at the Casuarina Curry, ordered drinks and waited. Kathy studied the menu, unable to commit to any one particular *roti prata*. Watching the flat bread as it was made was almost as much fun as eating it. From their table, they could see their skilled "*prata*" man, much like a pizza man, transform small elastic dough blobs into paper-thin sheets, snapping and flapping them through the air with a few deft flicks of his wrist. He then folded and tucked them into squares, tossed them onto a hot griddle and, with generous quantities of butter, fried them to a golden brown, the outer crust crisp, the inner layers soft and fluffy, ready to be devoured with a splash of spicy curry gravy or sprinkled sugar for the sweet-toothed. Kathy practiced the *prata* jargon — *kosong* for plain *prata, telur* to have an egg cracked into the *prata* before it was folded, *plaster* to indicate an egg cracked over the *prata*, or what turned out to be their favorite, the onion-stuffed *bawang*.

Shalini's eyes wandered across the décor, unique to this part of Asia. Clean lines, a lot of bamboo. Contemporary art with striking mini-malism. What struck her as most surprising about Singapore was the jux-taposition of its rich, age-old, eastern-influenced buildings that included temples and museums beside a serrated skyline of glass-and-steel build-ings, similar to a western city. In all directions large picture windows framed lush tropical rain forests of the "Garden City," a feast for the eyes, and unique, the way foliage probed between soaring skyscrapers.

Shalini was enjoying the diversity of people at the other tables, soaking in the energy that seemed to be bubbling up from this sea of hu-manity, when she saw something that startled her. Her heart skipped a beat. A sharp gasp escaped her, and the hair on her neck stood up. She tried to take her eyes away, to breathe…but she was petrified.

"Shalini, what's up? What happened?" Kathy turned her face in the direction of Shalini's unblinking stare.

"Kathy…" Her voice was barely audible.

"What do you see? What's wrong?"

"That birthmark on the arm of the person…" Shalini pointed at a man, his back to them, just three tables away. He sat innocuously, a black T-shirt on a muscular back and a khaki baseball cap covering short hair. There was nothing out of the ordinary about him, except a disturbingly familiar birthmark.

"What about it? Looks like any other birthmark. Does it remind you of some island I don't recognize?" Kathy was clearly mystified.

At that very moment, as if on cue, the man stood up. He was done with his meal and getting ready to leave. He would have to turn around and walk past their table in order to reach the restaurant's only door. Gathering his belongings, he flung a jacket over his shoulder. Shalini was still gazing intently at him when his glance caught her eyes. His face remained expressionless. She couldn't tell if he had recognized her or not. But she had.

How can he not recognize me? She thought desperately.

The man hesitated, stopped in his tracks and looked at Shalini with immense curiosity. He looked away, it seemed out of politeness, only to return again to study Shalini's face. Suddenly, there was a flash in his eyes.

"Shalini," he mouthed her name.

Under her breath Shalini whispered, "Ram..." Their eyes locked. Shalini blinked, several times, half hoping that what she was seeing was no more than an apparition.

"Hi there. I'm Kathy. You guys know each other? I didn't know you had friends in Singapore, Shalini." Kathy's presence of mind helped Shalini snap out of the awkwardness and regain some composure.

"This is Ram," Shalini said still mesmerized, craning her neck up to meet Ram's gaze, "Do you...live here?"

"Yes. Been here for some time now." Neither his voice nor his gaze wavered. Shalini could not trust herself to the same degree of composure.

"Hi Kathy. Nice to meet you." Ram, still charming, extended his right hand to exchange a handshake with Kathy.

"I assume you are visiting then?" He turned toward Shalini and offered her his hand. Shalini flinched at his touch. A sudden rush of questions as well as memories overwhelmed her. Where to start? She felt paralyzed. It was also obvious from Kathy's expression that Shalini had a lot of explaining to do.

"Um, yes. What about you?"

"As I said, I live here," he repeated kindly.

"Oh, sorry. Of course, you did." Totally flustered, Shalini could not even assemble coherent thoughts.

"What made you move here?" She bit her tongue immediately. Why did she have to ask that? How could it matter what he was doing in his life?

"This is a long way from San Francisco." He turned beet-red as soon as the words escaped — his turn to feel embarrassed. And Shalini was flummoxed by his knowledge of her whereabouts.

We went separate ways ages ago, she told herself.

And Shalini had worked very hard to erase him from her mind, and life. To make a fresh start. To wipe the slate clean.

"How do *you* know where I live?" Obviously it bothered her that he knew more about her than she did about him.

"I heard from friends..." He stammered.

Shalini didn't give him time to recover. "Do you live alone?" His discomfort gave her permission and courage to ask questions that would otherwise have seemed nosy. She couldn't help herself. There was no wedding ring, but that meant nothing. Why was it maddening, not knowing what his relationship status was?

Quick to deduce where she was heading, he smoothly changed the subject. "No, I don't. Talk about the world being small. Of all the places, we meet in Singapore. After all these years."

"I know..." Shalini plastered a smile on her face.

"You look beautiful...just as I remember."

She was so glad that they had made that quick shopping trip.

His compliment left Shalini tongue-tied, the flattery totally distracting her.

Stop being vain...

Unfortunately, the harm had been done. She lost her train of thought, stumped after asking that one critical question. Another long disconcerting silence ensued.

"Let me write down my phone number. If you have time give me a call and we can catch up over coffee?" He scribbled on the back of a napkin, his eyes searching Shalini's expression for an answer. Thankfully, this brought an end to an excruciatingly uncomfortable situation.

"I don't think there'll be time this week. We are taking the kids..."

"No worries. I understand." At that point he left abruptly, all emotions draining from his face, but not before Kathy noticed all she needed to notice, to sense that there had been volumes spoken between the lines.

"Whoa, whoa, whoa. What was that all about?" Kathy's eyes danced with the anticipation of a juicy story.

"An old relationship. But it was over before I met Amit," Shalini offered.

"Over? You call that over? I don't think so."

"Oh, c'mon, Kathy."

"How come you've never mentioned him before?"

"I had put him out of my mind. That had been the only way to deal with our breakup. Wasn't easy." That part had been true. Shalini had been successful in banishing Ram from her thoughts over the last seventeen years. Almost. She lowered her eyes, her face was flushed.

"Shals, that was intense. You guys can fool yourselves as much as you want, but there's definitely unfinished business here." There was more truth to what Kathy was saying than she could have guessed. Shalini's head hurt. She felt an intense need for fresh air. She could barely concentrate on Kathy's conversation.

"Let's order the *pratas*," Shalini suggested abruptly, still too stunned to offer any further explanations to Kathy. What was there to tell anyway? She was reeling from the shock of the realization that after all these years, she had failed to reset her feelings. By a long shot.

And it irked her to think that he might be with someone. A girlfriend, or worse, a wife. Or whatever. Hadn't he said he didn't live alone?

What is wrong with me? Why shouldn't he be with someone? I'm married!

"...onion and cheese *prata*, we'll skip the mushrooms that you don't like, and then chocolate *prata* for dessert. What do you think?" Kathy regarded her expectantly. "You didn't hear a word I said, did you?"

The unexpected encounter with Ram had taken all breath, all sense out of Shalini. It threw her completely off balance, a balance that had been as daunting as wire-walking, but one that she had painstakingly kept to stay sane. How was she ever going to regain her equilibrium?

"I'm sorry. But yes, whatever you suggest sounds terrific," Shalini said, with genuine remorse for her lack of mental presence.

"Shals, are you okay? You don't look well."

"No. No, I mean, yes, I'm fine." Making a note to herself to dispose of the napkin in the first trashcan, Shalini crumpled and stashed it in her handbag. And along with it she stashed in the back room of her mind her out-of-control thoughts, determined to give Kathy her complete attention. Or at least until she found her way back to the privacy of her own bed, where she was certain sleep would evade her.

Why was the universe playing such a cruel joke on her?

She didn't need this encounter. A delicately crafted internal state, or semblance of one, had been ruined. One that Shalini had somehow managed to create on that day in December 1991 when she accepted Amit's proposal to marry him, and in doing so obstinately convinced herself that she had closed the door of her heart to Ram forever.

●●●●

That night, Shalini slept fitfully, as she had anticipated. She was transported back in time to a place she never wanted to experience again, running from it all these years. Of all the random events that might have happened, why did it have to be this one? But then, was anything in the universe really random?

••••

Ram was an architecture student at JJ, second year into the program when Shalini first met him. His father, a renowned industrialist, was a widower who lost his first wife when Ram was only five. His father, having remarried a few years after Ram's mother's demise, had been able to find a replacement for a life partner, but not one for a mother. What his second wife couldn't give his son in affection, Ram's father substituted with all the material luxuries, hoping to fill the gaping hole left in his child's heart by the loss of his mother.

In her very first week on campus, Marzia and Shalini had been introduced to Ram in JJ's college canteen through the ritual of initiation that existing students at JJ practiced on incoming students. Not a fun experience, it was usually easier on new students who had "friends" from the upper grades. Ram had taken an instant interest in Shalini, and Marzia always credited her for how smooth their initiation process (or ragging) had been. Ram had taken Shalini, and Marzia because of her association with Shalini, under his wing, and they had been saved the harassment customary for newbies. It hadn't taken Shalini long to figure out campus politics.

Ram was a social being, always surrounded by a satellite of friends. A generous heart, and a seemingly bottomless purse, attracted good as well as pretentious friends. Boy friends and girl friends alike. Essentially, a lost soul at the time, Ram had appeared to most people, Shalini especially, as one who lacked depth. It was a façade he preferred to present to the world, as he concealed his pain behind a superficial and frivolous exterior.

His reputation preceded him. A rich man's son, obvious from the lifestyle he led; a womanizer to be wary of, Shalini had been told by every girl on campus, and a spoiled brat — she'd been quick to judge. Not her type.

••••

"Oh, stop it, Shalini!" she scolded herself aloud, squeezing her eyes shut and, with them, hoping to squeeze her brain shut too, unable to silence both body and mind. But irrepressible thoughts continued to torment Shalini's heart.

••••

Her head warned Shalini to steer clear of the danger that Ram represented. She pretended not to be interested in anything about Ram, yet was all ears when friends gossiped about his latest escapades. He was known to have dated every girl on campus, at least once, but was also known to change girlfriends as fast as clothing. Shalini was determined not to be one of them. Or one *like* them. Ram made several attempts to ask her out, but Shalini avoided each successfully. That only encouraged him. Not used to having his proposals rejected, it seemed to intensify his pursuit. She was determined not to make a fool of herself by falling for his famously smooth, much-talked-about tactics. When he persisted, Shalini, feeling reckless, devised a plan that would give him a taste of his own medicine — revenge for all the women whose hearts he had broken.

If she had only realized what grave danger her own heart courted as she executed her scheme: agreeing to go out with him in order to be the first to break his heart, instead of the other way around.

"Do you have any idea where Ram has been the last few days?" Shalini asked Marzia when her efforts to reach him by phone failed.

"I do. He has been most nights at Jazz by the Bay, apparently drinking like there's no tomorrow. Did you guys have another breakup?"

"Why won't he answer my phone calls?"

"You aren't listening, Shalini. He would answer your phone calls if he ever went home. He seems to have reverted back to his old crazy self. What was it that you guys disagreed on this time?" Shalini was surprised by the accusatory tone in Marzia's voice. How had this become her fault?

"Well...I was mad. I said some things that...not very nice things..." Shalini confessed.

"Like what?

"I called him an emotional coward...among other things...he was terribly upset with me over that."

"And why did you do that?"

"It started last Monday. He was supposed to pick me up. It was getting late. I had to take a taxi because it was too late to make it by bus. As I came through the main gate, I saw him pull up in his car. Veena was with him. You can imagine how I felt." Veena was Ram's ex-girlfriend who lived in his building.

"What was his explanation? You asked him for one, didn't you?"

"Not exactly. I was livid. He made several attempts to approach me, but I was beside myself. I gave him an earful...and stomped off."

"Then what?"

"I simply left for Pune. Without telling him."

"So why are you trying to reach him?"

"Because on the train I found out from Ruchika the real reason Ram gave Veena a ride that morning was because her mother had to be taken to the hospital. Apparently she attempted suicide. Mars, he was just being a good friend..." Shalini said.

"Oh Shalini...how many times have I told you...give people the benefit of the doubt," Marzia spewed, clearly fuming.

"I know. That's why I called you. I need to reach him. I have to talk to him. And apologize. Which is what I have been trying to do for the last seven days." By now Shalini was cringing with shame.

"So what's your plan? What do you want me to do?" Marzia asked, sounding frustrated.

"Mars. He won't return my calls. I have called him a thousand times. I have left a zillion messages with his maid. I'm surprised she still takes my calls…"

"Classes resume on the second of January. When do you plan to be back?"

"I can't stand it anymore. I am coming back tomorrow morning, by Deccan Queen. Will you be home?" Shalini asked, more than anything seeking forgiveness from her best friend.

Shalini's heart had panicked when she found out why Ram had been unable to pick her up as planned. Away from Ram, her week in Pune gave her time to sort out her tangled feelings. Her plan had backfired. There was no way she would ever break up with him just to give him a taste of his own medicine. She was trapped in the very web she herself had spun. Her pretense of not caring remained exactly that — pretense. The thought that she was responsible for Ram's lunatic drinking haunted her and nearly drove her mad.

Why couldn't she let it go? So he would think she was a terrible person? Why did she care? Torn between staying the course or surrendering to her weakening resolve, she convinced her parents that she needed to return to Bombay for New Year's celebrations with her JJ friends. The next morning she boarded the train.

Shalini was standing in line for a taxi outside what was then called Victoria Terminus, or VT station, later renamed Chhatrapati Shivaji Terminus, or CST, when a pat on her shoulder made her jump out of her skin. She half thought someone was trying to steal her handbag.

"Hey!" she yelped.

"Shhhh, easy…it's me." A crumpled shirt, unkempt hair and an unshaven face greeted her.

What have I done to you, she thought even as her heart leapt with joy.

"I know I don't look my best…" he said, reading her mind. "I hope it's okay I came…"

"I couldn't be happier," she blurted, relieved to see him but curious how he knew.

Marzia.

"Here, let me take your bag," Ram offered. "I brought my car. And, don't worry, I've been sober since Marzia came to the bar and told me that you were returning today."

They walked without any further exchange of words. He drove toward Joona Bangla, his eyes focused on the road. In front of the gate he stopped and parked.

Shalini looked at him. "Thanks. For picking me up."

"It's okay," he replied, brushing it off.

"How's your nose?" Ram had broken it a few weeks earlier when a batsmen accidentally whacked him during a practice stroke, unaware that Ram was setting up stumps right behind him.

"The pain's all right. But it looks pretty bad. See," he pointed to it before adding, "I think I'll need to get it fixed." Then he offered a weak smile.

"I like it. In fact, I think it's your most attractive feature," Shalini gently traced the new crooked line of his nose, "after your eyes."

"Really? Why do you say that?" He studied her suspiciously.

"It gives you the exciting air of someone, like a boxer, who has touched danger."

He laughed.

They were silent again, the tension between them palpable. Shalini started awkwardly, searching for the right words, her resolve to appropriately apologize to Ram unwavering. "I'm so, so sorry. I didn't mean to hurt…"

Instantly Ram aborted her effort, leaning over and kissing her before she could finish her sentence. That didn't stop Shalini from completing her quest without words, as she approached with the ferociousness of a feline, her tongue continuing to seek his forgiveness, her fingernails leaving through his shirt unrestrained marks of fervent emotion.

"God, Shalini..." Ram pulled back a few inches, still holding her face in his hands.

"What?" she whispered, his stubble leaving her with a tingling stinging sensation around her mouth.

"Please don't do this to me again..."

I won't, she promised herself, *I won't, I won't, I won't.*

●●●●

The restraint that Shalini had been able to exert, from thoughts and feelings half-buried over the years, collapsed. Just laying eyes on Ram that day, her body remembered the vivid sensations he was capable of evoking in her. The tremor that travelled to her pelvis when his fingers traced her collarbone, caressing it back and forth, lightly, tenderly. All she needed was to rest her head in the crook of his neck, snuggle up beside him, his fingers absentmindedly finding the edge of her shoulder. And she would want to devour him. She had never again felt that shudder, that tingling his touch alone could elicit. Not before Ram, never after.

She could still taste him, their lips searching in passion, her tongue exploring his mouth with an impatient eagerness, challenged to find his true depth, and in doing so scoffing at her readiness to believe Ram's much-assassinated character.

Why did this encounter have to happen?

Her head spinning, her mind overworked, Shalini tried to put an end to the turbulent thoughts as one might cut off power to an engine. But it was as though she held the key to the ignition but lacked the ability to turn it off.

••••

Ram had in fact had many relationships. He neither denied them nor made excuses for them. Shalini's expectation was that once she executed her perfectly scrupulous plan, dating and breaking it off, she would have the satisfaction of making a point. A point misplaced in a false sense of feminine justice. And there had not even been a semblance of satisfaction.

Apparently, the universe had a different plan. It teased her for a while, allowing her to believe she was in total control of her destiny, and when she was least expecting it, it pulled the rug out from under her feet.

"Will you go out on a date with me. Just once? I'll guarantee you a good time. If you aren't a hundred percent satisfied, I promise you I won't ever ask again."

Ram had accosted her on his motorbike as she was walking to the bus stop, classes over for the day. He had already attempted to ask her out many times in past weeks, and so far she had successfully ignored him or skirted the issue.

She kept walking. He'd turned off the ignition and was dragging his bike, still talking.

"C'mon. How many times should I ask you? What else do you want me to do? Do you always play so hard to get?"

That stopped her in her tracks. Suddenly furious, she spun around.

"I don't play. Do you understand? I don't take such things lightly. All *you* want is to have fun. Today it's me. Yesterday it was Anju, Raina, Shaalu, Preeti, Rim Zhim, Jhil Mil and whoever. What about tomorrow? Will I be just another conquest? One more name on your long list of have-beens?"

Ram looked shocked. Secretly she enjoyed the effect of her words.

"Now what? Nothing more to say, huh? Clearly, no one has spoken to you this way."

Ram lowered his gaze, climbed on his bike and turned the key in the ignition before attempting to kick start.

She began to feel twinges of remorse —- she'd been mean.

"So I was right. This is just a game for you."

Another kick, but the bike only sputtered weakly. Ram futzed around various bike parts, resignation written across his face.

Her own guilt, Ram's astonishingly passive response to her scathing words and his futile efforts to bring his bike back to life composed such a sorry picture, that Shalini found herself melting.

"So that's all?"

She could have kept walking, she didn't really need to wait, but instead put down her heavy satchel.

"Here, let me hold the bike. It'll make it easier for you to reach behind the silencer."

In silence Ram accepted her offer.

"Are you going to say anything at all?" she asked.

Ram was crouched on the ground, his fingers gingerly feeling around the hot metal exhaust pipe along the lower side of the back wheel. He glanced up at her as she stood opposite him, holding the bike's handles. "You've already decided who I am, what I am and how I am without even giving me a chance. Will it make any difference what I say to you?"

"You won't even defend yourself?"

"And you'd believe me if I did?"

It was Shalini's turn to be speechless.

"Okay, I'll go out with you," she said after a long pause.

"No, you don't have to. You've already made it clear how you feel."

"No, no, really. I'd like to go out with you."

"Are you certain?" Ram asked, still down on his knees.

"Yes. I am," she said demurely.

"You are crazy. And confusing. What was that long tirade about? You even stunned my bike into silence."

Shalini burst into laughter. Suddenly she was overcome with shyness — not part of her plan.

Violating the very basis of her strategy, Shalini found herself undeniably and uncontrollably head over heels in love. And there was nothing she could do about it. There was no logic to it. But then, what place had logic in matters of the heart? Shalini was living proof.

••••

What she had not been prepared for was his attentive, gentle and sincere side, his affection and thoughtfulness that rendered him irresistible.

"Where's Marzia? She has been MIA." Ram was walking Shalini to her bus stop. Shalini was not yet comfortable enough to accept a ride home from Ram.

"She has been skipping afternoon classes to go home to help her mother with tiffin delivery. Their old Fiat finally gave out. Taking the taxi isn't cost effective. And it's too hard for Ammijaan to take the bus, so Marzia's doing it instead."

"Until...?"

"Until they figure out a transportation solution, I guess."

Ram walked along quietly, lost in thought. "I have an idea. Why don't I have my driver take their Fiat to my regular mechanic? He's not God but he's really good. And if the car isn't fixable, I'll find them an affordable used car."

Shalini was touched. Even though Ammijaan may have had sufficient resources to fix or replace the car, she wouldn't have known where to start looking for a good mechanic, let alone another car.

What she hadn't expected was how funny Ram was. Or that he loved to read, and talk, and eat.

All she had heard was that he drank like a fish and smoked like a chimney, loved fast cars, and spent money like there was no tomorrow.

What she discovered on her own was that he never said no to a friend in need, doling out money to the point that some took advantage of him. He wasn't naïve but he was generous to a fault. It was no wonder her head and heart had been at odds. Logic continued to caution her to protect herself from succumbing completely to this charming but fickle lover. Her heart, on the other hand, stubbornly clung to the hope that somehow for Ram she was different. That what they had was unique. That somehow, *Shalini* was different. And that, unlike his prior girlfriends, Ram truly loved her.

Wasn't it true that he had not dated anybody else since they got together? Even when he could have, when they were officially on a "break"? And, that every time they called it off, or rather, *she* called it off, it was she who was being fickle, not him?

Her yearning for him burned to the core, incinerated her. She was consumed by a fervor that soon became obsessive and addictive. Sometimes it frightened Shalini how much she longed to be with him.

"Ram, I can't do this anymore. I need to take a break. From us."

"But why? What happened? Did I do something wrong?"

"No, it's me. I feel suffocated. I feel I'm becoming too dependent."

"And the problem with that is?"

"If you don't call, I panic. I don't like it. I don't like what it's doing to me."

"Shalini..."

"I don't think this is healthy, being so out of control."

"Because..."

"I didn't..." Shalini stopped herself from blurting *plan it this way*. "Please Ram. I'm sorry. This is who I am. How I am. I totally understand if you get fed up with me."

Shalini was consumed not only by her intense feelings for him but also because of them. Desire for him made her feel alive as never before. It also terrified her that emotions possessed such powerful control over her. Seesawing between extremes, she struggled between surrendering unconditionally to passion or heartlessly rebuffing it. She agonized, even as she thought these thoughts, about the turmoil she had put them both through. Ram had wanted commitment, with or without marriage. She had wanted freedom and rejected any notion of conforming to social rules. For a while, in the early months of their relationship, and until Shalini finally caved in to her heart's calling, they continued on a volatile path, the consequence of her own conflict and indecision, not of anything lacking on his part. Ram had displayed unusual patience with her vacillating positions.

How had she not seen through him? Why had she been so stubborn? Why had she questioned his intentions, his love? Why had the universe not stepped in then, when she most needed it to help her?

In the end, it was the very intensity of their desires, the unyielding nature of their romanticism and her pig-headed idealism that left Shalini with a lifetime of regret. And guilt. But the realization came too late, long after she could have done anything about it.

Mulish rebellion led Shalini to resign herself to what she had vowed never to allow. True to her personality, she swung from one extreme to another. Finally she convinced herself that marrying Amit was the right thing to do, because she was determined that she would slowly but surely sever all connections with her past. After all, hadn't she already taken the first few painful but crucial steps?

••••

A tumult of thoughts had Shalini so agitated that she could feel the heat emanating from her as tears and sweat drenched her face and body. She sobbed without restraint, as Ram's face kept appearing before her eyes, grieving for a life that could have been. That *would* have been had she not thrown it away.

It was still dark out side, only 5:00 a.m. Finally Shalini surrendered to instinct, picked up the phone, and dialed the number scribbled on the crumpled napkin that she had been incapable of discarding, however hard she had tried. Ram answered almost immediately, as if expecting her call.

••••

What she told Kathy the next morning was that she *had* to meet Ram. Kathy offered to take the kids to the Science Center to see a special traveling exhibit. Shalini told Aarush she had a headache so that she could stay home and not accompany them.

Kathy didn't ask her a single question that day or even after. But, with her acquiescence, she demonstrated her support, reassuring Shalini that she understood.

••••

Kathy's acquiescence reassured Shalini that she could keep to herself what happened that morning she met Ram. That she took a cab to the address he gave her when she'd called. That when he opened the door, they stood there, like statues, on either side of the threshold, not knowing where to begin, drowning in the liquid of each other's eyes. That after what seemed an eternity, Ram's outstretched arm gently pulled her toward him as he closed the door.

That he had taken her to the kitchen directly.

That when he asked, "Have you had breakfast?" she had replied, "No. Ummm, yes. Maybe. I mean, never mind."

That when he offered her a glass of water, they sat across from each other at the dining table, awkward silence charged with palpable emotion separating them.

That she had felt compelled to ask something, anything to break the silence.

"You still build buildings?"

"If you still paint paintings."

That she had burst into laughter, just like old times.

That she remembered a lot of words were exchanged but retained nothing of consequence that she could recall.

That somehow it hadn't felt necessary.

That she had no idea how they bridged the distance between them and ended up in each other's arms.

That it had felt like only yesterday, not thirteen years since they last held each other.

That Ram had reached out and traced her collarbone, from the edge of her shoulder to the base of her neck, as he always had.

That it sent the same shudder through her body even after the long years.

That she melted instantaneously, surrendering to him as if it were the most natural thing, the only thing to do.

That, later, as she lay in his arms, spent after trying to make up for years of suppressed and unexpressed emotions, they had still not uttered a single serious word of explanation to each other.

That when he noticed her eyes rest on a picture of him with someone on his nightstand, he offered no explanation.

That she asked for none.

That, in fact, she needed none, reluctant to break the spell.

That she left, not long after, like a ghost, mute in that final moment, his chest wet with her tears and hers bearing now a hole where her heart had once been.

••••

$\mathcal{A}$arush

Five

$\mathbf{H}$is cell phone's ringtone played a favorite tune, "Right Round" by Flo Rida.

It was noon. Aarush was still trying to rehearse in his head how he was going to present his plan to Lara. He had texted her that morning, asking to meet her after school, at her house. He chose her place as the location because it would feel more secure than his for them. These days he preferred not to spend more time than was absolutely necessary at home.

He looked at his phone — Lara calling.

"Hey, bug?" Aarush answered, his heart beating rapidly, wondering if somehow she had already read his thoughts.

"Aar, have you checked your mail today?" She sounded excited. Happy excited.

"No, I just got out of class. How come you're home?"

"Mrs. Black called in sick. Since that was my last class for the day, I came home."

"What about the mail?"

"Aar, I got an acceptance letter from UC Santa Barbara. I have a feeling you have a letter waiting for you too. Please, please, please go home and check your mail. I can't wait."

He had planned to grab a sandwich from the cafeteria, then head to the library to finish an assignment due tomorrow.

"Okay," he said, not offering any resistance. And just like that, in the snap of a finger, he lost all appetite. This would be bad news.

Rushing to his car, he headed home. He kept his car running outside the gate and vaulted toward the mailbox. There, along with other innocuous mail, lay the dreaded envelope from UC Santa Barbara. Dreaded? At that moment Aarush was almost certainly the only senior in the United States praying for a letter rejecting his application to college.

He tore open the envelope, almost tearing the letter inside, read it, reread it, the tension in his body escalating. He felt like a pincushion, stung by an onslaught of inescapable worries.

He dialed Lara's number.

"And…?"

"It's a yes." Aarush tried hard to keep all inflection, all emotion out of his voice.

"Oh-my-God-oh-my-God-oh-my-God," she said.

"I'll be there," he said and hung up.

There was no way he could go back to school. He had to talk to her right away. The news of their acceptances was only going to make his announcement more difficult. For both of them.

So much easier to simply stay on course with the route Lara and he had mapped out so carefully over the last two years...

Wasn't this exactly what he had hoped for not that long ago?

What was responsible for his inexplicable, preposterous desire to throw everything safe out the window and risk losing the only emotional anchor he had left in the world?

"Aarush!" Lara shrieked from her patio.

She dashed down the pathway toward the garage door as he pulled his loyal '97 Accord in and neatly parked it in front of the garage door, buying time, every extra second he could garner.

She leaped into his arms, hugged him tight, her legs flailing behind her as his embrace lifted her off her feet. Then he lowered her back to the gravel and gently released her grip.

"Lara, we need to talk."

"Yes, we do." She could hardly contain her happiness, or suppress her ear-to-ear smile. When she grasped that his grave and incongruous expression didn't reflect her own excitement, she froze, her body stiffening in his arms.

"What is it?" It hurt to see her face, moments earlier beaming with joy, now drained of color, pale with worry.

He took her by the elbow and led her toward the house. "Let's go to your room."

"Aarush...What is it? *What* is it?" Her face, a gray cloud, wore an expression of impending doom.

Aarush closed her bedroom door and turned around, pulling her, almost roughly, into his chest and holding her tight, as if to make her an extension of himself.

Help me, God! he screamed in his mind.

Words eluded him. Nothing he had rehearsed seemed right. He thought he had prepared himself for every possibility. That was supposed to have been his strength. It was why career counselors had suggested he become a lawyer, because he could think ahead and predict the workings of people's minds. Wasn't that the tool he had used to manage his father?

What he hadn't factored in was his own emotional strength, or lack thereof. His voice failed him, his vocal chords paralyzed, mouth dry. Many times he had been told that he was a man of few words but this seemed neither the right place nor the right time for restraint.

Lara craned her neck to peer into his eyes. Her face became a blur, his eyes boring through her, as if focusing on some magic point inside her head would somehow transfer from his to hers what he needed to reveal, without words. Glancing away, he tried to compose himself, but not before Lara witnessed the anguish on his face. With uncharacteristic strength, she forced herself out of his grasp.

"*What* is it? What *is* it? Tell me, please..." she implored, her voice shaking.

What he was about to say would hit Lara out of the blue. There was nothing she could have done to prepare, nothing either of them could have done. Truly, he had tormented himself over this, agonized over how to break the news to her, suffered with guilt about his plan alone, so as to protect her for as long as possible.

Like a water balloon that finally bursts, splashing words randomly he blurted out his news.

"I can't go to UC Santa Barbara. Or to any UC for that matter. Listen, Lara," he pleaded, "how can I best explain this to you? I've decided to go to India. I have so many unanswered questions. I need to find answers. I need to understand what happened to Mom. I need to find closure. I *need* to go to India. It won't be long, I promise. Only one year."

No reaction from Lara. Just a blank look, a deathly silence.

"I'll defer my admission and join you next year."

The longer she was silent, the more desperate his words and assurances.

But she stared at him as if not understanding a word. As if in not comprehending them, they would somehow stop existing.

At last she said, "But you promised we'd go to the first UC that accepted both of us…"

"But that was before Mom died."

"Isn't there any other way? So we don't have to be apart? India's too far. One year is an eternity."

"The year will fly, I promise." Another promise. He hated himself for uttering those words.

"Can I go with you?"

It wasn't practical and she knew it. She went limp as a corpse in his arms, a chasm suddenly between them.

"I love you, bug. I love you," Aarush whispered over and over, pulling her closer, a feeble attempt to bridge the distance his pronouncement had opened up. He was desperate to make things right. But how?

Eventually, her body slumped, limp with resignation, buckling over. His arms still held her up, but barely. Straightening, her eyes squeezed shut, her fists tightly clenched beneath her chin, her torso rocking back and forth, forehead pounding his chest, she succumbed finally to the wrenching panic that his decision ignited. She sobbed into his T-shirt, and he hoped the flood would wash and heal the wound his decision had inflicted.

He discovered that he was crying too — for broken promises, broken dreams, broken hearts.

●●●●

"Lara, just a minute," Aarush called out. Lara was about ten yards ahead of him. He had dropped to his haunches to tie a loose shoelace, deciding to tighten the other one as well, to avoid another interruption. As he shifted his weight from the ball of one foot to another, he could feel the warmth of Lara's closeness. His eyes noticed the uneven thickness of the soles of her shoes, her right requiring a one-inch lift to adjust for the uneven lengths of her legs.

"Aar, I think I saw a coyote." Lara ran back to where Aarush had stopped, her breathing rapid as she pointed into the trees with a stick she had picked up along the way.

"No, really?" He couldn't see anything but he heard a rustle and some furious activity before it was quiet again.

"I can't believe we are just half a mile from my house. It's such a contrast."

They were barely ten minutes into their hike. They had decided to try a different trail that Saturday morning, the Rhus Ridge Trail, in the Los Altos Hills. A hectic week of submission deadlines had confined them indoors all week, mostly Lara's house, and they were feeling the effects of Vitamin D deficiency — sunshine. An avid athlete before the accident, Lara often missed the high she earned with long distance running. Hiking had replaced that passion, and her enthusiasm for the outdoors had rubbed off on Aarush.

If Aarush were asked to be completely honest, he'd confess that he didn't love hiking as he did swimming, not enough to do it by himself. He enjoyed the togetherness of hiking and that it was "their" thing. He saw a side of her nobody else was privy to. Lara's eyes lit up with wonder as she pointed out birds and animals and trees that he hadn't previously noticed, and may never have noticed, amazed not just by her comprehensive knowledge, but by the pleasure it brought her.

Aarush planted a quick kiss on the side of her knee before getting up, laces now secured with double knots. She grabbed his hand, and with a stick in the other, they continued up the steep hill.

"It feels ten degrees cooler here," he said, as he tugged up the zipper of his red cotton jacket. He had almost left it in the car, but was thankful now for having brought it. The thick canopy of oak trees, with sinuous branches interlacing as they reached up and sideways, like interwoven warp and weft threads entwined to form fabric, created a tapestry of boughs and leaves that shaded the trail.

97

"I know. It feels like we walked into an air-conditioned space. The car showed 70 degrees when we got out. This feels like 45." Lara released his hand, tucked the stick under an armpit, and rubbed her palms to generate some heat.

"Let's pick up pace. That should warm us up." Aarush grasped her elbow and started taking long strides.

"You have longer legs," she said, laughing through her complaint. He knew she was only pretending. Lara was used to competitive sports, routinely getting her heart rate up and running. This, unfortunately, had been ruled out after the accident. The treadmill was not inspiring enough, so the gym was out as well.

When their high school soccer team was announced the year she repeated junior year with Aarush, reality finally sank in when she saw that her name was not on the list, not even among the extras. She had even been able to try out. But it had been an in-your-face reminder for her that that part of her life had changed forever. On Sophie's suggestion, and to distract Lara, they had biked along Foothill Expressway, to the Stanford Dish, the first time for Lara and Aarush. It was there that Sophie trained with her team players through soccer summer camp, and she was excited to be their guide. Lara enjoyed it so much that hiking soon became their favorite activity, as other couples might go on movie dates.

The steep slopes gave her the desired exertion, and Aarush enjoyed exclusive time with Lara at her happiest.

"I'm glad you have that stick. We may need it to scare those coyotes." Aarush pulled her closer, mocking fear. She laughed again, the sound of it company to chirping birds, secreted in the lush foliage sheltering their rather precipitous climb.

"That's my favorite color," she said, pointing with her stick to the bark of a tree.

"Brown? I thought you loved green."

"No, not the bark, silly. The moss wrapping around the bark. It looks like neon green velvet." She instinctively reached out and ran her fingers lightly over the soft fabric of nature.

Ah, Aarush noted, *neon green.*

No sooner had the thought struck him than with it the realization of their limited time together.

"Aar, what happened?"

Aarush went silent.

"Um...nothing." He glanced away, unable to look Lara in the eyes. After all, it was his decision, not hers, that was forcing their separation. He had no right to indulge the sinking feeling in his gut.

They were halfway to the top of what seemed an almost vertical slope when the soil became so dry and loose that even their boots failed to hold onto the ground. Lara slipped twice, and Aarush had to concentrate with all his might, carefully putting one foot in front of the other, with just the right shift in body weight to prevent sliding backward. Their calves and thighs were on fire as they climbed the first half-mile, both relieved when they came to a brief level clearing where they decided to take a break.

The view from their little rest area was breathtaking, a little window that peered out of the dense wilderness enclosing the trail, reminding them of their proximity to civilization. Aarush pulled Lara close as he pointed down into the valley.

"Do you think we can spot my house? Yours is hidden in those trees right there," Aarush said, indicating a spot south of the Foothill College Campus.

"And there, is that the top of the Hoover Tower at Stanford? Lara, look! I think that's the Dumbarton Bridge, and that other one there, it's the San Mateo."

He was fascinated by how far he could see from their elevation. All at once an immense sadness overcame him. He wished desperately that there existed a place where he could stand with Lara and see far out into their future. A future that looked as beautiful, safe and secure as this expansive valley guarded by protective mountains with the waters of the Pacific ducking under the Golden Gate to form the Bay Area that he called home. That was what he wanted — to be at home, wherever that was, or would be, with Lara.

"I hope Shakutai still works at Mahila Seva Gram," Aarush said aloud.

"Who's that?" she asked. The wind was blowing her brown hair, strands randomly frolicking about her face, framing her sea-green eyes, bright and smiling, as they gazed eagerly at him.

"She was the lady who looked after me until I was five."

She looks so irresistible, Aarush couldn't help thinking.

Her cheeks were red with the exercise, light sweat moisturizing her skin and radiating health. He gave in to an impulse to lean down and kiss her, his lips planting one on her forehead, then as she closed her eyes, on each of her lids, and her nose, before they found her lips. He put his arms around her and hugged her, her face buried in his chest.

"What will your day be like in Pune? How often will you go to tutor?"

The breeze dried their sweat, cooling their bodies and causing them to shiver again. They stood there, letting the sun soak in, each one pulling the other tighter and tighter into the warmth of their closeness.

"I'm not sure. Marziamaasi called this morning. She said my admission at JJ has been confirmed."

Aarush prolonged their embrace, not wanting to let go, wishing the moment could last forever. He closed his eyes to etch the memory of the precious feeling, their amalgamated bodies swaying to the music of wind and birds, the moment now safely tucked into the deep recesses of memory. He would call it forth, when he would most need it, when he was far away from Lara, and alone, missing her.

"What does that mean?" she asked.

"That I will attend school in Bombay."

"So what happens to the English tutoring at the orphanage?"

"They need it only on weekends, so it will work out perfectly. I'll buy a monthly pass on the Deccan Queen and go to Nana's on weekends. It's only a three-hour train ride between Bombay and Pune."

"Where will you stay in Bombay? The dorms?"

"No. Murtaza said the dorms there are nothing like what we have in schools here. Marziamaasi was appalled with my suggestion to look for living accommodations elsewhere. She insists that I live with them. They have an extra room."

Lara released her embrace, lowering herself to the ground and pulling Aarush beside her.

"They all sound so sweet, don't they? I'd love to meet them some day." Her fingers started tracing circles in the dirt.

"Wish you were with me instead," she added.

"Me too. But you know what? I plan to connect a Vonage box at their place with a U.S. number so we can call each other for only $25 a month. We can talk as much as we want for as long as we want."

Looking away, she didn't respond.

"What?" he asked.

She shrugged. "Nothing."

"C'mon, Lara...we'll talk every day...you won't believe how fast the year will fly by."

"How can you be so sure?" she asked, her voice charged.

"I just...know."

"A year is a long time. Phone conversations can't replace being together. Besides, you promised..." she said, her face flushed, her disappointment palpable.

"I thought you understood. We've already gone over this."

"I *don't* understand. Why can't you go for just the summer? Why does it have to be all year?"

"But..."

"I just know this is not what I wanted. Not what I thought *we* wanted. I want us to be together. You've already lost your mom. Doesn't it worry you that you might lose me too?"

"Lara..."

"I want to be with you through this. I feel like you are pushing me away." She was sobbing by now.

"I'm not, baby, I'm not," Aarush whispered into her hair as he pulled her in and gave her a long squeeze.

Her shaking body gradually quieted down. Slowly he released her, gently brushing away her tears.

"Let's keep going so we can get back down before dark. That stick won't be enough to protect us from the coyotes," he said as he took her by her shoulders, turned her around and pressed her on playfully back onto the trail.

Lara wiped her face with the sleeves of her T-shirt. His affectionate teasing, a weak attempt to lighten her mood, was not entirely successful, but distracting enough for the moment.

Squirrels chattered along the trail sides, scampering across their path, with no real purpose it seemed, but to give them company. When Lara pointed out a banana slug, it wasn't with her customary infectious excitement. Her misery, in spite of her effort to camouflage it with random tidbits, was impossible to ignore. She continued pointing out new examples, but Aarush couldn't keep up with her as he usually did, her voice blurring in the background as his thoughts went up in volume.

I'm going to miss you so much, he thought, his heart burning like leg muscles taking on the challenge, the intensity of their respective climbs. *It won't be long*, he swore.

In a strange way, having experienced the finality of his mother's death alleviated somewhat the pain of separation from Lara. At least this wouldn't be forever.

"It will feel like forever," she said out of the blue, as if reading his thoughts.

●●●●

The next two months fled by. But for the time they spent apart in classes not common, Aarush and Lara tried to spend every waking hour together. As their senior year came to an end, his departure loomed. They pushed the thought out of mind as far as possible, avoiding any conversation about it. Lara helped Aarush with shopping trips to Target, Walmart and the Stanford Mall. They packed his bags. Then his father weighed them to ensure they were within the baggage limit.

The evening before Aarush was scheduled to leave, Aunt Kathy and Uncle David threw a farewell party. The house was overflowing with music, food and friends.

"Hey, Aarush, Sophie told me you qualified for the *Jeopardy* show."

"Hmm." Aarush smiled and nodded. His eyes darted across the room, following Lara as she carried around a tray of appetizers.

"Excuse me, I'll be right back." He slipped around the dining table toward the kitchen where he'd seen Lara disappear.

"Aarush, man, you clocked a helluva time last night! Will you be able to keep up in India?" Nate, his buddy from the swim team. Fortunately, all the team were heading off in different directions, college admissions safely tucked in their pockets. Aarush was the one heading farthest and with the least likelihood of keeping up with the sport. Aarush didn't answer. Instead, they exchanged their usual high fives, pumped fists and back slaps. Just then he noticed Lara out of the corner of his eye as she emerged from the kitchen. He looked at her intently, trying to catch her gaze.

"I'll be right back. Hey, Sam, show Nate around, will you?" Aarush hurried toward Lara, avoiding eye contact with anybody else, determined not to be interrupted.

She held a plate of Aunt Kathy's signature sautéed garlic asparagus. He grabbed her free hand and gave it a squeeze, feeling just a teeny bit relaxed when he saw her lips curl upward in the hint of a smile.

"Hey," Aarush whispered. "You okay?" She did nod, but barely, the tension in her face and body evident.

"Here, let me set the asparagus on the dining table." Aarush took the plate from her and wrapped one arm firmly around her shoulder, not wanting to share her with anybody else.

The rest of the evening passed in a haze. All he remembered was that he didn't let Lara wander more than arm's length away, and definitely not out of sight.

He vaguely recalled words like "wish Shalini was here" and "cows on the street" and "noise pollution" and "travel" and "palaces in Rajasthan," etc., etc. He also remembered making an effort to nod, to smile, to be polite so as not to offend well-meaning guests. When the evening was over, though, he couldn't have been more relieved. Fraught with emotions, he desperately needed to get away from the crowd, to hold himself together, and even more importantly, to keep Lara from falling apart.

When all the guests finally left, Sophie, Lara and Aarush helped clean up while his father, Aunty Amy Jo, Uncle David and Aunt Kathy relaxed and chatted, enjoying drinks in the living room. Sophie had had an intense day of training and looked totally exhausted; eventually, she escaped to her bedroom and crashed.

"Mom, can I have Aarush take me home? I'm tired."

"Sure, honey. I won't be long." They heard the adults break into laughter as someone remarked on the irony of the situation — teenagers turning in for the night, with the adults wanting to keep going.

In the car, Lara's left hand clutched his right as they drove the ten minutes to her house with hardly a word. Aarush pulled into the driveway and cut the engine. They looked at each other. He leaned toward her and kissed her lightly on her lips.

"Do you have to go?" she asked.

"Maybe I can wait until your Mom comes back." She smiled as he jumped out and opened her door. Then Lara let them into the house. They went straight to the couch in the living room, painfully aware of the gloom presented by their last evening together. They sat there, side by side, staring at the flat-panel TV.

"Remember?" she giggled suddenly.

"No. What?" Aarush teased.

She snuggled closer. "You lousy pretender!"

He turned her face toward him, and they kissed, gently at first, and then with urgency, their mouths conveying what words could not.

"How can I ever forget?" he said.

"Neither will Mom." They laughed, blushing at the memory of

being caught in the act.

They snuggled under the same red blanket of their first kiss. He ran his hand through her hair, caressing, as she rested her head on his shoulder. His fingers traced every feature of her face, forehead to collarbone, soothing her as he memorized, until finally she fell asleep. And, eventually, so did he.

Aunty Amy Jo did not disturb Aarush when she returned that night. She called to inform Amit. Aarush woke to the comforting sight of Lara cuddled against him on the couch, a heavier, bigger additional blanket thrown over the red one, both of them still fully dressed. He lay still, not wanting to disturb her, as rays of morning sun lit up the living room, the sound of birds, already busy in trees, and a loud rooster in the distance announcing a new day, a new chapter.

••••

There was bright light, not so different from the white flash that had just penetrated his eyelids, pouring through the only open door into a long dark corridor at the orphanage. He could see a cold stone building, Victorian, a remnant of colonial influence from more than a century-long British rule in India. There was a central courtyard for group activities, surrounded on all four sides by two stories of rooms. One of the north corner rooms, probably the coldest one, (and that was a good thing) was furnished to handle toddlers and infants. In the hot sultry weather, reliably unreliable power supply meant that ceiling fans were of no use. The stone walls kept the rooms reasonably insulated. The north location also ensured that the windows of the room did not fall in the direct path of the east-west trajectory of the sun. Aarush was still little, just under five, which guaranteed he had a few more months in his "deluxe room" before he moved up to live among the older boys in hardier surroundings. But Aarush never graduated. And for that he was the happiest of boys.

Through that diffused, white light pouring through the solitary open door letting into the corridor, his almost-five-year-old mind registered the clear image of a tall, moderately built woman bending forward, ducking to avoid the low door frame, crossing over the threshold and coming toward him. In fact, that image, including the halo around her head, remained etched in his memory. He compared the thrill that ran through his body at that moment, of finally being the one who had been "matched" akin to meeting an angel. His angel.

●●●●

What he remembered from that day was probably not exactly what happened. Probably not even remotely close! But did it really matter? He preferred remembering it the way his mind had saved it, colored with time; had even brightened some colors as they faded over the years, sometimes even taking liberty to modify the lines. Always making the picture more romantic, more magical, as if from a movie. Transforming and merging what was and what he wanted until he could no longer distinguish the original lines from the new. Why would he care to judge what he did with this picture? It was his to own, after all. So what if he had exaggerated, romanticized…even dramatized to suit his needs?

The only fact that mattered was that he had got what he had longed for, hungered for. Even prayed for.

He fixed his eyes on a distant point in the empty blue sky, out through the oval window, high over the clouds, thirty thousand feet above the earth, as he remained lost in thought.

●●●●

Aarush had made his entrance into the world at 3:13 a.m. on May 27, 1992. There had been complications during his birth mother's pregnancy that had resulted in a premature delivery — eight weeks.

It was around the time when he turned thirteen that he remembered his mother, Shalini, and a conversation. She told him all she knew about the story of his first four years, 330 days of his life. It wasn't much but enough to entrance.

She had started with the place of his birth. "You were born in Sassoon General Hospital in Pune to a wonderful young girl, Rushi." He concentrated with all his might, not wanting to miss a word.

"She was only fourteen, a child herself, not in a position to care for another child."

"Even Shakutai remembers how your mother used to frolic and play in the courtyard at the Seva Gram, innocent and carefree." Shakutai, the *ayah* responsible for the children during their waking hours from 8:00 a.m. to 5:00 p.m., had been Aarush's primary caregiver at the Mahila Seva Gram, which, in addition to being an orphanage, was also a women's shelter.

It provided a safe place for pregnant unmarried women, a serious taboo in India, to live through their pregnancies, the intent being to provide medical care and proper nutrition to both mother and child. These expectant mothers would usually stay on until they delivered their babies and then another week to nurse their newborn, before they went home to rebuild their lives, the babies left for the Shakutais of the world to nurture while social workers tried to place them with prospective adoptive families.

"I know she loved you, Rushu, and she did what she thought was best for you." His mother's face had been hard to read as she spoke. Aarush didn't feel much sadness over what she had been telling him. On the contrary, he was so thrilled to be Shalini's son that he could only think how thankful he was with his birth mother's decision. But, why was his mother so emotional? Distraught even? Aarush never felt much curiosity about his birth mother. Or father, for that matter. He always credited this to the fact that he had been blessed with such a wonderful family.

"Ma, aren't you happy that she gave me up for adoption? How would I have ever met you and Dad?" Aarush nuzzled closer to her and buried his face in her chest.

He had few, but definite, memories of his time at the orphanage — Shakutai singing songs and telling stories always in the local Marathi dialect, usually about characters from the *Mahabharata*, but mostly with the intention of painting a picture of a magnificent *Aie* ("mother" in Marathi) or a mother figure. He remembered her chanting a *Ganpati stotra* to them and having them repeat it after her, one phrase at a time.

"*Ganpati tuzhe naav changale...*" He still knew that one by rote.

"You must pray to Lord Ganesh for protection and Saraswati for knowledge."

As she related stories about deities to the children, the face of every heroine in Aarush's mind was always the same. That of Shakutai.

After all, she was nearest to any form of divinity. She predicted their hunger and provided for their rumbling tummies, changed their soiled clothes, even dispensed teaspoons of a sweet, magic, pink syrup that pretty much took care of all discomforts ranging from tummy aches to raging fevers. Aarush was her biggest fan.

"Most importantly, pray that you'll all be blessed with an *Aie*," Shakutai insisted. And so he did.

Not that he had any idea at the time exactly how a mother would be any different from what he already had in Shakutai. It just seemed that this mysterious person held some exotic, much desired but unknown, almost sacred quality that made her worth praying for fervently. For the most part she remained an elusive fantasy, especially when they overheard the older boys in the courtyard, who seemed less willing to believe Shakutai than he and his friends.

How was it that he had been matched to Shalini and Amit?

"The minute I laid eyes on you, I told the social workers that I wanted you," his mother said. "It was love at first sight."

Aarush knew this was not true. Still, he liked to believe that he was none other than Disney's Woody from *Toy Story*, the chosen one from among equally wonderful, beautiful and lovable toys.

There was nothing unreal about the fuzzy, hazy, glowing halo surrounding his mother's face. Or the dreamy quality of her features when

Aarush gazed at her. And that Aarush would be the first to acknowledge that his eyesight had something to do with it. Premature birth and low birth weight had caused a condition called Retinopathy of prematurity (ROP), leaving him with poor vision. Shalini was to find out later that ROP's definition included terms like *disorganized growth of retinal blood vessels* and *retinal detachment,* that this disease was at Stage 2 in her son's eyes, and that this in itself didn't cause blindness but could lead to it.

More important to her was the fact that it was the same disease that had afflicted her favorite musician, Stevie Wonder. Something about that knowledge reassured her, and she mentioned it proudly, as if it was a feature and not an affliction, that somehow placed Aarush in an exclusive group with certain privileges. Privileges that she hoped would not hold her son back from leading a fulfilling and prosperous life.

Recurring ear infections had left Aarush hard of hearing. He was barely making coherent sentences at an age when his peers were exchanging long stories, true and invented. Because of his hearing limitations, he only picked up occasional words. Most of reality lived in his head. His mother liked to call it his inner vision, a loud, busy and vibrant inner vision.

When Aarush looked back, what everybody thought were his handicaps turned out to be his greatest assets. For how else would he have enjoyed the special treat of having his new, exclusively-for-him Mom, hand-hold him through all the surgeries and therapies that he would need during the first decade of his life?

Because she was such a hugger, her heartbeat was what Aarush first became attached to. He swore that he could tell her heartbeat from anyone else's, even blindfolded. It had a distinct cadence. He could still hear in his head the even, reassuring rhythm of her heart as she held him close after the first surgery to insert ear-tubes. He also remembered how it had picked up pace and started pounding when she was told he might have to go through this surgery several times, many times. He could still bring to mind the feelings that arose when her voice suddenly went from being dull and far-away to crisp and loud, as he awakened from the effects of anesthesia. Abruptly his world was scary, intimidating, unfamiliar. His mother, realizing what had happened to him, was the first to lower her voice. She hummed his favorite lullabies, rocking forward and back, soothing him. How desperately Aarush wanted her to do that…right here, right now.

And her smell…how could he best describe it? It was a sublime combination of the first drops of monsoon on parched earth and the scent of bursting *mogra*, or jasmine, with a touch of citrus. Earthy, woody, fragrant, and fresh. When Aarush had his first laser eye surgery, they had patched his eyes. So, even as he came out of the effect of general anesthesia, he couldn't see a thing. But he could smell. How comforting it was that he could recognize her scent anywhere.

••••

"We have started our final descent to Chhatrapati Shivaji International Airport," a gentle Korean-accented voice crackled over the PA system.

It was almost 2:35 a.m. Bombay time, and the entire economy class cabin had been fast asleep. In that silence, even this soft voice was jarring enough that it pierced through Aarush's deep sleep and with a start brought him back to reality. It had been a twenty-hour flight from San Francisco, with one refueling stop in Seoul, to Mumbai. Or Bombay, as his mom insisted on calling it.

The white fluorescent overhead lights that simultaneously flashed on along with the FASTEN SEAT BELT signs, penetrated his heavy eyelids. He squeezed his eyes to suppress the glare, felt his body stiffen with frustration, even aggravation. He wasn't quite ready to leave dreams of his mother.

As the stewardess gently nudged him to stow the tray table in preparation for landing, Aarush tried desperately to weave frayed images together, willing his mind not to let go of the warm comfort they gave him, resisting the panic that he found himself drowning in, his chest tightening with the dull weight of emptiness.

"Please fasten your seat belts, stow your tray tables and make your seat backs upright…"

Aarush stubbornly clenched shut his eyelids. Longing to return to the safety of the world that he had just left behind.

As much as he tried, to weave the few lingering images from his dream, he failed to hold onto them. He would have other dreams, but not *that* one.

••••

As Aarush collected his meticulously filled customs form, his backpack and his thoughts, he couldn't shed the one thing he did not want to carry with him — the searing pain in the recesses of his heart.

How could this have happened to him?

To be cheated of not one, but two mothers in a single lifetime?

"*Kamsanmida*," Aarush said, thanking the Korean stewardesses as he stepped off the plane onto the arrival ramp.

••••

.

$\mathcal{S}$halini

Six

"Shals, anything you need? I need to go back up one last time. I forgot to get the box of *suttarfeni* we picked up yesterday for Uncle." Marzia deposited her handbag, two pillows and bottled water on the back seat of Saleem's Innova, which he had graciously offered for their Pune trip, and hurried back to the elevator. Ahmed, their driver, was going to take them to Pune. As much as Shalini prided her own driving skills, she was relieved, for once, not to have to deal with the chaos of Indian traffic, which was like dodging random bullets.

"No, I don't think so," Shalini called out as Marzia disappeared into the waiting elevator.

"Ahmedbhaiyya, can you show me where the cigarette lighter receptacle is?"

Shalini opened the passenger side door and scooted into the seat. Using the car adapter, she plugged her iPod into the car's stereo. With music taken care of, pillows to cozy up with, roasted peanuts and *chevdo* to snack on, Shalini and Marzia were ready for their four-hour drive on the expressway from Bombay to Pune.

Shalini called her father while she waited in the car for Marzia to fetch the forgotten *mithai.* "Good morning, Pappa, we are just leaving Marzia's place. We should be there by 9:30 a.m."

It was only 5:30 a.m. They had decided to leave early in order to beat commute traffic. But it was taking Marzia longer than seemed necessary to come back down. Shalini glanced at the cell phone for the time, then back at the elevator door, wondering what could be taking her so long. Finally Marzia emerged, her brows drawn together, forehead creased in a frown.

"I have had it! It's impossible to leave these grown men and trust them to take care of themselves, let alone the house. The way they behave, you'd think I was going away for a month. Ahmedbhaiyya, *chalo chale,*" Marzia said, obviously aggravated with Saleem and Murtaza. Shalini bit her lip to suppress a smile. Marzia had some more colorful things to say, and Shalini let her vent.

"Let's stop at the Food Mall after the first toll booth. I love the chai and *vada pav* they sell." For Marzia food always worked as a great distraction.

"I'm looking forward to the *kharvas* at Dutta's on the way back. Too bad it's hard to cross over from one side of the expressway to the other. I could eat that both ways. Saleem and Murtaza give me so much grief about my food whimsies when we travel together, that I've stopped asking. I'm so glad you invited me to go with you." Aggravation gave way to a smile at last.

Ahmedbhaiyya pulled out of the parking lot and onto the main road, following Bombay's coastline along their left, the sky still dark, as if the sun were unwilling to rise from its bed where the sky met the Arabian Sea, reluctant to reach its sleepy arms to shine over the west coast of India. They had their windows rolled down, and as the car gathered speed, the warm breeze laden with the familiar smell of fish blew through their hair.

"Lovely, isn't it?" Shalini asked. "Bombay seems like such a different place at this time of the day."

In the distance fishermen unloaded their morning catch. Within minutes the car left behind their flurry of activity, rolling along the semicircular Marine Drive, rhythmic strobing of street lamps still, the "Queen's Necklace," as it was still fondly called, the name reminiscent of pre-independence colonial times.

"It does. It's a hardworking city. Only those determined to slog can survive here. And the rules apply to one and all — actor, laborer, stockbroker, or even a beggar," Marzia mused.

"How is your latest project coming along?" Marzia was now into interior decoration, which, as satisfying as it was creative, came with its own people challenges.

"What can I say?" she sighed. "The Singhania's oldest daughter-in-law is the most difficult client I have ever had. If it weren't for the fact that times are slow right now, I would be more than happy to have her out of my life. She can't make up her mind. On anything. I have to keep giving her new options, more choices. There's always some reason why it's not quite right — too bland, too gaudy, too expensive, not the color she likes, or not something she thinks she will like in ten years. Who in the world thinks like that? Ten years? C'mon, I said, get serious, ma'am. Do you even know if you'll be alive in ten years?"

"Nooo, tell me you didn't really say that?" From what Marzia herself had described as typical client relationships, this would definitely signal the end of one. And Saleem worked for the Singhanias. Not only were the Singhanias a renowned business family, they were also well known as terrible employers. Shalini shuddered at the thought of the consequences of Marzia's probably justified but imprudent outburst.

"No, I didn't. But was I glad to tell her I couldn't be reached for the next few days!" Marzia laughed, clearly amused by the look of horror on her friend's face.

"Phew," Shalini chuckled, reaching for her phone, which had just beeped, indicating an incoming text.

"Who's that so early in the morning?" Marzia looked at her wrist-watch.

"Amit," Shalini said, "checking in. I told him we were planning to drive down together."

"Does he know why?" Marzia studied her, curiosity written on her face.

"No." Shalini inhaled deeply and looked away. "It's mostly in my head. Yes, we have been arguing, disagreeing. At times it's been really ugly. But it's me who wants out. Even though, in the heat of the moment, it seems more like Amit's the one who has had it."

"Have you guys considered counseling?"

"He won't hear of it. He doesn't think we need it. I have tried it for myself."

"And..."

"I don't know, Mars. I wish I had an easy answer. Any answer."

"So what *is* it that you want to talk to Narsi Uncle about? I thought you had a plan."

"I have questions for him first." Shalini knew she was deflecting, but what else could she do?

"About what?"

"Memsaab, it will be a good idea to roll up the windows now," Ahmedbhaiyya said. They had just entered the Dharavi slum area. It was past 6:00 a.m. and the streets were busy with hawkers setting up their stalls. The area was infested with a combination of little street urchins and homeless kids — the former industriously selling miscellaneous wares, like plastic flowers, soft felt squares to wipe down windows, cheap plastic toys or other such items while the latter, naked and disheveled, often with malnourished babies hanging from their little bony hips, begged for alms.

Shalini's chest tightened at the sight of one boy trying to sell cheap photocopied versions of popular English novels as their car came to a stop at a traffic light in the heart of Dharavi. The persistence with which he knocked on the glass separating them unsettled her. She tried, unsuccessfully, to break eye contact with him to indicate her lack of interest in his wares. Instead, she went into a trance as she stared into his beautiful evenly tanned chocolate brown face with its perfectly formed features — a sharp regal nose even plastic surgery couldn't possibly reproduce, a slender neck holding up a perfectly round head topped with an unruly mop of dirty, sun-bleached hair, eyes twinkling in anticipation of a sale — a book he most certainly could not have read.

"Shalini, about what? What answers could Uncle have that you don't?" Marzia mechanically rolled up her window, not letting Ahmedbhaiyya's interjection interrupt her train of thought.

"Oh, Mars, I don't know." Shalini's eyes moist, palpitations reverberating in her chest cavity, she continued to look at the little boy, intrigued by his perseverance. She rolled down her window.

"*Kitne ka?*" Shalini asked, pointing to Dan Brown's *The DaVinci Code*, a poorly reproduced, pirated copy.

Ahmedbhaiyya expressed his disapproval, "Tsk tsk, memsaab, others will follow, and whom will you refuse?"

Shalini fished out a few hundred-rupee bills and exchanged them for the copy from the little fellow's hands. Quickly she rolled up the window, unable to take her eyes from his face, now transformed with joy, having made his first sale of the day. As their car rolled past the light and his face slowly receded, the throbbing in her head, booming drums, deafened her ears, the start of a splitting headache.

"Do you know how many times I have looked into eyes like his and wondered if that's what happened to my child?" The physical pain brought some relief from the emotional turmoil that she would inevitably have to face head-on.

"The orphanage? My baby? What happened after? Pappa is the only one who knows." She could not any longer maintain her fragile composure. "My nightmares follow me with more vengeance than my shadow.

At least my shadow leaves me alone at night."

"Oh Shalini, don't do this to yourself." Marzia gathered Shalini into her arms. "Shush, dear."

She held Shalini and rocked her until they were well out of the slum area and approaching the tollbooth guarding the expressway.

Eventually, Shalini broke the silence. "I have tried to be a good wife. I gave up everything that mattered to me, that I believed in, that I wanted to be, to redeem myself from my biggest mistake." She spoke in a low voice, though she was beyond care of being overheard by Ahmed-bhaiyya or anyone else for that matter.

"You *have* been an amazing wife. Why, you've supported Amit through his research and teaching career, taken on all responsibility around running the house, paying bills, and even raising Aarush, pretty much single-handedly. Amit is gone twenty days of every month, and that's been the case for as long as I remember."

"But that's not everything that defines a good wife. I haven't been able to love him like I should, Marzia. I have tried, though, I really have."

"It seemed like you guys bonded tremendously after Aarush came into your lives, didn't you? I have seen you happy with him, Shalini."

"But don't you see, that's exactly the problem, Mars. We needed Aarush to bring us closer. Now Aarush will leave soon, and then what?"

"That happens to all of us, believe me. Marriage is hard work, any way you see it."

"Hard work isn't what I'm scared of. Even in adopting Aarush, I failed Amit. He always wanted to have kids, and many kids. But I couldn't."

"That was because of medical reasons. You couldn't control that."

"No, Mars. It wasn't medical. That's what the world thinks. You think. Or rather assume."

"What do you mean?" Marzia stretched the seat belt in order to turn around in her seat, as if her entire body needed to receive whatever Shalini was going to reveal next.

"We had a hard time, intimacy-wise, especially the first few years. I talked to you about it, remember?"

"I do. But then I thought it got better. When you stopped talking about it, I thought..." Marzia's voice trailed.

"Talking didn't help change anything."

"You mean you never had medical issues around getting pregnant?"

"No."

"Then..."

"I didn't lie to anybody, technically," Shalini said, even as she realized she was contradicting herself. "I came back from the doctor one day. The doctor said there were no obvious reasons for infertility. That we'd just have to do it more often. Increase the frequency. Time it. Those were our early days together. I was uncomfortable talking about it. Besides, I had a hard time making myself do it, Mars. I was still deeply in love with Ram, and it was a struggle. Misplaced loyalties." She felt herself blush with shame as she recounted the tale.

Marzia took Shalini's hand in hers. "My poor baby."

"Amit somehow assumed that I *had* a problem. I just went along with it. It was convenient."

"Go easy on yourself, Shalini. You do understand that even though you didn't quite explicitly tell him what was going on in your brain, there *was* a problem. It may not have been a physical problem but definitely an emotional one."

Sweet friend, Shalini thought. *She loves me so much, even now, she's willing to rationalize and support my untruths.*

"I couldn't get pregnant because I didn't want to."

"So, you decided to adopt? Is that how you convinced Amit?"

"Actually Amit brought up adoption. My depression was undiagnosed. There were weeks when I'd lay in bed, unable to accomplish even basic tasks. Amit insisted it didn't matter to him how we built our family. He was a huge support during the adoption process. In fact, he did all the paperwork and all the running around that was required. "

"I wish you had talked to me, Shals," Marzia said, gently stroking Shalini's hand.

"You were so far away. I didn't want to worry you. You had your own life to deal with. Besides, I had already put you and Ammijaan through enough."

"Don't say that. We did what anybody in our place would have done. It was a mistake. A mistake that came from a place of love."

"Mars, it's been a mistake that I have paid for with a lifetime of lies. And guilt. In trying to make it right, I have made it all wrong. That's the problem. The only thing that has been right in my life is Aarush. He has helped me, at least partly, redeem myself."

"Oh, my poor baby, I can't bear to see you suffer like this." Marzia's eyes brimmed with tears.

The car stopped and with it their conversation. Ahmedbhaiyya had pulled into a gas station to fill up the tank. The Food Mall was right around the corner, but both Marzia and Shalini had lost their appetites.

"Ahmedbhaiyya, can you please bring us chai in takeout cups?" Neither of them wanted to get out, gloom weighing them down.

"The only thing that would give me any relief is to know that my baby was adopted by a good family. I just want to know that he is doing fine. I think of him every single day. I had all of one week to spend with my baby, to nurse him and hold him to my breast, before I signed papers giving up all rights to him. I begged the orphanage to let me give him one gift, his name Rushi — a sage. I knew he would need the strength of one."

Every muscle in Shalini's chest clenched in pain. She reached her trembling hand into her purse and found an anti-anxiety pill to swallow with the chai that Ahmedbhaiyya had just handed. There were men, women and children, lining up separately outside the restroom at the gas station, chattering and laughing, a stark contrast to the somber stillness inside the car.

"Is that how you picked Aarush's name?"

She nodded. "I want to know that Rushi's fine."

"Shals, you have to have faith and believe that to be true. You know that we can never find that out. The Indian legal system keeps all adoption information under seal."

"I know. But maybe Pappa knows or he can use his connections. This same Indian legal system is also ever willing to break rules if we bribe them with enough money."

"Is that what you plan to talk to Uncle about?"

"Yes. And about Amit, of course."

"What exactly are you going to tell him about Amit? That you can't have sex with him?" The ludicrousness of the idea produced laughter. And they laughed uncontrollably until tears rolled down their cheeks. It was the kind of laughter that fed itself and generated more, not because of inherent humor but because of the emotional relief it provided in a hopeless situation that seemed to offer no easy solution.

●●●●

Their Innova rolled along the high speed, six-lane expressway, a newly constructed private venture that had reduced the commute time between Bombay and Pune from between five to thirteen hours, to a three- to four-hour drive through the Western Ghats. Bombay was located at sea level, with most of the densely populated land reclaimed areas of the Arabian Sea. Pune, on the other hand, was south-east at an elevation of 1,840 feet, and required an ascent on two-lane roads through beautiful, picturesque mountains, often through tunnels, where invariably children in passing cars hooted at the top of their lungs to hear their own voices echo back.

Which end of the five- to thirteen-hour spectrum your trip ended up taking depended upon different calamities, natural and man-made — frequent landslides triggered as much by rain during monsoons as by controlled rock explosions, part of continuous road construction; road accidents because of sleep-deprived and drunk drivers alike; stalled old lorries, like stubborn mules, plonked down in the middle of the road, having finally given up, pushed beyond their limits; or something as innocuous as an overenthusiastic father, deciding, with no thought or awareness of the consequences, to randomly park his car to admire the view of the valley while his children delighted in feeding droves of monkeys that sat along the low wall bordering the freeway. The new expressway, a toll road, had been a godsend.

Soon after their car started the climb into the Ghats, Marzia fell asleep. This was Shalini's favorite part. She leaned against her window and gazed into the mountain range, trying to find shapes in the outlines of each peak. When the car reached the top, they passed through the town of Lonavala, a favorite picnic location halfway between Bombay and Pune.

Ram and Shalini came here often on his Yamaha motorcycle, mostly on Fridays. After finishing their week's submissions, leather jackets zipped up to their necks and helmets secured on their heads, they'd leave early in the afternoon and arrive in Lonavala when it was still daylight. They'd park the bike at the base of the trail called Duke's Nose, the name derived from the shape of the precipice, which from a distance looked like a distinguished hooked nose.

They'd sit there, side by side, as Shalini looked forward to her favorite part of the outing — Ram reading poetry to her. Poems he'd written himself or the week's selection from among his favorite poets. There was an Emily Dickinson poem...

> *I'm nobody! Who are you?*
> *Are you nobody, too?*
> *Then there's a pair of us — don't tell!*
> *They'd advertise — you know!*
>
> *How dreary to be somebody!*
> *How public like a frog*
> *To tell one's name the livelong day*
> *To an admiring bog!*

Before starting their climb back down to the bike, they'd stand together and watch the sun set behind the mountains in the distance, Ram sheltering her with his hands crossed over her chest, his chin atop her head, as Shalini faced the valley, her arms wrapped backward around his waist, the sound of crickets growing louder, wind sweeping their hair in all directions, bringing with it the sweet smell of earth moistened by light showers.

It was the very same spot where she revealed to him that she was pregnant with his child, and unknowingly changed the course of their lives altogether.

As usual, it was a Friday. July 1990. Ram had just finished reciting a poem he'd written. Shalini had a hard time concentrating because she was consumed with thoughts of how to announce the conception of this life, his child, inside her. She was nervous. She knew this was no small deal. But strangely, she felt no fear. Instead, she was bubbling with excitement. To her romantic, impractical self, this was the ultimate sign laying to rest all doubts she had about her love. Their love. Whether naïveté or simply the optimism of youth, Shalini was convinced her news could only make Ram exuberant. As she was. Of the many possible scenes she fantasized, Ram getting on his knees to proclaim eternal love and propose marriage was part of every single one of them.

"Ram, I have something to tell you," Shalini said. They were sitting on a bench-like rock protrusion halfway up the trail. He stood, laying the sheaf of papers on the grass at their feet and using a small rock as a paperweight. Then he sat back, this time straddling the rock so that they faced each other. Shalini took his hands in hers and gazed into his eyes.

"Ram, my love, I am pregnant." There. Short and sweet. A smile on her face. Her heart racing in anticipation. She squeezed his hands, waiting for a reaction.

"What?" he gasped after a long moment, dropping his hands from hers. "Did I hear right?" He stepped down from the rock, Shalini followed him.

She almost giggled in relief. He looked so cute, frazzled and flabbergasted. She felt delighted by his sweet surprise.

"Yes, darling, you heard right." She reached again for his hands, a slight uneasiness growing inside her when he didn't immediately respond. She needed him to hold her, to be in physical contact with her. Finally, he pulled her close.

She could not have been happier. Together they would figure out how to proceed. Yes, they would have to deal with her parents. And his.

She had gone over and over it in her head, how she would break the news to her father.

"It's all going to be fine," Ram murmured, her face pressed against his chest.

"I knew it would be once I told you," she said, not looking up.

"How far along are you?"

"Not sure. I haven't been to the doctor. I don't know whom to see. I've missed my period. Twice."

"So it's possible you are not pregnant?"

"No. I have never missed my periods, ever. They've been regular since I first started at thirteen."

"Then we need to see a doctor as soon as possible." Shalini hugged him tight, moved by his concern.

"Will you go with me?" She was scared and embarrassed and hadn't told a soul yet. Having told Ram, she finally felt safe.

"We need to find somebody who is reliable and trustworthy. I don't want you to be in any danger," he said, anxiety lining his voice.

"Why would I be in danger? Women get pregnant all the time. What we first need to do is talk to our parents. They'll help us find the right doctor."

"We shouldn't tell anybody, Shalini! We can handle it between the two of us."

Ram's body was now tense, and Shalini started getting exceedingly nervous.

"How can we handle this on our own? I can't hide a growing abdomen for too long."

"There will be no growing abdomen. We need to find a doctor who will perform a safe abortion. We can't possibly have this baby."

"What? What did you just say? Did I hear right?"

"Is there even a choice?" he said.

Shalini went cold as ice. *Oh, Ram,* she thought, *how can you even think this way?*

It was the last thing she had expected. She said nothing. Fear squeezed her heart as her thoughts desperately flipped, like a fish on a dry dock, in disbelief. How was it that Ram and she could think so differently?

Shalini had no recollection of what Ram said beyond that point. His voice was a buzz in the background. A surreal feeling enveloped her — disbelief, desperation to stay true to herself, her desires, her instinct . One thing clearly nonnegotiable — there would be no abortion.

Shalini took a few steps away from him, trying to make sense of what had just transpired, when her foot accidentally knocked the stone off the papers. She heard a fluttering, but neither Ram nor she made any attempt to stop the pages from flying away.

And with them, just like that, they watched their innocence disappear too, their lives taking a turn they could have never foreseen.

Shalini couldn't say what it was that disappointed her most: Ram's apparent lack of strength to take responsibility and follow through the consequences of his actions, or the cold-hearted way he had minimized the culmination of their love, as if it were merely an error made on a blackboard that could easily be dusted off.

The following months were a blur. Shalini confided in Marzia, who convinced her to take Ammijaan into confidence as well. Ammijaan drove Shalini to an OB-GYN and got her started with prenatal care. She began to wear the *abaya*, on Ammijaan's suggestion, to hide her growing belly. Shalini couldn't fail to notice whispering neighbors gossip about her apparent conversion to Islam, but this was far better than rumors about an impending pregnancy out of wedlock.

The life growing in her womb and the subsequent changes to her body preoccupied Shalini's mind. In the beginning, Ram visited regularly. She remained immovable in her decision to carry her pregnancy to term, while he was convinced otherwise. They argued bitterly, so much so that Ammijaan eventually prohibited Ram from visiting. Then he sent letters to her begging and pleading her to see his point of view.

Darling Shals,
I love you. You have to know that. Please understand this
has nothing to do with our love or my intentions to marry

you. We are just too young. I need to settle down before I can commit to a family. I am a child myself and so are you. How in the world are we going to look after another child?! We can get through this, Shalini. Together we can. Please listen to this one request. Please, Shalini. If you love me, you will do this for me. There isn't much time left. Please trust me. Trust my love. Our love. Don't be stubborn.

Love always,
Ram

When pleading didn't move her, he seemed to hope that threats of a permanent breakup might work. She'd get calls from a drunken Ram, simultaneously proclaiming his love and questioning her love for him. But she remained defiant, refusing to communicate with him unless he relented. She felt profoundly let down. She could still hear his last words ringing clear.

"You continue to believe this is your decision exclusively when truly it is *our* decision," he pleaded

"I carry the baby in my womb, if you don't know that already," she said sarcastically.

"You are beyond stubborn. Your romantic choice to have this baby has consequences that I don't think you have quite thought through."

"Let's just agree to disagree on this point and leave it at that. If your romantic choice is not to support me through this, just leave. I do have free will, you know."

"You want freedom? Then have it. Just know this was your choice and yours only." Then he stomped off.

Her maternal instincts were stronger than ever and she was determined to move mountains to protect her unborn child. Sacrificing her love for Ram seemed a small price to pay for the love she felt for the life that was completely dependent on her. Looking back, she was amazed by her resolve and clarity, against all logic, to go forward with what seemed an irrational and supremely idealistic decision.

Shalini's limited attendance, apparent conversion to Islam and

Ram reverting to his old wild behavior patterns only fueled people's imagination, rumors of their breakup circulating the college campus.

That October Shalini came up with an excuse not to return home to Pune to celebrate Diwali. When, under another pretext, she didn't show up during Christmas break, her father surprised them with a visit. She should have known. He landed at Ammijaan's doorstep minutes before Shalini and Marzia returned from campus. They had stopped to eat *pani puri,* her pregnant state having prompted relentless cravings for *chaat,* savory snacks served on roadside carts, which made them later than usual getting home. That fateful December evening when Shalini's father rang the bell, Ammijaan opened the door expecting to see the two young women.

"Why are you girls late today?" she asked, unlatching the chain lock before completely opening the door.

"*Namaste Behenji.*"

"*Hai Allah, Salaam Bhaijaan*, what brings you here?" Ammijaan exclaimed, holding on to the door, as if she had turned to stone.

"You don't look pleased to see me?" Shalini's father smiled as he suggested she invite him in.

"Oh, I am so sorry. Please come in. The girls should be back soon."

Not minutes later, Marzia, dressed in a pink *rida* and Shalini in a floral one, walked in.

Shock and disbelief covered Shalini's father's face. His jaw dropped and he was speechless, if only for a minute. "Is that why you don't want to come home anymore?" he whispered, his head in his hands as he sat down, unable to bear the distress of what he was witnessing.

"Pappa," Shalini cried as she ran to him, kneeling before him. "This isn't how it appears." A tight knot formed in her stomach, competing for space with her baby, as she uttered her beseeching words.

It wasn't how it appeared. It was much worse.

••••

Shalini glanced at Marzia as she snored lightly, mouth open. How Shalini longed for such peaceful sleep. Tears rolled silently down and she made no attempt to hold them back.

••••

Shalini confessed every sordid detail to her father, still kneeling, her face buried in his lap, sobbing uncontrollably, as she blurted everything, including Ram's desire to terminate the pregnancy and her inability to see eye to eye with him. Ammijaan kneeled by her side, her hand firmly around Shalini's shoulder, lending her strength with her unconditional support. Narsidas sat silently, his expression indecipherable.

Shalini was certain he wished she had converted to Islam. In comparison, it would be a far easier to explain, less painful problem to have.

After a torturous silence, he turned to Ammijaan, "Have you taken her to a doctor?"

"Yes *Bhaijaan*. I sincerely apologize for keeping you in the dark but hope you understand it was not for me to tell. As I promised you, I have taken care of Shalini. I did what I would have done had it been Marzia in the same situation."

••••

"You do understand that your decision to have the baby is honorable but not practical. I wish you had confided in me sooner. It's too late to do anything now," her father said bluntly.

"What do you mean?" It came as another unexpected blow to her when she realized he might actually be insinuating his agreement with Ram's suggested course of action.

"Do you understand what pressure you put your mother and me

127

under with your choice? An unwed mother is not something you can pull off. Definitely not in Pune. Not even in Bombay."

"So what are you suggesting?" Fear numbed Shalini. She couldn't believe what she was hearing.

"We need to find a place where you can safely, but discreetly have the baby and then give it up for adoption."

"Give my baby up? Are you serious? You can't make me do this!" Shalini became hysterical. Now she really was falling apart. *Not you too...*

"Shalini, do you have any idea, any understanding of reality? You may think you are immune to social rules and expectations, but your mother and I are not. Can you even imagine what we will go through if this becomes common knowledge? And have you even thought about the child? He'd be..." she had never seen her father this excited, this afraid.

To Shalini, there was no difference between terminating her pregnancy and giving up her child. She felt beyond horrified.

Her confidence began to crumble as she gave it deeper thought — how could she support her child? She realized in no time how unrealistic it was to give birth, to take care of a baby, to earn money to support a child single-handedly, all without her parents' help. She felt responsible for putting her parents through enough turmoil with the choices she had made. How much further could she test their strength? She labored over all possible options to keep her baby. When she ran out of ideas and realized that the most selfless act would be to give the baby up for adoption, it practically drove her insane. After hours of counseling and pregnancy-safe depression treatment, the doctors helped pull Shalini together, and guided her into making the stoical decision, apparently in the best interests of her child — to give him up.

The wound left by that single choice festered for the rest of her days.

●●●●

Her father approached Mahila Seva Gram in Pune, both a women's shelter and an orphanage offering a safe place for unwed mothers to deliver and give up their babies for adoption.

Freedom was what Ram had given her, and she had asked for it. But why did it feel like abandonment? The line between freedom and abandonment was fine indeed.

She spent the last month of her pregnancy in the cold stone building of Mahila Seva Gram, writing and sketching to fill the gnawing emptiness of desertion, eventually giving birth to Rushi at Sassoon General Hospital on January 29, 1991.

As far as school officials in JJ were concerned, she was recovering from a severe case of jaundice and would return after six weeks.

••••

The sudden silence of the car's engine stirred Shalini back to consciousness. Somewhere after crossing Duke's Nose, she had dozed off. Marzia also sensed the end of the journey and woke up.

"Are we here already?" She stretched her arms and rounded her back like a cat, a yawn escaping her. Ahmedbhaiyya had stepped out and opened the trunk, and was unloading their luggage. Shalini checked her cell phone.

"It's only 9:00. We made it in great time. Pappa won't be back from his walk. He wasn't expecting us so soon."

"Does Vimalbai still come? I am dying to have her *adrak* chai," Marzia said.

Shalini went to the front door, only a couple of steps from the gate of the Mistry house where their car was parked, and rang the bell.

"*Aga baya tai, ya aat ya, kashe ahat?*" Vimalbai welcomed them with a huge smile, wiping her brow with the corner of her *saree pallo*, as she swung open the door for them.

"Vimalbai, how are you? I want your chai, Vimalbai" Marzia

squealed in delight, and her infectious excitement immediately filled the house. Vimalbai got busy in the kitchen, happy to indulge.

"Pappa *yeteelach ata.*" Father wouldn't be long.

"I'll call him on his cell phone and let him know we're here," Shalini declared.

"*Phone visarlet ghe-oon zayla, tai.*" Vimalbai pointed to the cell phone that he had forgotten to take with him. Just then, as if on cue, it started ringing.

Shalini crossed over to the living room coffee table and glanced down to see who might be calling.

Probably her aunt at this time in the morning. She would surprise her and answer the phone.

But at that moment Shalini registered the caller's name flashing on the phone. It stopped her in her tracks.

••••

Aarush

Seven

"Hello, is this Ms. Lara Vintner?" Aarush said, using a gruff serious voice.

"Yes, this is. May I know who's calling?" Lara answered, her polite voice lifting his spirits already.

"Uh…I am Mr. Mackey from Whole Foods, ma'am."

"What is this regarding?"

"I am sorry to inform you, uh…Ms. Vintner," Aarush had a talent for impersonating voices, "but are you aware that we have video surveillance cameras in all our stores?"

"No, I don't. I mean, I didn't think…um…I don't…do you?" He could sense from Lara's voice that she was clueless where this conversation was taking her, but that she was nervous all the same.

"Yes, we do. And unfortunately, we have several recordings taken over many days, that show you've been stealing fruit."

"Noooo, I haven't!" Her voice went faint, as if she were passing out at the accusation, almost forcing even *his* wicked heart to confess at that point.

"Yes ma'am, you have. The cut fruit all over the store is for tasting only. The recordings over these different days indicate that you have been rather generous with your tastings, haven't you?" He sounded wonderfully authoritative, even to himself.

"I can't believe this! You are actually accusing me of stealing when all I have done is taste your fruit. I…I…" She was furious. He imagined her face red with anger, the green centers of her big wide lovely eyes shining with fury.

"When we counted the number of peach slices alone, it seems that you've consumed five entire peaches. Even your conscience will agree that five peaches can't be called tasting. Especially when our recordings have noted that you never once bought anything yourself."

"My mother buys all the fruit. I can't believe this is happening. I love your peaches. And Aarush had warned me to stop. Oh, what am I going to do?" Lara's voice had crescendoed.

"Ma'am, please calm down. We can make a settlement and prevent this from getting ugly. We want to offer you a chance to come in and pay for what you have consumed before we file a case with the police." Barely managing to keep his voice level, his tone composed, Aarush was tearing up with laughter.

"Okay, I will." Her voice was so forlorn he couldn't take it anymore. *My sweet peach, Lara,* he thought with affection. "And you've been bloopered in the morning! This is Don Bleu from K101.3," he said with flourish, imitating their favorite FM radio host.

Pin-drop silence. He wondered if he had lost the call.

"Lara…"

"AARUSH…you rascal…I am going to kill you!!"

"Am I good or what? I got you bad, didn't I?" he said, without any pretense at modesty.

"I can't believe you'd do this to me!" She was still adjusting to the shock, unsure whether to be relieved that she wasn't actually going to be charged with theft, or mad with Aarush about his practical joke.

Luckily for him, she softened and chose instead to be delighted to hear from him. It was his first call to her using the Vonage connection he set up in Murtaza's bedroom, eight long days without her voice.

"Can I save this number you called me from?"

"Yes, bug. This is it. My dedicated Lara line."

"So…tell me. How is it? How are you?"

"So far so good. I miss you, terribly. Other than that, all's terrific."

"Let's do the One Good–One Bad thing that we decided."

On the morning of his departure to India, when Aarush had awakened to find himself on the Vintners' living room couch with Lara in his arms, he hadn't budged, wanting her to sleep a little longer. When she finally stirred, she was so overcome with emotion that she clung to him like a koala, refusing to let go. He didn't want to let her go, either. But the phone rang, and Aunt Amy Jo hollered down that Amit had just sent a reminder. Aarush had to leave immediately if he was to make his flight.

In order to take Lara's mind off of his impending departure, Aarush came up with a modified version of his and Sophie's True-False-True game. There was no guessing in the One Good–One Bad game, but he hoped this would give them both something to think of for each other, to help take their minds off of the missing.

"Great idea. You go first," he suggested.

"No, you go first."

"Okay. Let me see. My One Good is that I get to have Murtaza as my roommate."

"You mean you don't have your own room?" She sounded surprised. And why shouldn't she be? They all had their own bedrooms in

Los Altos, taking such things for granted.

"But that's the good thing. He is so cool to share it with me. It doesn't bother him at all."

Aarush had been genuinely touched by Murtaza's absence of any displeasure at having to share his already limited real estate. The room had no space for more than one twin bed, so in anticipation of Aarush's arrival, Marziamaasi and Murtaza made plans to mount a bunk on top.

"So does that mean he's there right now as you talk to me?"

"No, bug. He went downstairs to talk to Tulsi. Pretended like he had some work. He understands. He's cool."

"Who's Tulsi?"

"She's a second-year student at JJ. If you ask me, I think Murtaza has a crush on her. He swears otherwise. He's using me as an excuse to pursue her. Says he'll have her show me around, et cetera, et cetera." Aarush smiled.

"Is she cute?"

"She is. But nobody could be cuter than you, my bugga." It amused him to hear jealousy in her voice.

"Okay, what about the One Bad?"

"I went on a forty kilometer bike ride this morning. With a group called Pedal Pushers that Murtaza bikes with — first time without you."

Lara was quiet.

"Your turn now. Tell me your One Good–One Bad for this week?"

"Well...my favorite red blanket was drying in the sun two days ago and Penny tore it. Accidentally, of course. She was chasing a squirrel. Flipped a prickly cactus pot that pulled on the blanket and ripped it!"

"Uh-oh, that's too bad," he said, fond memories of their first kiss and many subsequent ones witnessed by that blanket flashing down his private memory lane.

"But I now have a good reason to pull out the moss-green chenille blanket that you gave me before you left. It *is* my favorite color. And it's from you." Her voice gradually dropped to a whisper and he could barely hear her last few words.

"That's good. What's your One Good?" He could hear her sadness and wished he could hold her.

"That is my One Good, dummy." She laughed good-naturedly, raising his spirits.

"Aar, Mom's waiting in the car, and I have to go. She's taking Soph and me to the city to watch a matinee of *The Fiddler on the Roof*. When can we talk again?"

"I will be in Pune every weekend. I start English tutoring at the orphanage next Saturday. That rules out weekends because the Vonage connection is in Bombay. How about your time 7:00 a.m. every weekday morning? That's 7:30 p.m. weeknight for me, at least until daylight savings ends in fall."

He could hear the distant honk of a car on her end of the line.

"Okay. I'll wait for your call. I have to go. Love you."

"Love you too, bugaboo."

He continued to lie in bed, staring at Murtaza's sky-blue ceiling, glad to have finished a conversation on the upbeat with Lara. Surveying the room, he tried to embrace it as his new home. Marziamaasi had hired a carpenter to construct an identical twin bed like Murtaza's, which they planned to stack on top of his, a makeshift bunk bed only without a ladder. The carpenter had shown up only twice since he had been paid for the job two weeks ago. A not-quite-finished bed lay in a pile of sawdust downstairs, in the Batliwalas' assigned parking space. Aarush was both amused and amazed at the unflinching confidence displayed by Marziamaasi that the missing carpenter would show up, however much it frustrated and upset her everyday that he didn't. Until then, Aarush continued to sleep in their guest room. Plans around Aarush permanently occupying the guest room had changed after Saleem Uncle's mother suffered a stroke, very recently, and would need to be cared for once she was released from the hospital. She would be staying in the guest bedroom.

"Hey, Aarush. A couple of my friends were planning to meet up at Chowpati corner for *kulfi*. Do you want to go for a ride?" Murtaza peeked into the room to see if Aarush was done with his call.

"I'm beat, Murtaza. Maybe another night?" He was still getting used to the late-night social scene in Bombay, where it was completely routine to start an evening at 9:30 p.m.

"No problem, man. See you in the morning. I'll drive you and Tulsi to JJ."

Aarush smiled knowingly at Murtaza.

"What?" He asked, blood starting to color his cheeks.

"I can take the bus, you know. " Aarush raised his eyebrows questioningly. "With Tulsi," he added, to cause Murtaza further discomfort.

Murtaza had offered to give Aarush, and hence Tulsi, a ride every day of the previous week, and Aarush noticed he had become a convenient ruse in Murtaza's courtship.

Murtaza mock-wrestled him as Aarush rolled with laughter.

"I'm cool, dude. Use me as much as you want," Aarush said as Murtaza pummeled him with a pillow.

••••

Murtaza attended St. Xavier's College and was in his second year of the bachelor of arts program. An active member of the IMG (Indian Music Group) at their college, he spent most of his time participating, organizing and furthering the cause of Hindustani and Classical Music among the youth. What that really meant was that Murtaza almost never attended any lectures.

So it wasn't strange that he had offered to drive them on Aarush's first day at JJ. Marziamaasi, Tulsi and Aarush folded their bodies into Murtaza's little Maruti and headed to college an hour before classes were scheduled to begin.

"Joshikaka, Joshi-kaka..." Marziamaasi called out, rolling down her back window before the car had come to a halt. She was trying to get the attention of a man in uniform — khaki pants and shirt with a white Gandhi or Nehru *topi*, the signature cap made of *khadi*, pointed in the front and back with a wide band and named after Mahatma Gandhi, who introduced it during the Indian Independence movement, and which was further popularized by the first post-independence prime minister, Jawaharlal Nehru.

The man turned around to reveal a face etched with lines, surprising Aarush, for his straight posture and quick gait had given the impression of a much younger gentleman. Joshikaka squinted in their direction. Immediate recognition lit up his face and he almost ran toward Marziamaasi.

"Marziabeti...is that you?"

"Yes, Joshikaka. Look who I have here. This is Shalini's son, Aarush."

They had all just stepped out of the car and were standing crowded together.

"Shalini's son?" His smile lost its brightness, his eyes became wistful.

So he knows about Mom, Aarush thought.

"Yes, Joshikaka. Aarush has come from America. He is going to study here at JJ."

"*Arre wah!*" Joshikaka, pulled Aarush's cheeks affectionately, bobbing his head with joy. Aarush was both touched and a little surprised.

"Aarush, this is Joshikaka."

That much Aarush had already figured; he waited politely for Marziamaasi to further enlighten him.

"I have known your mother and this Marziabeti...since they were your age..." Joshikaka reminisced, patting Marziamaasi on her back. "I have even watched over Murtaza when he was that little..." he continued, leveling his hand against his knees. He turned to Tulsi, who was trying hard to vanish in the background.

"Tulsibeti, I was wondering why I didn't see you on the bus today. I didn't realize you knew the Batliwalas," he said.

Tulsi was tongue-tied. She and Murtaza blushed, and Aarush realized then that except for him, their budding romance was a secret.

"Tulsi is going to show me around campus," Aarush said to ease the awkward silence.

"Here, come with me. I *have* to show you something. It's hanging in the principal's office. Your mother's award-winning painting. Come… come…" Joshikaka took hold of his hand, pulling Aarush along, and the rest followed.

It was still before hours, and the campus was relatively empty. Joshikaka unlocked the principal's office and let them in.

There, behind the principal's desk, hanging on the wall, just below the ceiling, and framed in a detailed and intricate rectangle, was a picture of two fishing boats anchored in calm waters. But there was nothing calm about the thrashing strokes, the thick vivid paint depicting the sky and the shore.

Aarush had seen many of his mother's paintings over the years, even been inspired by many, but he had never seen one that was so raw with emotion. The brush strokes were definitely tender and gentle around the boat, even the reflections exuded tranquility. Everywhere else they changed their nature completely. It seemed as if she may have simply reversed her brush and used the hard wooden tip, letting her emotions take over, etching into the paint an impossible entanglement that was like a ball of wool gone awry.

What was she feeling? Seething passion? Or seething anger?

He missed her so keenly in that moment that his insides hurt. He wished to ask her questions that he used to when they'd analyze and discuss each other's paintings. He felt her unmistakable presence in that room, and simultaneously her undeniable absence from this world. His esophagus tightened and it was difficult to swallow his own saliva, let alone voice any reaction.

"Beautiful…" he heard Tulsi's voice, almost a whisper.

"*Marve'l*, that's what she called it," Marziamaasi added, her voice thick with emotion.

●●●●

That night, Marziamaasi set dinner in traditional family style, a three-foot diameter stainless steel plate resting on a low stand, so that they all sat on the floor and ate from their designated section of that single large plate.

"We don't sit cross-legged, Aarush. We fold our feet under us to one side, like this…" and she demonstrated how, "…to show respect."

"Here, take a pinch and put it on your tongue," Murtaza said as he offered Aarush a little crystal bowl with white powder that he soon realized was salt, a customary way to begin the meal.

"Whoa, do we start with dessert?" Aarush said in delight when Marziamaasi brought out his favorite, sweet, creamy rice pudding topped with nuts and cardamom.

Everybody, including Uncle Saleem, Murtaza, Tulsi and Marziamaasi laughed. Aarush noted that Murtaza had somehow successfully convinced Tulsi to stay for dinner.

"Yes, dear, we do. We alternate sweet and savory courses," Uncle Saleem explained. "Wait till my Ammi comes home from the hospital next week. She'll tirelessly instruct you on how not to create *nadi-gallis* in the *thaal*," he continued.

"What does that mean?" Aarush asked, unsure as to what rivers and lanes could mean in the context of food on a large plate.

"Oh, all it means is when we eat courses like DCP, Shalini's absolute favorite by the way, we shouldn't let soups and liquids travel from our assigned part of the *thaal* into anybody else's," Marziamaasi explained.

"What's DCP?" Tulsi asked.

"*Dal Chawal Palida,* layers of white rice baked with seasoned *toor dal* and a spicy soup with long thin pods of drumsticks, served on the side — one of those indulgent comfort foods marked by its simplicity and feel-good quotient. Ammijaan made it for us every Thursday. It's a good break from all the meat we eat the rest of the week. I am so glad Murtaza and Saleem also savor it as much. Makes for an effortless cooking day, like today."

Marziamaasi and simple cooking just didn't seem to fit together. Even on an "easy" cooking day, they had already eaten home-made minced lamb samosas as the savory course, followed by a custard-based ice-cream pudding, and a delicious charcoal-smoked eggplant *bharta before* she served them DCP. If this elaborate meal was effortless, Aarush wondered what a meal that required "effort" would entail.

When they were finally done, Aarush helped clear the dinner setup. The timing couldn't have been better. He seized the opportunity to catch Marziamaasi alone. "Tell me more about Joshikaka. He seems so fond of Mom. Does he know she's dead? I didn't quite follow everything you guys were saying."

"Everybody at JJ knows about Shalini. And Ram." As she uttered the words, Marziamaasi glanced up at Aarush, a look of alarm on her face, as if she had said something she shouldn't have.

"Who's Ram?"

Marziamaasi took a deep breath, wiped her hands with a kitchen towel, and sat down at the breakfast table.

Murtaza was busy with Tulsi, and Uncle Saleem had retired to his bedroom. Marziamaasi and Aarush had uninterrupted time, just the two of them.

"I think it's time I told you what I know," Marzia said, her voice tightening.

And with that Aarush felt his gut tighten too. He pulled out a chair and sat down across from her, sensing that there was a great deal he didn't know.

●●●●

"I don't think she has told me everything yet," Aarush was on the phone with Lara. "I think she stopped when she knew I needed time to digest all she had just told me."

"It's okay that your Mom had a boyfriend, bug. Why does that shock you so much?"

"Because I don't think she ever got over him. I get this feeling that everybody around me knows something about their love story that breaks their hearts. You should have seen Joshikaka's face every time he mentioned Mom. And Ram, that's his name. Why didn't she ever mention him?"

"Why would she? It would probably only make her feel sadder, wouldn't you think? People don't usually talk about old boyfriends. Especially after such a long time."

"I guess. Joshikaka talks about Mom and Ram as if they were his own kids. When Mom was a student at JJ, Joshikaka had been in a hit-and-run accident. Nobody came forward to help him. He had been left to die on the road, when Mom, on a motorbike with Ram, apparently recognized him. Ram gathered his limp body, ignoring everybody's warnings, and rushed Joshikaka to Bombay Hospital where he used his father's connections and paid for Joshikaka to be treated immediately. Had it not been for them, Joshikaka stood no chance of survival."

"Wow…what a story."

"Mom's painting has been hanging in the principal's office, in her honor, since the 26/11 bombings took her life and Ram's."

"What do you mean her life *and* Ram's? How does he come into that picture?"

"Mom had gone to the Taj to meet Ram that day, not some lawyer, like she told Dad."

"Oh my goodness," Lara gasped.

He was quiet, lost in thought, as he tried to recall every single word from his conversation with Marziamaasi.

"Why do you think? Maybe they were just meeting…you know…people do reconnect," Lara suggested, keeping the conversation going.

"Why didn't she just say that to Dad? Why make up a story about a lawyer? I asked Marziamaasi if she had any idea what was so important about that meeting that Mom needed to postpone her return."

"And what did she say?"

"That Ram was coming down from Singapore the morning of the 26th, and all Mom told Marziamaasi was that she had an urgent need to meet him."

"But she never explained what that need was?"

"No. That's when Marziamaasi called it a night and said she was beyond exhausted. I had so many questions, but it felt rude to push her. Besides I'm still trying to make sense of what she's told me so far."

"You need to rest your mind, bug. It's all good. I know it's hard when you have so many unanswered questions, but you might never find out everything. You know that, darling, don't you?"

What he did understand was that Lara was trying to manage his expectations. He felt restless.

"I'll talk to you later, okay?" He said abruptly, wanting to hang up, frustrated with the physical distance between them, and having nothing more to say.

"You okay?"

"I'm fine. Love you." He knew he sounded impatient but he couldn't help it.

"Love you. Lots. Call me tomorrow?"

"Yes. Bye." He hung up, ending the conversation with uncharacteristic haste. He couldn't help himself that day and offered Lara a silent apology.

That night he slept fitfully. He couldn't wait for Marziamaasi to continue his mother's story. And he was convinced Marziamaasi wasn't finished, never mind what she might have hoped Aarush believed.

••••

"Nana, I didn't see Shakutai at the Mahila Seva Gram yesterday. Do you know if she still works there?"

Aarush had taken the train Friday evening to Pune. Saturday afternoon he tutored three fourth-standard kids, two girls and a boy. It had been frustrating. The kids were still getting to know him but they were in awe of him. While he wrote on the blackboard, they sat on the floor, cross-legged, painfully quiet, hardly responding. Nani had said that it usually took a month before they started to show results. Aarush assumed it was his accent.

He sat across from his grandfather, who was reading the newspaper.

"I believe she does. She might have been out sick." Nana said.

"Do you think she'll know anything about my birth mother?" Aarush asked. Nana set aside the paper, removed his reading glasses and studied his grandson.

"Have you always felt the need to know, my child? Or is it only now that your mother has passed away?"

"I'm just curious. I've never thought about it before. It didn't seem relevant. But now it does. When I asked Dad, he said that the Indian family court keeps everything sealed and there was no way to find out any information about my birth parents. Is that true?"

"It is, *beta*. How would it help anyway?" Nana's tone held a controlled impatience, as if he was trying to restrain himself.

For Aarush, it was disconcerting.

"But I've heard bribing can get you anything here, and you are so well connected in Pune…"

Nana completely snapped. "Do you think that's what my expertise is? Bribery and exploitation so that you can get the information you seek? First your mother and now you!"

"I am just asking."

Aarush moved to the edge of the seat.

"Mom made the same request? She wanted to know about my parentage too?" Aarush found that very interesting.

"Of course not. She wanted to know…" and he stopped abruptly, his face still red.

"She wanted to know what?"

"Never mind. It doesn't matter anymore. She took matters into her own hands. If only…" Nana said, his mouth a thin resolute line, his eyes faraway.

"What do you mean she took matters into her own hands? Does this have to do with her meeting Ram at the Taj?"

"How do you know anything about Ram?" Nana asked, horror

replacing his rage.

"Between Joshikaka at JJ and Marziamaasi, I have heard his name and have figured out that much. I know she had gone to the Taj to meet him when they were assaulted by terrorists."

"Hey, Bhagwan. Does your father know this too?" Nana's face had changed from a furious magenta to a dismayed red to an appalling white, like one of those mood-light fixtures you see in high-end restaurants, cycling through neon colors, one to the next.

"Dad? No, I don't think so. At least I haven't talked to him about it. But why is it all such a big secret?"

His last conversation with his father had been brief. Amit had said he planned to visit Aarush in the course of one of his business trips to Asia. Aarush had been thrilled. Neither of them was a phone talker, and Aarush missed his father's quiet, soothing presence.

"I don't have an answer for you, *beta*. Besides, now that Shalini's gone, it's even less relevant."

"He was an old boyfriend. So what? There is something more to this than meets the eye. I want to know what it is. Nothing about my mother is irrelevant to me." So it was Aarush's turn to get excited.

At that moment the doorbell sounded, bringing their conversation to a convenient end. For Nana.

It was Shireenmaasi. She stayed until it was time for Aarush to catch the train back to Bombay, and when she offered to give Aarush a ride, Nana eagerly accepted.

Aarush was disappointed but determined to continue with his line of questioning the following weekend. He wasn't about to let either Nana or Marziamaasi off so easily. After all, he *had* come to find closure, and they were jolly well going to help him find it.

●●●●

"Can I give you Two Bads and Zero Goods this week?" he asked Lara.

"Of course, my poor bugga. What happened?"

"I don't think the kids at the orphanage understand a word I'm saying. And I'm frustrated with Nana and Marziamaasi. They're both withholding information from me, and they insist it's irrelevant now that Mom's gone. I didn't get to meet Shakutai, either. Make that Three Bads."

"Oh, dear. The kids are probably just shy, getting used to a new teacher. Don't you remember how we felt on our first day in a new grade? It can't be too different for them."

"That's true."

"Where your granddad and aunt are concerned, go easy on them. Remember, they're grieving too. And next Saturday, just ask the matron on duty what Shakutai's work hours are."

All solid points, he was happy with her sympathetic attention as he licked his wounds. "Fine. But only because you insist." Humor returned to Aarush's voice.

"Okay, there must be something good that happened over the weekend. Can't and will not accept a Zero Good. C'mon, Aar..."

"Well...let me think...Oh, I know...the carpenter finally showed up while I was in Pune, and I now have my own bed, stacked above Murtaza's." It surprised him, the turn in his mood, and he was once again thankful to have Lara in his life. To vent, to count on, to love.

"Okay, bug. Enough about me. You've helped me feel better already."

And it was his turn to make up for their last call.

••••

$\mathcal{S}$halini

Eight

$\mathcal{S}$halini stared at the ringing phone unable to decide whether to answer or not.

Why was Ram calling her father? What could he possibly want from him? She remembered her last conversation with her father, when she had transferred his old contact list to the new phone. Even then Shalini had her doubts and remained unconvinced with his explanation. There was something missing...

Wait, she thought. *Maybe he's trying to reach me? That made*

146

sense. Ram didn't have her phone number. Pappa's was the only one Ram could reach her through. He must have heard she was visiting. Where did he live now?

In fact, Shalini *had* never given Ram any of her contact information. Not in Singapore when they met, not after. It hadn't even occurred to her. She carried his phone number in her cell phone, close to her heart, reassured by the knowledge that he was only a phone call away. She had never called him. But she had imagined it many times. Many, many times. She had imagined not just calling him, but another rendezvous. Pictured all the details — how she'd greet him, touch him, taste him, one more time. How she would tell him all the things that she had wanted to reveal but couldn't. Yes, she had visualized it all. A tremor ran down her spine.

That's it. He has to be trying to reach me. It all makes sense.

Father was the only person through whom he could contact her. Shalini hadn't really kept in touch with any of her college friends. And Marzia, loyal to Shalini, had severed all contact with Ram since their split-up in 1991.

The idea that Ram might be thinking of her made her heart skip several beats. Perhaps it wasn't just she whose mind was consumed with thoughts of her former love. It wasn't long before her initial suspicions around a Father-Ram conspiracy were replaced with hopeful romantic anticipation as a meticulous, step-by-step analysis of possibilities allowed her to reach what she decided was a rational conclusion — Ram was trying to contact her; was obviously making an effort to locate her; so was naturally, maybe — just maybe — obsessively, thinking of her. Even as she tried to manage her expectations, Shalini couldn't help feeling elated. The honest truth was that she was bordering on the dizzy, the euphoric.

Caution, she chided herself, though only half-heartedly. There could be other reasons, innocuous reasons. Besides, Ram was married, he had a family. She couldn't, *shouldn't* be thinking about him like this. Not now. Not anymore. After all, she was a married woman.

Oh, but what could she do? She loved him. God, how she loved him.

And that had not been more evident since their unplanned meeting in Singapore. At the time, Shalini had tried hard to explain Singapore as the closure they both needed. For a while, she had even fooled herself into believing it. Finally, they would be putting to rest a precious relationship that not only had ended bitterly, but without mutual forgiveness. Divine intervention in the form of a chance encounter had helped bring it to its proper conclusion; they could make peace. Except that, on her return to the United States, she realized that it had been anything but a closure. Rather, it began the unraveling of her relationship with Amit, shaky from the beginning. She questioned the very foundation of their union.

Would it have been vastly different, she wondered, had she faced her problems? Had she not shoved under the carpet all that she didn't wish to see; had she laid bare her past to Amit and not spent seventeen years battling the guilt of having kept secrets from him; had she sought out Ram, at least once, before giving up their child and plunging into a lifelong marriage contract with a relative stranger; had she not been so stubborn, so foolish, *so* reckless as to have turned a deaf ear to the pleadings of her own heart, allowing pride stand in the way of reason and prudence and, most importantly, love? Would she have been any less bound up had she chosen otherwise? How different would life have been?

She stood transfixed, unable to decide whether or not to answer the cell phone.

Ultimately, the decision was made for her. The ringing stopped. She had waited too long. Or perhaps, long enough.

"Who was that? Why didn't you answer?" Marzia asked.

"I didn't recognize the caller," she lied, buying time to sort out her thoughts, her emotions.

••••

"*Arre*, Marzia, I'm so glad to see you. It's been so long since you visited us here in Pune." Narsidas's smile extended from ear to ear. He was awfully fond of Marzia, and with good reason. She was so easy to be fond of.

Marzia flew into his arms. "Narsi Uncle…"

"You girls should have called me. I could have cut short my walk." He gave Shalini a warm and long hug.

"Shalini thought about doing just that. But you forgot to take your phone with you," Marzia explained.

"Oh, did I?" Narsidas patted and checked his jacket pockets.

"It's there, on the coffee table. In fact, you missed a call." Marzia gestured to where the phone lay on the glass tabletop a few feet away.

Shalini kept quiet, worried that if she spoke her voice would reveal emotions that she was still trying to sort out.

He picked up the phone and glanced at it. She studied his face as he scrolled through the call log. She had no idea what exactly to expect, but felt a definite uneasiness when he calmly dropped the phone into his pocket. Shouldn't he be at least a little surprised? After all, it couldn't possibly be even *remotely* routine to receive a call from Ram Rugge?

"Tea is ready. And so are the *pohe*," announced Vimalbai as she set the table.

She served a savory breakfast cereal made with water-soaked flattened rice seasoned with oil, turmeric, salt and nuts, a trademark Puneri Maharastrian specialty. Unlike Bombay, the capital of Maharashtra, which had a diverse population hailing from all over India, Pune was a city with a dominant Maharashtrian influence. Shalini's parents, in spite of having roots in the northwestern Indian state of Gujarat, had become completely Maharashtrian in their way of life. A welcome variety for Marzia's taste buds. "Vimalbai, you are simply the best!" she said in delight.

Thank goodness, Shalini thought, *for Marzia's talkative nature.* It made it less conspicuous that the cat had got her tongue.

They settled down at the round dining table, its glass top covered with a white, lace-like, though plastic, table cover. Once Marzia became focused on the taste and flavors of the food, the only sounds that could be heard were the clinking of silverware on steel bowls, noisy slurps as they sipped hot tea from their saucers, and on Vimalbai's antiquated radio in the kitchen Lata Mangeshkar's voice singing "Is Mod Se Jate Hain," from the '70s Bollywood movie *Aandhi*.

Still tongue-tied, Shalini feigned a voracious hunger.

"How is your jet lag?" her father asked, watching her.

"Not bad," she mumbled, her mouth full, not taking her eyes from her plate.

"Uncle, can you please take me to the place where you get the famous Pune *bakharwadis*?" Marzia asked.

"Of course, it would be my pleasure, Marzia. I have been a loyal Chitale's patron for the last thirty-five years. They will gladly make a fresh lot for you, *beta*."

"Shalini, are you okay? You seem very quiet today."

"Uh-huh. Just tired," she replied.

"You were fine not that long ago, Shals." Marzia reached out and touched Shalini's forehead with the back of her palm.

Shalini decided to dive in, head first. Why wait for a *muhurat*, an auspicious moment? This was as good a time as any.

"Pappa, I have a question for you. A request, actually. Can you find out what happened to Rushi?"

"What do you mean?" Father's eyes popped. Her question had struck him like a bolt from the blue.

"Exactly what I said. I know you are going to say we can't — legally. I am asking you if you can use your connections to bribe someone in the Family Courts to tell us where Rushi is," she added harshly. She couldn't help it. She was certain by now that her father was keeping something from her. Wronged in so many ways, her aggressive, unforgiving mood seemed justified to her.

"I can't. You know that. That's an unreasonable request," he said it with a finality that felt like a slap across her face. She noticed that his expression was angry — so unlike her father.

Maybe she shouldn't have brought this up in front of Marzia....But what was there that Marzia didn't know?

"Oh, Pappa, come on. Don't say no. You can do anything. Please, Pappa. I promise I won't ask you for anything after this." Her voice had begun to tremble under the strain.

"That is a chapter you closed the day you gave him up. It would be wrong to disrupt him from the life and family he has settled in."

"But Pappa, I won't disrupt him. All I want to know is that he's doing fine. Please..."

"What *is* fine? Fine has so many definitions. What's fine for him may not be fine for you and vice versa. You have to let it rest. Besides, does Amit know anything about Rushi?"

"Why does that even matter?"

"The less you know, the less you will need to lie to him."

That hit a nerve.

"Okay, so I'm a liar. How are you different?"

"Shalini, this discussion is over. I understand you are upset, but right now, you are crossing all boundaries. I will not entertain you talking to me in this manner." He was furious, but nothing was going to stop her. She felt desperate.

"You are a liar too. What are you hiding from me? Why are you in contact with Ram? Why is he calling you on your phone? How come it didn't surprise you to see his missed call? Last time when I asked, you said you were not in touch with him at all. What's going on?" She stared accusingly at her father.

"SHALINI!" he roared. She had never heard his voice so loud, so outraged. She stood up, physically stunned, pushing aside her unfinished *pohe* and tea, and charged to the bathroom, angry tears streaming down her face.

••••

When Shalini was a little girl, she could hardly wait for her favorite Ratnagiri Alphonso mangoes to arrive from the Konkan coasts and flood the marketplace. She would drive her mother crazy with impatience, pestering her with the same question, "Have the mangoes arrived? Did you buy mangoes?"

To which her mother would suggest, "Stop thinking about the mangoes. They'll come sooner that way."

Well, Shalini tried. She really did. But the harder she tried *not* to think about them, thinking about them was all she could do. Not only did they consume all of her imagination, she became an expert at living in a pretend world. Her mouth watered as she fantasized, her senses overwhelmed with the anticipated delicious smell emanating from the ripening fruit as her taste buds responded to what seemed real to her, the juicy rich smooth texture of the deep red flesh of this King of Mangoes.

It was no different now. Shalini strived to banish thoughts of Ram, but the more she endeavored, the more he occupied her mind. Monopolized it, took it over entirely.

●●●●

Eventually, Shalini calmed down. She was convinced that this was the first time Marzia had been left inarticulate, silenced by the nasty interchange. Shalini and her father were known for their calm and peaceful demeanors, with an abhorrence for conflict. Shalini emerged from the bathroom, her composure returned, and except for her red face, no hint of having had a meltdown. Her father, too, regained his poise. Marzia's presence had compelled family serenity.

One thing the morning's showdown had made clear, though, her father was not going to budge in his decision not to help her obtain Rushi's file. Shalini was her father's daughter, after all, and she knew when his mind was made up. She had got her headstrong doggedness from those same genes. If he decided not to be amenable, she was equally determined to be obstinate and tenacious. She would find Rushi and, if needed, she would move mountains. It had become a matter of life and death, the only way to lay to rest her inner demons. They were driving her into such an insane state, she was convinced they would eventually get the better of her if she didn't do something about it soon.

After lunch her father retired to his bedroom and Marzia to the guest room. Shalini lay on the living room couch, her spirits at an all-time low, feeling hopeless, full of despair. All she could see before her was a dead end.

How could she get the information she sought? Who would help her? Even more importantly, who was *willing* to help her?

Suddenly, out of the blue, the answer to her predicament came to her.

"Shakutai, that's it. She's the solution," Shalini said aloud.

Shakutai had been the orphanage midwife assigned to take Shalini to Sassoon General Hospital when she went into labor with Rushi. She had also been the one responsible for the care of all babies and toddlers under the age of five. Coincidentally, Shakutai had cared for Aarush until he came to Amit and Shalini just before he turned five. In fact, Shakutai was the only memory that Aarush had held on to from his early years at the orphanage. The Shakutai connection between Rushi and Aarush had been the most ironical twist.

Shalini regretted her cowardice at feigning lack of recognition when Amit and she had encountered Shakutai along the corridors the day they arrived to pick up Aarush. She hadn't expected the woman to still be working there. She could only hope that Shakutai would understand her dilemma, her conflict, her turmoil, and forgive her.

Sometime in the last few months of her mother's life, Shalini vaguely recalled her mentioning Shakutai and how she continued to work with dedication at Mahila Seva Gram.

She is my only hope, Shalini prayed. *She will know what happened to my Rushi. At a minimum, she can tell me what kind of family has my baby.*

That much Shalini knew for certain. Rushi had been taken. She had looked furtively, heart in mouth, for a Rushi, any Rushi, when they picked up Aarush. She had labored over her decision to adopt from the same place where she had given up her child. Finally, it was her desperate need to stay connected, in whatever way, with the place where she last laid eyes on her child that drew her back there. Shalini had even asked the new matron in charge then, "Is there a child called Rushi here? Should be five years old by now."

"Rushi? There has been no Rushi here since I was hired for this job three years ago," the matron replied, puzzled by the question.

Shalini resolved to go to Mahila Seva Gram the very next day and track down Shakutai.

••••

The instant Shalini saw her father slide his cell phone into his pocket without so much as a flicker of expression, it struck her how unprepared she had been for what was to follow. For one, there was definitely something that was being kept undercover, something that was going on without her knowledge. But most significantly, she was completely unequipped to handle the deep sense of disappointment and disillusionment that overcame her. Disappointed not only in how life had failed to meet her expectations, but disillusioned with what felt like her own unrelenting desires. Hadn't she got what she wanted?

Nobody had forced her to marry Amit. Sure, it had been a strong suggestion by her mother, but then she had made many other suggestions throughout her life that Shalini had firmly refused. In Amit's case, it had been Shalini who had made the final decision. Just as she had decided against terminating her pregnancy. It wasn't as though no one had warned her about the emotional consequences of giving up an essential piece of her being. Father, Ammijaan and even Ram in his own way had cautioned her and pleaded with her to consider other options. In all fairness, her father, at Ammijaan's suggestion, had even offered to talk to Ram's family and fix up their marriage. But Shalini had been so full of anger and resentment that she turned a deaf ear to all of their proposals. Instead, she went on obstinately, trying to build a meaningful life without Ram and Rushi. And in her selfish, pig-headed struggle, she had inadvertently exposed Amit to collateral damage.

And now, after all she'd put everybody through, all she could think of was something as frivolous as Ram's romantic interest in her.

She couldn't have felt more ashamed, mortified by self-indulgence and humiliated by the way she pressed her father for more favors.

How could one person, one little insignificant woman, damage so many lives and fail so miserably?

Marzia and Narsidas left for Chitale's soon after their afternoon siestas, around 4:00 p.m., to buy snacks that Marzia wanted to take back with her. They had either noticed Shalini's need to be by herself or had decided that she was best left alone. They made no pretense of asking her to join them. She couldn't have been more grateful for their timely impoliteness.

That night, the disturbing chatter in her head brought on the worst headache of her life. She could have sworn that somebody was splitting her head in two, exactly where she parted her hair. The pain was so intense it made her stomach churn with nausea that threatened to completely turn her insides out. The pain was relentless. Her chest tightened and her heart pounded against her ribs, ready to explode. Physically and emotionally, she was a complete mess. Shalini popped more Advils that day than she was willing to confess, hugged herself and curled up in fetal position, unaware at what point sleep released her. Her only memory was a vision of being carried and comforted in what she was certain were her mother's arms.

••••

Shalini opened her eyes, bright sunshine pouring over her. She could hear mynas singing in the trees outside. Disoriented, she stared at the white ceiling. She even panicked momentarily as she tried to re-member where she was, the day, and why she was on a couch that looked vaguely familiar but which she couldn't immediately place. In less than a minute, she sighed in relief when she realized that after all she had not lost her wits. Before long, and with her mind's frenzied effort, she cleared her murky confusion.

I am in Pune. In my parents' home.

That explained the couch and the mynas. She recalled the pre-vious day's unpleasant events. She remembered how miserable she had been before falling asleep. It struck her, with great relief, that her head-ache was gone. The singing mynas lifted her spirits, as if announcing the promise of a new day. Just then she cheerfully remembered, with renewed anticipation, "Shakutai..."

She rose with purpose and headed to the bathroom, showered and dressed. It was still early, just 6:00 a.m. Too early to head to the or-phanage, though she was ready.

She decided to make up for the previous day's despicable be-havior and put water to boil on the stove. Then she poured it over finely ground Peaberry Madras coffee spooned into a stainless steel decoc-tion strainer. It would take about fifteen minutes for the coffee to drip through. It was called "filter coffee" in the Mistry household, her mother's morning ritual, the first thing she did before bathing. In the time she took to complete her morning ablutions and emerge from the bathroom, the coffee would have dripped and would be ready for her father. Then she would take two stainless steel, five-inch tall glasses, pour three quarters of the black coffee into one, a bit of milk and a teaspoon of sugar. A glass in each hand, she would stream the concoction from one glass to the other, pouring from a height of about two feet, so that the ingredients would not only mix together, but would also create foam. She would do this a couple of times and soon the aroma of fresh coffee permeated the house. Shalini couldn't recall a single day when she didn't wake up to the smell of coffee.

She had made up her mind to give her father a break from Vimal-bai's daily Nescafe, by emulating her mother's morning tradition. And in doing so, she meant to offer a truce.

It amazed Shalini to discover what a difference a good night's sleep made to her ability to think and to her disposition. As bleak as everything seemed the previous night, this morning she felt infused with optimism, however guarded. She couldn't wait to head to the Seva Gram. She had no intention to let her father in on her plans. He wouldn't cooperate, anyway. But she'd take Marzia into confidence. She had only a few days to achieve what she wanted before her flight back scheduled for the twenty-fifth.

"Good morning." Marzia walked into the kitchen, her hair rolled and knotted at the nape of her neck. "Ummm...coffee. Is Narsi Uncle up yet?"

"He hasn't stepped out of the bedroom. Probably decided to avoid his pain-in-the-neck daughter."

"Who's a pain in the neck, *beta*?" Her father came over to where she stood next to the stove and wrapped his arm around her shoulder, pulling her close. She was overcome with emotion as they made, tacitly, peace with each other.

"Filter coffee...just for you." Shalini turned and handed him the two glasses, each with half the coffee and foam rising to the rim.

"My lucky day. Favorite coffee made by my favorite daughter." He smiled as he took a sip.

"Mars, here's your cup. Let's sit at the dining table. We can make some toast if you'd like. I have asked Vimalbai to make *upma* for breakfast."

Upma, a savory South Indian breakfast preparation, was made with cream of wheat, or *rava,* and vegetables for flavor.

"Thanks, but I think I'll wait for the *upma.* What are our plans for today?" Marzia asked.

"Let's decide. Pappa, how are you placed this morning?" She

157

wanted to carefully choreograph their day in order to avoid discussions that might lead to conflict.

"I have work at the bank. And I have to pay some bills."

"Well, then I can take Marzia to Lakshmi Road during that time. We can check some things off our shopping list, huh, Marzia?" Shalini glanced at Marzia and she nodded her approval.

"*Theek, beta.* Let's meet at home for lunch." He seemed pleased with the plan.

Easy, Shalini thought.

"We'll be back by noon. In plenty of time for lunch." Her mind was already working out details. Marzia, blissfully unaware of Shalini's plans, sipped her coffee, happy to let someone else decide the day for a change

Probably relieved, Shalini thought, *that her hosts are back in each other's good favor.*

••••

"I thought we were going shopping?" Marzia looked puzzled as Ahmedbhaiyya turned according to Shalini's instructions, and stopped at the closed gate. Shalini rolled down her window and signed a register held by a watchman. The gate and the boundary walls loomed before them, like a fortress, hiding the interior structures and their inhabitants from the outside world. In no hurry, the watchman ambled leisurely and unlocked the gate.

"What is this place? Where are we going?" Marzia asked.

It occurred to Shalini that Marzia had never had an opportunity to visit Mahila Seva Gram.

"Rushi and Aarush's first home," she said.

"No! Really? Is this where you...?"

A look of wonder came over her face.

"Uh-huh," Shalini answered quickly, easing Marzia out of any discomfort, so that it was not necessary to articulate the obvious.

The car entered through the open gate and Ahmedbhaiyya dropped them at the entrance to the main building, a circular driveway connecting three large stone buildings, the center main building at five storeys being the widest, with those flanking it only two storeys. Shalini felt a heaviness descend in her. Memories of her two previous visits to Seva Gram played a terrible game of tug-of-war in her mind, the later visit ultimately losing to the trauma of the first. Had it really been that long? It seemed like it was only yesterday...

"You are?"

"Mr. Mistry. Narsidas Mistry. Mrs. Dandekar asked me to meet with you."

"Yes, yes. I was expecting you, Mr. Mistry. And this must be Shalini. Please come into my office. I need you to fill out some paperwork for your daughter."

The matron in charge had beckoned Shalini's father to enter her office from the reception area where they both stood patiently waiting their turn.

"Will she be...?"

Shalini had no recollection of the conversation that ensued, but she could still remember every physical sensation that dreary January morning in 1991. Her face was flushed, surely a side-effect of pregnancy, but also with shame, heat emanating from her body as if it were a hot summer day, in spite of her father's knitted sweater, woolen scarf and earmuffs' evidence of the cold winter morning, typical that time of year in Pune. The reek of the antiseptic liquid disinfectant Dettol as a lady mopped the floors in the hallway, simultaneously both hygienic and hospital-like, and in a strange way also reassuring, reminding Shalini that she had come to give birth. The sound of an unseen toddler wailing, cosseted in one of the rooms down the hallway, which sent a bolt of pain into her heart as her own unborn baby kicked as if on cue, engulfing her in guilt for the crime she was about to commit.

Shalini shook herself from memory's trance, the sight of the driveway evoking the familiar shame, wondering, as she and Marzia stepped into that same reception area, if her crime was obvious to one and all who laid eyes on her. Several people were waiting in line for the matron in charge. There were no chairs, so like everybody else, they too stood in line.

"What are we doing here?" Marzia, having overcome her initial state of wonder, now had questions for Shalini.

"I want to meet Shakutai. I hope she still works here." Shalini looked around, distracted, trying to keep her answers to the point, unable to control the urge to peer into the corridors leading to the room, her room, where she had spent the last few weeks of her pregnancy.

I wonder what's the story of the unlucky girl in that bed today?

"What purpose does that serve?" Marzia asked, unconvinced.

"She was my midwife. Rushi was her charge when I left."

Outside a woman draped in a *nauvari*, a nine-yard saree, was drying clothes on parallel clotheslines tied from pillar to pillar in the central courtyard, mostly triangular pieces of white cloth that served as reusable diapers for babies, taking each piece, wringing out the extra water and flapping it a couple of times in the air before neatly pinning it to the line — a sight Shalini had seen when she had come to pick up Aarush.

She took in a deep breath. Her stomach turned. *What is it? Could it be the smell...*now she knew why she felt sick every time she ran a load of whites!

"That was eons back. What makes you think she's here?" Marzia said.

"Mummy had mentioned she was still working with toddlers when she volunteered here. If three years ago she had dedicated a minimum of fourteen years to these kids, it's highly likely she's still here." Shalini was trying to stay upbeat, but she knew Marzia's doubts were valid.

"Okay. It's worth trying, I guess," Marzia said supportively.

Suddenly, a commotion in the matron's room caught their attention — a loud exchange of words followed by the matron rushing out of her office, her face red. "Security! Security," she summoned.

A guard, sitting lethargically on a stool outside the entrance to reception, abruptly stood to attention and strode in wearing a look of grave self-importance.

"Definitely the most exciting moment of his day," Marzia chuckled under her breath.

"Wonder what happened." As much as Shalini wanted to find humor in the situation, she was worried the mishap might put the matron in a non-cooperative mood.

Just what she didn't need...

The urgent situation, whatever it was, produced several more members of the office staff materializing out of nowhere. The matron excused herself and left. Shalini's heart sank. Staff members cleared the area, telling people to return the following day.

But, desperate times called for desperate measures. Shalini accosted a staff member, the one who looked most approachable, and pleaded, "Ma'am, I have come from America and am leaving tonight. I wanted to meet Shakutai. We adopted our son twelve years ago. She was my son's caretaker, and I just want to say hello."

In retrospect, it was probably best that the matron left in a fit. She may not have favorably entertained Shalini's request, especially if she had decided to check her file, which would have been required procedure. The preceding confusion and the missing matron worked in Shalini's favor. The lady examined the two of them, finally taking pity on them. She told them to wait to the side as she disappeared behind a door. Shalini could hear her holler down the corridor, "Rajani, Shaku *la bolav. Saang, pahune alet bhetayla. Amerikehoon.*"

Shalini's heart was pounding so anxiously that she didn't notice the crowd dissipate, leaving Marzia and her alone, in the waiting area. She had hoped with every cell in her body to have the opportunity to meet Shakutai, but never once had she actually expected their encounter to happen with such ease, without having to put up a fight. It was like the surprise of preparing to strike a blow, only to find her fist punch sailing through thin air.

That Shakutai still worked there, had been sent for and could appear at any moment, left Shalini feeling completely edgy. Marzia must have sensed her nervousness because she took Shalini's sweaty hand into hers and gave it a tight squeeze.

••••

"Did you get your shopping done?" Father asked, a bright smile on his face. Marzia and Shalini were sitting in the living room when he walked in the front door.

Marzia came to their rescue. "No, Uncle. I didn't find a thing I liked."

Shalini had tried to clean up and make herself presentable before her father returned, not wanting to risk his suspicion. Her goal required a certain amount of scheming, and it was imperative that he remained unsuspecting.

They had lunch together, and afterward her father and Marzia retired to take a nap. Again and again Shalini replayed the emotionally charged reunion with Shakutai that morning, ruminating on every word they had exchanged.

"Shalini *bal*," she had said as soon as she laid eyes on her, recognizing Shalini instantaneously.

Seventeen years had hardly changed the woman. She still stood straight and walked briskly, a picture of health, belying her seventy-two years, the only signs of age a generous addition of a number of lines to her face.

Each line a merit badge for every child she has cared for, Shalini thought.

"It's these kids that keep me young," she said shyly, pleased when Marzia expressed disbelief at her age.

"How are you? And how is my Aarush?"

Shalini was impressed with her knack for remembering names

and people. After all, she must have seen and known hundreds of adoptive parents and children in her long association with the orphanage. But Shakutai made no mention of Rushi, and she wondered if it had anything to do with Marzia's presence.

What could she ask her about Rushi anyway?

"Aarush is in his last year of high school. Same as twelfth standard here," Shalini said.

She fumbled in her handbag for her wallet, where she carried a relatively recent picture, the one with Sophie from Singapore.

"Look...this is Aarush from a few years ago."

Shakutai examined the picture closely. Shalini didn't tell her that he now looked quite different even from that photo, that he was a foot taller and had sprouted facial hair. She thought it best to let her enjoy this Aarush who was already a transformation from the five-year-old child Shakutai had trusted into their care.

"What a handsome young man. Lucky fellow. He got to go to America. Hope he has turned out to be a good son."

"He has been more than good, Shakutai. He has turned out to be my..." Shalini's voice faltered and she left the sentence incomplete. Marzia gripped her by the elbow, offering strength.

"I am so sorry about your mother. We all miss her here at the Seva Gram. She was so dedicated. You were blessed to have her in your life." Shakutai's unintentional change of topic helped, and Shalini regained some composure.

"I miss her too. Shakutai, I...um...have a question for you. Please don't tell me you can't answer it."

"So long as it has nothing to do with Aarush's parentage, I am happy to answer any questions."

So Shakutai was asked this often...

"Good, because it's not about that at all. What happened to Rushi?" she asked, mincing no words.

Shakutai looked at Marzia and then back at Shalini, her expression startled.

"It's okay. I have no secrets from Marzia," Shalini said.

"You know I can't."

"Please, Shakutai, please." Shalini grabbed her hands, despair clutching her heart. "All I want to know is that he is fine and happy," she implored.

"Shalini *bal*. I can imagine how you feel. I have spent almost twenty years at the Mahila Seva Gram. And have lived more than seventy. Take advice from this old woman who has seen it all. Free yourself of guilt. We are all products of this Universe and She has a plan, a divine plan that we are designed to be part of. Destiny chooses who we give birth to and the same Destiny decides whom we raise. Not all of us are fortunate to give birth to and raise the same life. Trust that your child is where he is meant to be."

Shalini was sobbing by now, Marzia standing beside her, holding her. Shalini refused to let go of Shakutai until she gave her something, anything.

"Please, please Shakutai. Give me one clue where he could be? Nobody understands my feelings. I am human too. I made a mistake. All I want is to find peace. I won't disrupt his life, I promise."

Shakutai had to help her. She was her last resort, her only resort, couldn't she see that?

Shakutai inhaled a long breath and paused. And either because she felt sorry for Shalini or realized that if she didn't tell her something, there'd be no escaping from her, she spoke:

"Rushi's case ran into legal problems. There was a wonderful family from Australia who had fallen in love with him. I'm not sure what happened with that adoption. Had something to do with his birth certificate and missing signatures. He wasn't technically free for adoption… something like that. Ask your father. He was called in to fix the problem. *Tumche vadeel dev-manoos nighale*," she said, with much hesitation, her voice barely audible.

As Shalini replayed the conversation, scrutinizing every word, searching for clues, she came to the frustrating realization that she had just come full circle. Everything pointed to her father. He had all the answers. Shakutai, sweet as she was, had said a lot, but revealed little.

••••

Having reached a dead end on the Rushi front, Shalini felt the burning need to investigate the Father-Ram angle. She rationalized a reason for calling Ram, to confront him directly.

It isn't like I am calling him to set up a date.

How many times over the last four years had she resisted the urge to pick up the phone and call him? But now it was different. She had urgent queries…about him being in touch with her father. She wanted an explanation. She *deserved* an explanation. It annoyed her that her father wouldn't, despite irrefutable evidence, even acknowledge his connection with Ram, let alone shed light on their relationship. What *was* it? His behavior and reactions had been so out of character that, the more she replayed them in her mind, the more it drove her over the edge.

Since her father refused to talk about it, she would ask Ram. She had every justification.

Something far beyond curiosity had gripped her, exposing Shalini, the proverbial cat, to the not-necessarily-favorable consequences of her inquisitiveness. But was that going to stop her? No.

Shalini noticed her father's cell phone charging on the computer desk. An ingenious thought came to her. She walked across the living room to the desk, next to the dining table, and picked up the phone. Guiltily, she searched through the call log. No Ram Rugge. That was strange…

No listing for Ram in his contacts file, either. He had deleted all of Ram's information from his phone.

She should have handled the whole Ram phone call better, with more tact. What was she going to do?

••••

165

Aarush

Nine

"How was your afternoon with the kids?" Nana had arrived to pick Aarush up from the Seva Gram. It was his second weekend with Raakhi and Chaaru, the two girls, and Hari, the boy from last week.

"Much better, thank goodness. Last Saturday, I started to get serious doubts about my teaching abilities."

"What was different, you think?" Nana's interest was infectious and Aarush couldn't wait to tell him all about the afternoon.

"I think it was the first half hour. I had them close their books and put them away. I told them that we would practice spoken English instead of written."

"I would think that would be even more intimidating."

"I know, and it was. They completely clamped up. I wanted us to get to know each other. So I told them I would talk first. And I went ahead and told them all about me."

"That was brilliant. What did you tell them?" Nana's eyes were shining with excitement and interest.

Nana reminded Aarush so much of his mom, the same eyes, the same expressions.

Was he only imagining it? He shook himself out of his reverie.

"I made fun of my own accent first. They thought I was really funny because they laughed, nervously at first. But when I continued to crack jokes, impersonating different voices and accents from different parts of the world, they rolled like there was no tomorrow."

"I think these children are used to very traditional, strict and old-school ways of teaching where teachers never smile, always look stern and angry, and seem ready at the drop of a hat to discipline with corporal punishment," Nana offered. "Fear-based," he added.

"Maybe that's why they refused to open their mouths last week. Today, I couldn't get them to keep quiet. Next weekend, I'll have to get them somewhere in between if they are going to learn anything."

"Did you give them any homework? Or are you going to be their favorite and only teacher who gives them none?" Nana asked with a twinkle in his eye, clearly proud of his grandson, his face revealing his feelings.

Just like Mom, Aarush thought with a pang of loss.

"Oh, I gave them some homework. We ended up mostly talking about me today. So I asked them to write two complete sentences about their favorite activity for next week's discussion. They were thrilled. Each one said, 'Thank you, Mr. Kamdar,' at least a dozen times. They are so sweet and polite."

Aarush had quickly realized that he would have to get used to the formal address. However much he tried, he couldn't get them to call him

167

by his first name.

It had been a good day. The children had bonded with him. Now they felt like *his* kids, *his* responsibility.

"Well, it couldn't have been a better afternoon." Nana patted his hand as they sat side by side in the back seat of the car. Hosgé, a trusted family servant for three decades, drove them back to Nana's house.

"Any news about Shakutai?" Nana asked as they stepped out of the car.

"I asked the matron. She said Shakutai was recovering from cataract surgery and would be returning on Thursday. I'm glad she still works there. I'm looking forward to meeting her."

Aarush decided not to bring up their unfinished conversation from the previous weekend and instead enjoy a pleasant and untainted weekend with Nana. It had been tough adjusting to his demanding and still unfamiliar routine at JJ, and he was in no mood for conflict.

••••

Homesickness had started to set in. Aarush missed Lara. He missed his dad. He missed Sophie and Aunt Kathy and Aunt Amy Jo, even Penny. He missed his faithful Honda Accord, his bed, his bathroom. He missed the quietness of his house in the mornings just as much as he missed his rowdy swim team buddies. He missed Jamba Juice, Mikado sushi, Fraiche frozen yogurt, even the Caramel Cream Frappuccino prepared just right *only* at the Starbucks located in the strip mall off El Monte.

The only way Aarush found he could deal with the missing and longing was to keep himself so busy that it left him no time to think. The hardest time was at night when he tried to go to sleep. He must have counted at least a million sheep.

Classes started with gusto and teachers loaded them up with

assignments; two unfinished ones Aarush had brought with him to Pune — making it a strenuous week. He was getting used to working in limited space in a shared bedroom, and without Lara's help. He began to realize just how much he had taken her help for granted. The initial excitement around his move now behind, everybody had settled into their respective routines. Murtaza no longer dropped them at school though he would gladly have done so, but Marziamaasi received a letter from the principal at St. Xavier's, informing her that her son may not be allowed to take his final year university examinations if his attendance didn't show a significant improvement. That had put an end to Murtaza's musical ventures, his unsupervised "freedom," and unfortunately, his courting efforts with Tulsi.

The first couple of days, Tulsi and Aarush took the bus together. However, their classes and schedules didn't always match, so Aarush had taken to finding his own way to school. Amit had insisted that he not worry about money, and use a cab instead of the bus.

"It'll save you a lot of time, which I promise you, will be better spent on your homework."

It took Aarush exactly two days to understand the wisdom in his father's words. It may also have had something to do with the novelty of shoving and pushing and fighting his way through long, painfully slow-moving lines at the bus stop having worn off, especially when his arms were overburdened with rolls of canvas and art supplies.

••••

"How was last week at JJ? How do you find the classes? And the teachers?" Nana asked as they sat in the living room. Aarush had picked up the remote control and was flicking through channels, trying to find one in English.

"It was okay. I like the assignments that the teachers gave out. I just don't always follow what they say, though. They switch to Marathi or

Hindi a lot."

"Have you made any friends?"

"Not really. My classmates are all nice. They smile and seem friendly enough. But I haven't really found a buddy."

"Maybe once you have a group project, it will force a group interaction. Those offer unique opportunities to get to know people and often the best times to find friends. At least that's what Shalini used to say."

"What else did Mom say?" Aarush asked. He switched off the television, his interest piqued by the mention of his mother.

"She always had a lot to say. You know what a chatter box she was." It was heartening to see Nana finally talk fondly about her, instead of being rendered speechless with emotion and grief.

Time does help, Aarush thought, tucking the thought safely away, as one hides that extra twenty-dollar bill, to be retrieved in an emergency.

"She told me how happy she was about you and Lara," Nana teased.

"Really? I can't believe Mom told you about Lara." He was embarrassed — *and* pleased at the same time.

"Yes, she did. She told me how pretty, smart, and caring Lara is. And, most importantly, how much she loves you. Shalini said she and Lara couldn't be more different, and yet she reminded her of herself at that age. That Lara is absolutely devoted to you. Is that true?"

"Hey, Nana. Let's not change the topic, okay? I want to hear stories *from* you, not the other way around."

There was no way that Aarush was going to discuss Lara with Nana. He was self-conscious enough, knowing that his mom and granddad had been discussing his personal life.

"Okay, *beta*. Tell me what you want to hear about Shalini," he laughed, "I have thirty-seven years and ten months of stories. I wouldn't even know where to start."

Aarush knew exactly what story he wanted to hear. But he hadn't seen Nana in this frame of mind for so long that he didn't have the heart to disrupt it.

All in good time, he told himself.

"How about when Mom first moved to Bombay? Did she ever mention Joshikaka to you?"

"Ah yes, Joshikaka. She admired that man. She used to say that, had he been tested for his knowledge in architecture, he would have done better than most students at JJ College of Architecture. In fact, he routinely helped Ram with his assignments, especially with constructing detailed miniature models of buildings. She always insisted he was as deft as a one-armed paper hanger. Does he still work at JJ?"

"He does. Marziamaasi introduced us on the first day. I wasn't going to bring it up because the last time I did, you weren't too pleased with me. But since you mentioned him, may I ask you to tell me more about Mom and Ram? It seems like, here in India, no one who has known Mom can ever talk about her without mentioning Ram."

"Ram..." Nana closed his eyes as he let out a long sigh.

"It's one of those love stories that wasn't meant to be, I guess. But then, how could we have been blessed with you? And Shalini and Amit made a life together that can hardly be minimized. There's a grand reason why everything happens. And, though I can't see it yet, Shalini and Ram's being killed in the Taj fiasco must also have something good that will come out of it. Your Nani was such a believer in karma and destiny. How I wish she were here today. She would have known how to handle our complicated situation in a pragmatic manner."

"What complicated situation? Do you mean me? Am I a complication for you?"

"Gosh no, Aarush! How can you even think that? Where would I even begin to tell you what makes this situation so convoluted?" Nana looked troubled, and Aarush, for one, was sorry to see worry darken his brief light-hearted demeanor.

"Start anywhere, Nana, but please start. I am in no hurry to hear it all at once. You can tell me in small chunks, if that's easier."

He sensed strongly that Nana really did want to talk. He seemed like a balloon being inflated to its breaking point, as if one more puff of air and it would burst. A little release might help lessen the pressure and with it the burden he was carrying.

Nana got up from his reading chair, came over to where Aarush was settled on the couch and sat down next to him, pulling him closer. It had been a long time since he had snuggled up with his grandfather, though it felt like only yesterday that Nana recounted Aarush's favorite stories about the *Chambal Ke Daku*, Dacoits of Chambal. Aarush could have sat forever in the comfort of his grandfather's warm embrace.

"I do think it's time I told you my side of the story. About your mother. Because, everything about her is relevant. I owe it to you, *beta*."

Aarush's heart fluttered in anticipation, with part fear of the unknown and part excitement.

••••

"You've been here almost a month. Do you feel adjusted, sonny boy?"

Aarush was thrilled to meet his father at the airport. He arrived on an Air India flight from Malaysia. Nana had driven up from Pune to meet Amit, as he only had a two-day stopover in Bombay, not enough time to make a Pune trip.

"More or less," Aarush replied.

In some ways it felt much longer than a month, and in other ways he still felt like a newcomer, a novice.

"How is school treating you?" Amit looked equally happy to see his son.

They walked together, Amit's arm wrapped around Aarush's shoulder, beaming smiles on their faces, to Murtaza's car in the airport parking lot.

Aarush felt sorry for Murtaza, convinced that they were taking advantage of his generous offers to be their airport shuttle, and at insane hours too.

"Murtaza's friend Tulsi has pretty much ensured that if anybody at JJ even so much as dares to disturb me, they'd have to face Murtaza's wrath, so I'm in really good hands, Dad." Aarush smiled and winked at Murtaza.

Murtaza glared at Aarush, and as they loaded Amit's baggage in the trunk, he attempted to kick Aarush's shins. Aarush laughed silently, successfully dodging Murtaza's embarrassed fury. Immediately, though, Aarush reached out with his closed right fist, mouthing the word, "Respect."

Murtaza returned a fierce look, for a brief moment, before softening and extending his right fist, lightly interlocking their knuckles: Aarush had been forgiven. "Last time," he warned Aarush with a scowl.

"That's wonderful, Murtaza," Amit said, oblivious to the entire silent exchange.

"Dad, I have tomorrow planned out for us. I want to take you to JJ and show you around. I have a submission due in one class this morning that I have to attend. Otherwise, I plan to bunk the rest of the classes," Aarush announced, proudly delivering his Indian college lingo.

"Good plan. What happens after our JJ tour?"

"Murtaza has no choice but to attend all his classes." Aarush looked pointedly at Murtaza, who grimaced in assent, while they sat in the front of the car, "Else he would have gladly taken us around. So I plan to be your official guide and take you to all my favorite spots. The highlight will be Not Just Jazz by the Bay for dinner with Nana, Marziamaasi, Saleem Uncle and Murtaza. Oh, and Tulsi, of course."

Abruptly Amit went silent at the mention of Not Just Jazz by the Bay. There was no response from his father, so Aarush turned around in his seat.

There was a distant look in his eyes. "Dad...? We can do something different if you don't like what I suggested."

"Oh no, son. I like your plan." Amit shook himself out of his trance and repeated, "I like it very much, actually."

The incongruence between his father's facial and verbal expressions confused Aarush.

"Oh, and don't let me forget, Lara has sent something for you," he added, some brightness returning to his face.

Before going to bed, Amit gave Aarush the parcel from Lara. Inside he found a UC Santa Barbara T-shirt with a note pinned to the front,

> *This T-shirt is a great find*
> *That I hope will serve to remind*
> *Just like UC Santa Barbara*
> *Awaits your Lady Lara*
> *With all her heart, soul and mind*
>
> *I know, I know…it's lame!!!*
> *But I love you, bug. XOXO*

All Aarush dreamed of that morning was a marching band of Chambal dacoits, looking exactly like the Air India mascot Maharajah, with their outsized mustaches, striped turbans and aquiline noses, welcoming him on a beach in southern California, trumpet, trombones, drums and all, with Lara dressed like Jhansi ki Rani mounted on a horse, and everyone wearing UC Santa Barbara T-shirts.

A hot sultry breeze blew through the room's open window, confirming that it *had*, indeed, been a dream. That here he was back in reality, in dear old Bombay, Lara's gift rolled under his chin and both hands clutching it.

••••

"That's hilarious. I need to read up about Jhansi ki Rani now," Lara laughed.

Aarush had just finished describing his dream to her.

"I'll bring back books for you."

"When will that be, Aar?"

174

"Christmas, perhaps?"

"That sounds like a long time from now."

Aarush knew right away it was imperative he changed the topic. This wasn't going in the right direction. He wanted Lara to keep laughing.

"Hey, tell me what's going on at your end. How's Soph?"

"Oh, did I tell you she tore her meniscus as well as her ACL in her right knee last week during a soccer match? She's so bummed because now she has to sit out the rest of the summer. Six weeks minimum recovery time after the cadaver transplant."

"No way. That's too bad. I'll give her a call."

Meniscuses and ACLs, as far as Aarush's knowledge went, were knee ligaments, and several of his soccer friends had suffered similar injuries. He knew enough to appreciate that this was no trivial mishap.

"Your call will help. She's really down. Especially because she blames it on our Half Dome climb from last weekend."

"You did Half Dome again? How come you didn't say anything about it when we talked last week? Did you remember to take gloves this time?"

Aarush and Lara had ascended the almost nine-mile steep climb of Half Dome, possibly the most familiar granite formation in Yosemite National Park, less than a year ago. After a rigorous approach from the valley floor, including several hundred feet of steep granite stairs, they had scaled the final pitch of the nearly vertical and slightly rounded granite with the aid of post-mounted steel cables. It had been a menacing climb, and Aarush had worried about Lara when he realized there was no way he could help her if her arms gave way. It was their first time, and gloves had not occurred to them.

"I remembered. Mom, Aunt Kathy and Soph decided on this trip last minute. I thought of calling and telling you but then knew you'd be worried."

In retrospect, he *was* glad that she hadn't told him. He would have been sick with worry.

"Glad that it all worked out well. I can't imagine the moms doing the cables, though."

"They did, Aar. They were amazing. But my One Bad for the week, bug — I got stung by a bee at that ledge before the cables. What they call Quarter Dome?"

"Oh, no. Where did you get stung?"

"My ear, of all places. Luckily, it was after I had already descended. I missed you a lot at the top."

It had been memorably special when the two of them had made the climb together. They were both exhausted, mostly because of the anxiety of the final sharp ascent, and relieved to have made it in one piece. They sat at the top, Lara on his lap, as close to the edge as they safely could, the hard breeze drying their sweat. It was both quiet and noisy — quiet because neither of them spoke, words too limited to describe the sight, sound and feeling of the earth from that elevation. And noisy because the strong winds roared in their ears, deafening them to even thoughts. Literally on top of the world, it was a feeling they treasured, the togetherness of having achieved a difficult goal.

Suddenly, sadness enveloped him. Under different circumstances, he and his mother would have been on this last climb. They had always done stuff like that together. The unfairness of life felt unbearable.

"Bug…are you there?" Lara asked when it seemed the line had gone dead.

"Yup."

"We missed you both. Aunt Kathy completely broke down at the top. She was inconsolable." So she had guessed his thoughts.

He remained silent.

"How was your Dad's visit? How did he like your college?"

"He was impressed by the fact that Rudyard Kipling was born on JJ campus during his father, Lockwood Kipling's, tenure as the school's first dean."

"Wow, I didn't know that. What else?"

"We went to this restaurant where Dad and Mom met for the first time. It was really entertaining to hear the story from Dad's point of view and then from Marziamaasi's."

That night over dinner, Amit's reaction on their way back from the airport had made complete sense to Aarush. They ended up having a good evening, reminiscing at Not Just Jazz by the Bay, their first time together without Shalini.

"Was it sad to see him leave?"

"Yup. It felt too short. But he said he'd visit again in the next couple of months. For the first time, I'm glad his work requires him to travel. And maybe next time, you can fold yourself into a little parcel and surprise me," Aarush suggested, only half-kidding.

"I wish I could do that," she giggled.

"What about Nana? Any further progress on your mom and Ram's story?"

"Mom had packed a box with some personal belongings and left it with Nana-Nani before she left for the U.S. It was collecting dust in the attic. I climbed up and brought it down at Nana's suggestion. We plan to open it together. This weekend."

"Is it a big box?"

"Not too large. About the size of a laundry basket. Nana had just finished recounting all that happened around Joshikaka's accident. That's when Nana first met Ram and realized that Mom and Ram were more than just friends. Mom, of course, didn't think anybody could tell."

"I can't wait to hear about the contents of that box. I can't believe you haven't opened it already. How do you think your dad will react to all this?"

"I don't know. I don't even know if it's worth revealing any of this to him."

"You're right. What purpose would it serve, anyway?"

"And I'll meet Shakutai this Saturday too."

"Lots to look forward to. Call me as soon as you can, okay?"

"I will. Have to go. Love you a ton. Love your limerick skills, by the way. Keep them coming."

Murtaza had peeked into the room for the third time already.

"Love you too. Big hug. Bye."

●●●●

"Your given name at birth was Arun. We all called you Aru because you had the most gorgeous eyes. You were our quietest, least trouble-some child. Everybody's favorite. You never complained. Even as a baby. Barely a whimper to remind us that it was time to feed you." Shakutai's eyes were moist as she reminisced. Aarush was so engrossed, he didn't want her to stop even to breathe.

"How did I become Aarush from Arun then?"

"By the time your parents met you, your eyes had deteriorated. Because of vision issues, you had developed a habit of squinting your eyes. I overheard Shalini and Amit talk to the matron when the paperwork was being drafted. Shalini was excited about the name Aarush because it means the first ray of the morning sun, the beginning of a new day. Which indeed it was for all three of you. The two names were so close, you hardly even noticed the change."

Lara will love this story, he thought.

"My poor hearing might have helped in the transition too," Aarush chuckled.

She burst into laughter with him. He was glad Shakutai saw the humor in what he said as well. She reached out, gently stroking his cheeks with her palms and then cracked her knuckles on her temples. Aarush had seen Nani do the same thing each time he left for the airport to return to the U.S.

"*Nazar kadthe ga mazhya balachi. Agdi sonya sarkha aahes,*" Sha-kutai said.

Shalini had once explained the ritual done to ward off the evil eye.

●●●●

178

Shakutai had waited for Aarush to finish his afternoon session with the young trio of Raakhi, Charu and Hari. On Saturdays she was usually done early, leaving by 3:00 p.m. Aarush told Nana he would call for the car because he was unsure how long he would need with Shakutai. He had worried that, after all the waiting and anticipation, they might end up running out of conversation in the first few minutes. In his practice conversation with Lara, Aarush hadn't gone beyond pleasantries. Where did one start after a dozen years, especially when those years spanned the period from toddlerhood through puberty to young adult?

He needn't have worried at all.

"I hope that *chunt* Hari is behaving himself. He is a busybody but a good learner. Wants to be an astronaut. Has since he first started talking."

That's how their conversation had begun.

"How come he hasn't been adopted yet?" Aarush couldn't help asking. Luck, destiny and fate took on completely new meanings for him after Shakutai related their stories.

"It wasn't meant to be. Hari acquired polio as a child. That was a huge detractor, mostly due to lack of knowledge. He was treated and has completely recovered. But now he is too grown up. As a child gets older, chances of being placed drop significantly."

"Why?"

"Most families want babies. Babies don't have memories and are like fresh clay, easy to mold, less adjustment issues. The other reason is that couples who come to adopt babies usually have not been able to have one of their own. So they want to experience raising a child all the way from the beginning."

"What about Raakhi? And Charu?"

"They are orphans but both are not free for adoption."

"What does that mean?"

"They have parents who visit them but occasionally. They are so poor that they are unable to care for their children. Since our Seva Gram is not only an orphanage but also an institution for women in distress, we admit children of women who are encountering a whole spectrum of

179

problems, ranging from being destitute or having been widowed."

"They must feel lucky to have parents who can visit, who come to see them," Aarush said, trying to imagine being in their shoes.

"I'm not sure, Aarush. They look crestfallen every time a friend gets adopted. I think it actually makes a bad situation worse. There is no hope of a new day for them."

"What was my story?"

"You were one of our exceptions. Shalini insisted she wanted a boy who was approximately five years old. Nothing else mattered, not even when it was disclosed to her that you had serious vision issues. We weren't aware of your hearing issues at the time."

Aarush hummed and tapped his feet to the tune of "I Gotta Feeling" by the Black Eyed Peas while he waited in the main building reception area for Hosgé to come pick him up.

••••

"Are you in the mood to go through the box?" Nana asked Aarush hopefully.

"Totally up for it. Lara was surprised that we didn't go through it last week." Aarush was still enjoying the cheerful feeling left over from his conversation with Shakutai.

"You talk to Lara regularly?" Nana asked, smiling, his eyes concentrating on untangling the knot of jute tied around the dusty cardboard box.

"I do. She's a great listener. Talking to her helps me feel better, think better."

After their conversation last week, Aarush was already feeling comfortable talking about Lara with his grandfather. Nana had ceased to be the conservative, old-fashioned, stereotypical Indian grandfather Aarush had decided he must be.

"That is a great characteristic in any person. Especially in a close friend."

Aarush had taken over the knot. He pulled out his keychain with its pocket penknife and was about to cut the rope when Nana added, "I would love to meet her one day."

Aarush looked up at him. "Really? I'm sure Lara would love to meet you too. You will have to visit us in Los Altos then," Aarush said.

For some reason, Nana had resisted visits to Los Altos. He always made excuses about the flight being too long for his old body and having nothing to do for the long periods that he felt pressured to stay after spending the substantial amount on the tickets. Finally a bribe. "Even better, we should invite her to visit us. Do you think Lara would enjoy a vacation in India?"

Aarush grinned, excited by the suggestion. Coming from Nana, it might actually fly with Aunty Amy Jo.

Today is indeed turning out to be an exceptional day, Aarush thought cheerfully.

"Are you kidding me? She would love to. Will you talk to her mother? Maybe over Christmas?"

Nana nodded. "It would be my pleasure." Aarush was thrilled.

"Cool." Aarush could hardly restrain his grin and he noticed that Nana seemed in the same ebullient mood.

It took Aarush several attempts to cut the jute with his blunt knife and open the box. Within moments they found themselves sneezing as years of disturbed dust wafted up from the box.

"What's this?" Aarush asked as he pulled out a plastic bag containing random items.

"That scarf is Shalini's. She wore it often. In fact, I'd go so far as to say that she wore it almost every time I saw her. Around the head, or neck, or even sometimes twisted like a rope as a belt around her waist. She was very creative with that square piece of cloth."

"What about this shirt? It looks too big to be Mom's."

"Here, see this." Nana directed his attention to what had caught his eyes — the label of the midnight blue shirt. In black marker, there were these handwritten words....*"To the love of my life. Hope to keep you warm. Always — Ram, May 22, 1990."*

"I don't get why they broke up. All you've told me are the wonderful times Mom had with Ram and Marziamaasi and the rest of her college buddies. What happened, Nana?"

The more Aarush uncovered his mother's story, the more obvious it seemed that she had loved Ram, intensely. He couldn't imagine walking away from someone that precious and irreplaceable. He was thinking of Lara.

There was a metal bracelet. "We'll need a magnifying glass for this," he said as he squinted to read what appeared to be English lettering finely engraved on the inside. When he glanced up, he noticed Nana staring at the contents of a Ziploc bag he'd just discovered.

"Is that what I think it is?" Aarush asked, feeling squeamish at the sight of fine brown hair and tiny nail clippings.

Nana's demeanor, which had started off bright and cheerful, gradually lost its luster with each item that they pulled from the box, the contents of the Ziploc bag plunging him into despair.

"Nana, are you all right?" Aarush helped him sit down on a chair. "What is it?"

"My poor, poor child. I don't think I ever really understood her pain." He looked shattered. It was disturbing to see his otherwise strong, rock-solid and stoical grandfather reduced to a broken state.

"What pain? Tell me, Nana, please."

"*Beta*, it's time I introduced you to somebody," he said, and Aarush could hear profound resolution in his voice.

••••

Shalini

Ten

Shalini looked through her phone list for Ram's number, the one he had given her in Singapore four years earlier. Staring at it, wanting to call but lacking the nerve to press "Call."

Her father was still resting. He usually napped until 3:30 in the afternoon. It was 3:10.

From her phone list, she punched the number into her father's phone and made the call. Singapore was two hours ahead of India. After four rings, just when she was about to hang up, she heard a deep male voice.

"Hello."

Shalini's heart skipped a beat. She said nothing, not sure it was Ram. Shalini was about to terminate the call, when he continued.

"Pappa, can you hear me? Hello?" So she needn't have doubted. She disconnected.

Almost immediately, the phone rang. She was certain it was Ram and expected to see the same number flash back, but her father's friend Chandubhai, popped up on the screen.

Bad timing. Ram would get a busy tone.

In haste, she "ignored" the Chandubhai call.

Within moments, Chandubhai called again. *Persistent man.* Shalini wondered if it was an urgent matter. This time she answered.

"Hello," she said.

There was only static on the line. Her pulse was racing. She wasn't sure if Father's phone plan allowed call waiting. She didn't want to miss Ram's call.

"Hello. Chandubhai?" Shalini paused, but only a second before disconnecting. She wasn't taking any chances.

She waited and waited. But the phone did not ring. How could Chandubhai call at that time? Didn't he know that Pappa rested until 3:30? Couldn't he have waited a little longer before trying to reach him?

Frustrated, she sat back down on the living room couch, working out her disappointment, when it struck her — "Of course, Chandubhai knows that Father won't answer the phone at this time. He probably takes an afternoon siesta himself."

She hurried back to the phone and looked up the entry for Chandubhai in her father's contact list. It wasn't the same number she had dialed but the country code was Singapore.

Darn it, she thought. *Pappa is smart. Wicked smart.*

But she couldn't help smiling at his cunning and was both proud and amused. So, he had saved Ram's contact under his best friend's name.

She had ten more minutes to make another attempt. She redialed.

This time the line was quiet, nobody spoke. Ram must have recognized her voice and was afraid to give himself away, if he hadn't already.

"Ram?" she asked tentatively.

"Shalini."

"Hi. I'm sorry. It was me."

"I figured," he said.

"Why didn't you say something when you recognized my voice?"

"You didn't, either."

"I'm sorry." She began to feel agitated.

Why am I apologizing? It wasn't I who kept secrets, she thought.

"Is Pappa okay?" he asked.

"Uh-huh." *And do you even care if I am? We haven't talked to each other in four years and all you care about is Pappa?*

"Shalini?"

"Yes?"

"You called."

"I did."

"Why?"

"Why?! You and Pappa are in touch with each other. Unbeknownst to me. And you ask me why?"

"You don't need to get excited, Shalini. Is there any law that says I shouldn't stay in touch with your father? Because of what happened between us?" His voice was serious but calm. Shalini regretted her outburst.

"I didn't mean it that way."

And Shalini was crestfallen. She wanted Ram to be eager and excited, talking to her. Not grim. How had the tables turned?

Dialing Ram, she had felt justified and naïvely confident. She expected him to apologize and confess to what he and her father had been hiding from her. How in the world had it gone from that to Shalini questioning her own motivations, as if she were the one overstepping boundaries? Why was it all so wrong, so mortifying?

Shalini cleared her throat and made a second attempt.

"You're right. But I'm curious. Why are you?"

"Have you asked him?"

"I've tried. He tries to give the impression that it's not something you guys do regularly. But the phone bill shows otherwise." She was instantly sorry for revealing that she had snooped.

"Shalini, what is it you want?"

"I want you."

Shalini couldn't believe what she had just said. It was the most honest thing she had said or thought or confessed, ever. She felt light and free.

There was silence. A long silence. Out of the corner of her eye, she noticed her father walk out of his bedroom. Still on the phone, she opened the front door, and escaped into the front yard.

"Ram...are you there?"

"Yes."

"Say something."

"You have a good life, Shalini."

Though she wasn't sure where he was going, she was relieved that he was talking at least.

"Don't mess it up," he continued.

"What do you mean?"

"You have a family. A devoted husband in Amit and a wonderful son in Aarush."

Offended by his patronizing tone, she also felt cheated by how much he knew about her life and how little she knew about his.

"Ram, please..." *Why am I begging? What am I, in fact, pleading for?*

"Shalini, I know I am repeating myself. Don't spoil what you have. Haven't we lived long enough to see that life takes more than love and fresh air?"

"Why does it have to be this way, Ram? I love you. I made the wrong choice seventeen years ago. Do I have to pay for it for the rest of my life?"

"He has a reputation, he's a good provider, a great father...Shalini, there is nothing that Amit can't give you. "

"What do you know about that?"

"Whatever Pappa has told me over the years."

"Oh, Ram...It's like I'm desiring *roti pratas* at Casuarina Curry in

Singapore, and you suggest I stay with Los Altos Grill's lamb sirloin?"

"Well, it's local wholesome food. Good for your health."

"But don't you see? It's not just for indulgence's sake that I love Casuarina Curry. And the only thing Los Altos Grill has on its menu is a grilled vegetable platter. Good for somebody, I'm sure. But it isn't working for me. I have tried to love the Grill, believe me. I have. I am grateful to have been taken care of, but is that all? Can I not follow my honest desires?"

"There are plenty of other options where you live, aren't there?"

That was a stab straight into her heart. "Ram, what is it with you? Are you suggesting that I look elsewhere? Why are you reducing me to a shallow and superficial woman? Do you really believe that?"

He did not answer, his silence callous.

"Is it because you're afraid I will disrupt your life and family? I am not that selfish. I would never do that. All I want is to tell you how I feel about you. And always have. And try as I might, I can't run away from that."

But he remained unresponsive, deepening her pain.

"Please say something, Ram. Don't be so heartless."

Shalini was pacing up and down the front yard, on the verge of a nervous breakdown, tears flowing freely by now, as she started losing control. The hair on her arms stood up, and she shivered, even as the afternoon sun beat down.

"Shals, who is it? What's going on? Is that Amit?" Marzia tapped her urgently on the back.

With a flash of her hand Shalini indicated that this would take five more minutes, to please leave her alone. Both Marzia's face and her father's, who stood watching from the doorstep, were pale with concern.

"Where do you think this will lead us? Even if, say hypothetically, I were available?"Ram asked.

Shalini almost hurled in relief. At least he had finally spoken. "I haven't thought that far. Thinking ahead has never been my strength, and you know that better than anybody else. All I can tell you is how I feel. Can I do just that much, please?"

"It will only make life harder. Impulsive behavior hasn't worked out for either of us. You owe it to your son to make it work with Amit, don't you think?"

"It's because of Aarush that I have stayed in this marriage for as long as I have. I am done with my job there. He has become a fine young man ready to leave home soon."

"God, Shalini. Don't do this," he groaned.

"Do what? I am trying, finally, to live honestly. And quit running away from my own feelings." Her confidence spiked as he showed signs of faltering.

He exhaled, sounding exhausted. "I am coming down from Singapore next week."

"Can I meet you? Please?"

"I don't think it's a good idea, Shalini. We were taken by complete surprise in Singapore. It wouldn't be right."

Shalini dropped to the grass, her guts twisting in anguish, wondering how Ram could possibly exhibit such uncharacteristic righteousness bound to rules made by society. The same rules that he believed, *they* believed, were lacking in moral integrity, because all they served was society at large and not the individuals concerned. What had happened to love and truth? Or was it simply that he did not feel for her as she did for him?

"There's so much I want to talk to you about. I never even told you about our baby. Our son. Rushi. That's what I named him. If I could have, I would have left him with your last name…"

By now she was sobbing uncontrollably. She had never felt so depleted. Marzia, desperately worried, came to her where she was sitting cross-legged in the front lawn and forcibly took the phone. Shalini offered no resistance.

"Hello, Amit…Amit?" Marzia's face froze as Ram identified himself.

"Can I have her call you back? She's not in good shape right now," Marzia said into the phone, adding under her breath, "and hasn't been for a while."

"Why are you so upset, *beta*? Is everything okay? Whom were you talking to?" her father asked as Shalini returned to the house with Marzia, her face red from crying.

"Chandubhai," Shalini answered, glaring at him accusingly, aware that her cruel sarcasm was unreasonable.

••••

Her father's cell phone rang not twenty minutes later. Shalini was in the kitchen with Vimalbai, trying to keep herself busy, making tea. Without a word, he handed the phone to Shalini. She looked at the caller ID. It was still Chandubhai.

"Hello," She said as she walked out through the kitchen back door into the backyard.

"Are you okay?"

Shalini smiled. "Now I am." She really was okay. *He had called back. He must still care for me...*

"You understand what you're suggesting is playing with fire."

"I am already ablaze, Ram. It can't get any worse for me. In fact, I'm trying to make it right. Finally. I do realize, though, that it's not the same for you. I've had time to think about it. And I don't want to disrupt the good life you've made for yourself and your family. I understand if you don't want to see me."

"About Rushi..."

"Oh, never mind that. I thought about that too. Those are my demons, and only I can fight them. Pappa won't help me trace his whereabouts. He's adamant. And no point in me burdening you with a choice you were against from the beginning. I will get out of your hair, really. Just know that I love you, and the only way I can prevent myself from drowning in my own emotions is to let them out. That's why I'm telling you. I'm really, really sorry. In every way. For everything."

Shalini paused to take a breath, her words overflowing, convinced that she was not only destined but deserved to suffer. Knowing that afterward she would cry bitterly at least for now she was determined to display nothing but dignity.

"Are you done?" he asked calmly.

"Done with what?"

"Talking."

"I'm sorry."

"Will you be able to meet me at the Taj on the twenty-sixth? My flight arrives that afternoon. I should be checked in by 4:00 p.m."

"Taj Lands End or Gateway?"

"Gateway."

"Are you sure, Ram? I don't want to cause trouble."

"What sort of a person would I be if I knew you were hurting and I was not even willing to see you?"

••••

So Shalini called her travel agent to change her return to the twenty-eighth. Then she called Amit and Aarush.

It was only three days longer. Surely they'll survive, she thought.

"I have extended my trip by a few days. I don't plan to tell Pappa," Shalini confided to Marzia. She still resented him for not helping her locate Rushi.

"I'm happy that you will be with me a few days longer. But what exactly are your plans? I assume that you'll come to Bombay with me. I have to leave latest by tomorrow afternoon. I do need to get back to work. That Singhania lady has left me ten messages already. Allah help me." Marzia rolled her eyes toward the heavens.

"I'll leave with you tomorrow. There is really nothing much left for me to do here, anyway. I'm going to look up Raghunath Patil. Do you remember him? He was at JJ and used to hang out with Ram?"

"Who? That hooligan who was the son of our chief minister back then?"

"Yes, that Raghunath. I heard that he is now a very powerful politician, a member of parliament, and has influential connections. I hope to get his help to open Rushi's file."

"Shals, I love you and I completely understand your turmoil. But you taking things in your own hands scares the hell out of me. I don't feel comfortable with you dealing with politician types. You never know what sort of expectations they have for the favors they grant." Marzia looked genuinely concerned.

"I'm left with no choice, can't you see?"

"Why won't you work on Narsi Uncle? He might give in. He would do anything for you."

"Marzia, you saw his reaction when I asked. I even begged. I know Pappa. He rarely refuses. But once he says no, there is no way in the world you can change his mind. It frustrated Mother all her life. In fact, she complained that he never refused me anything. That I was the lucky one. His favorite. If only she were alive to witness this startling exception."

"What if Raghunath doesn't recognize you?"

"Then I hope to have Ram help me. But I want to leave that as my last option."

"But Ram's in Singapore. How can he help? You think a call will be enough?"

"It may or may not be enough. The good news is Ram's coming to Bombay on the twenty-sixth."

"Is that why you've postponed your trip? Are you going to see him?"

Shalini nodded, trying to look matter-of-fact, but the blood had already rushed to her face.

"Shalini, you didn't tell me. What did he say?"

"Nothing, but since you let him in on the fact that I was in bad shape, he wanted to see me." Shalini could not contain her happiness. Grinning broadly,

"I never thought I'd ever see such joy in your eyes again, my dear friend," said Marzia as she gave her a hug.

191

"So you're fine with me camping a few days longer at your house?" she asked, her eyes twinkling with unrestrained joy.

"No way, Shalini, I'm going to charge you a steep fine for late checkout..." Marzia hugged her once again, both of them giggling like girls.

••••

Sunset Heights, Bandra. As always, to ward off jet lag, Shalini had gone for a run, finding her way back up the steep, winding road around Dilip Kumar's bungalow. Beads of sweat glistened on her face, her T-shirt wet. She was listening to the song "Zara Zara" from *Rehna Hai Tere Dil Mein* on her iPod. It was where Ram lived, alone. She took the elevator and stepped out on his floor. He was waiting for her at the door.

"Remember, you once asked me what turns me on," Shalini said, "and I told you I wasn't sure? Well, now I know. Music. The right kind. Completely capable of rattling me and my senses. Like this song..."

And she plugged one of the earphones into his ear. Ram pulled her close and guided her inside the apartment, shutting the door behind them. She looked into his eyes. They looked intently, neither one of them blinking. Shalini felt that she was drowning in what seemed an infinite depth, a kaleidoscope of sorts, a perpetual pattern of reflection inside a reflection inside yet another reflection. The music continued to play in their ears, the tangled wires of the now split earpiece keeping them close. She could hear her heartbeat and imagined him having serious difficulty hearing the song over her pounding heart. Ram brushed his fingers over her collarbone, and Shalini almost passed out with the sensation it elicited. His breathing had gone ragged, so that made it the two of them. She couldn't stand it any longer. Like a magnet, his pull on her was so strong, she could only abandon herself to it. Her lips found his. She felt an urgency to explore, to taste, to feel as though she might never have the opportunity again. Ram wrapped his hands around the small of her back and pulled her even closer. Shalini felt the coolness of his metal bracelet against her skin. Their bodies moved to the lilting rhythm of the song still playing, one earphone in each ear. Her arms were around his neck, her fingers running through the close crop of hair at his nape, their eyes at all times locked and lost in each other's depth. The emptiness inside Shalini at the pit of her stomach, aching for Ram to fill her up, couldn't have been more urgent. She felt his hardness and closed her eyes as a moan escaped her throat. His fingers caressed the skin on her back under the T-shirt, outlined her face, tucked a wayward strand of hair and kissed her forehead, her eyelids, the tip of her nose. They kissed again and without hesitation started undressing each other. It seemed the most logical and natural thing to do. Again, an urgency took over, and they jettisoned whatever was in the way, their bodies merging until there was no thirst left unquenched, no hunger left unsated, no emptiness left unfilled. Tender. Burning. Explosive.

Shalini woke up, startled, her heart racing, her head giddy and her body tingling. Abruptly wide awake, she lay there, not sure whether or not to be happy, that what she had just experienced seemed so real, or that it was only a dream. In the early days of their marriage, Amit had accused her of being sexually unresponsive, which she believed to be true over the years. She replayed the dream over and over, overcome with guilt for feeling so invigorated, so aroused, feelings she hadn't known since Ram.

So I'm not frigid after all, she smiled as she examined her reflection in the metal post of her bed.

●●●●

On the nightstand next to her, her phone lay charging. She was in Marzia's guest room and it was 4:00 a.m. on the twenty-sixth of November.

Today was her big day.

●●●●

She thought back to the last few frustrating days. It occurred to her that she couldn't really keep the fact that she was postponing her trip from her father. He was sure to call to check on her safe arrival. She would have to come up with a good reason to explain extending her visit to India.

The previous Thursday, when she had announced her decision to leave for Bombay with Marzia, her father had rightfully asked, "Why are you leaving so soon? Your flight isn't until the twenty-fifth."

Shalini decided to keep it brief. "I have work in Bombay."

"Let me join you. I have an unwell friend that I have been meaning to check on for some time," he said.

Her heart sank. If her father accompanied them to Bombay, there was little she would be able to hide from him.

"Okay. Sounds good. Did Marzia tell you where she's going?"

It was Thursday morning. They planned to leave by 1:00 that afternoon. Shalini decided to reveal her plans to her father bit by bit. Letting him know about the change in her travel dates could wait a few days. She knew he wouldn't stay in Bombay beyond Sunday. His bridge group met every Monday, and he never missed if he could help it.

"She said she had to pay a quick visit to Saleem's great-aunt who lives in Kalyani Nagar. You were on your walk with Shireen this morning when she left."

"Oh. I guess that means she won't join us for lunch. Her great-aunt won't let her go without eating," Shalini said.

"That's what Marzia told me. She asked that we not wait for lunch."

"*Dwaarika* then?" Shalini suggested with a grin, letting go of any trace of the resentment she still carried.

"Sure, *beta*." They smiled at each other.

●●●●

Shalini rolled over in bed. Still only 4:30 a.m. There was now no hope of sleep. *What should I wear tonight…*

Ram hadn't seen her in four years. The last time they encoun-tered each other, Kathy and Shalini had just come from shopping, dressed in new outfits.

She was wishing that she could climb into the attic, without drawing her father's attention, and gather up the scarf and bracelet from her treasure box. So it was only a dusty cardboard box, it contained all her treasures, those that she deliberately did not take with her when she married Amit and left India. They would have prevented her from cutting the cord to her past. But she couldn't get rid of them either, hoping that time would help fade their meaning. But it never did.

How she would have loved to wear that scarf!

••••

It was a Friday afternoon, one of those that otherwise would have been spent in Lonavala, at Duke's Nose. Ram's bike was with the me-chanic, waiting for a part replacement. Instead, they took a local train-bus combination to Juhu, to spend the afternoon at the beach. Folding their jeans up to their knees, they walked in the sand, hand in hand, from one end of the beach to the other and back. There were other beach walkers, couples in love as they were, serious athletes pushing limits, overweight but determined middle-aged aunties in salwar kameezes finding pleasure in an afternoon walk and talk with friends, pensive dog-walkers and the like. At least three different groups were playing soccer, and hundreds of pigeons had formed a thick carpet, concealing large swaths of sand. The air was filled with the chatter and laughter of humanity. Ram hailed one of the hawkers selling peanuts served in newspaper cones, strolling up and down the beach carrying their merchandise in brightly painted crates, probably retrieved from trash bins having completed their origi-nal purpose of transporting mangoes. He was paying for their treat when Shalini noticed a bunch of runaway balloons escape over the ocean.

"Look, Ram, look," she squealed in delight, so wonderful was the sight of that splash of color against the pale blue, cloudless sky.

Her cry distracted not only Ram but the hawker as well, and three additional sets of eyes joined the multitudes who had already spotted this unexpected and wondrous sight.

It would have been impossible for Shalini to describe the collective joy she sensed among the several hundred of them, each individual utterly unlike but united in a singular moment of shared wonder.

That magical moment, like all magical moments, did not last long enough. People soon returned to their activities.

"It's a feeling that has to be felt. A feeling that stays forever, no?" she asked Ram, as they dragged their feet through the sand, instinctively heading out toward the roadside *Bhel* stall, departing the beach on this joyous note.

"Like the sweetness of a hard-won Cricket World Cup victory," Ram answered in agreement, attempting to put his feelings into words, as if in doing so they could somehow extend the pleasure, the moment.

A wailing sound only a few yards away drew their attention toward a skinny, grimy, brown body in torn shorts. As they passed the crying boy, they realized that he was young, no more than eight or nine.

"*Kay zhala?*" Shalini asked another equally grubby boy who seemed to be hovering around him, looking worried.

"He was responsible for those balloons that got away. He's afraid his mother will beat him black and blue if he returns without balloons or money."

"How did they break away?" Shalini asked. The bamboo pole to which the balloon boys usually tied their goods seemed pretty firmly planted in the sand.

"A group of hooligans were kicking and teasing that stray dog over there. He tried to save the dog and accidentally let go of the balloons..." The wailing grew even louder as the child squatted in place, totally inconsolable.

"How much do you sell each balloon for?" Ram asked the sobbing child.

"Two rupees, *Saab*," he replied between hiccups.

"Here, this should take care of those balloons. I planned to buy them for my girlfriend, anyway." Ram handed him a hundred-rupee note.

The expression on the boy's face was priceless. Shalini hugged Ram, smothering him with kisses, not caring about the gawking eyes and her public display of affection, his easy generosity and presence of mind filling her heart with love, with pride.

They resumed their way back to the main road toward the nearest bus stop.

"*Saab...saab,*" a voice called. It was that same scrawny boy but this time he was accompanied by a young woman wearing a tattered saree that barely covered her body. She had brown unruly hair that she held down with a square piece of cloth, folded along the diagonal.

Ram and Shalini stopped and smiled at them. Once the child had caught his breath, he said, "My mother wants to thank you for your kind gesture."

The woman removed her make-do scarf and handed it to Shalini. And without a word, smiling self-consciously, she pulled her little boy close to her, and trudged away.

Shalini had never loved the Universe or Ram more than she had that day. She took that ragged piece of cloth home, washed it and hemmed it. Every day she wore it in some form or the other, or at the very least, she carried it with her in her handbag as a reminder of her belief in love and humanity.

Until she lost faith.

••••

Shalini checked the clock again, her emotions getting the better of her. Still only 5:30 a.m. How much longer could she toss about?

She quickly jumped out of bed and padded softly into the hallway.

There was no sound of movement. She went back into the bedroom and quietly picked up her towel and fresh clothes. The guest bedroom did not have an attached bathroom, so she needed to use the one down the hallway. Shalini flipped on the hot-water switch, then put her toiletries and clothes on the bathroom counter and scuffed over to the kitchen. As she put water on the stove to boil for a cup of morning tea, her mind kept returning to the dream. Nervous energy built within her. Unconsciously she touched the small of her back, beneath her shirt, the sensation of Ram's engraved bracelet on her skin all too real, still producing a tremble.

●●●●

"Shalini, I have a gift for you," Ram had said, a box tied with a ribbon in his outstretched hand.

"But…" she had protested. Mixed feelings of excitement, anticipation and hesitation confounded her.

It was their unspoken agreement that Ram and Shalini would not exchange "conventional" gifts. Firstly, because Shalini lived on a tight budget and Ram had a reputation for being a lavish gift giver. She knew that she could never match him, not even come close. Secondly, she wanted him to understand that she had fallen in love with the tender, thoughtful and sensitive person hiding inside him, not the flamboyant, pretentious and brazen Ram he presented to the world. Mostly, though, she wanted Ram to stop running from himself, from his pain, from looking for love in all the wrong places — to discover instead all the good within that was obvious to her but to which he seemed blind. Considering his father provided Ram's only role model, and was limited by his own circumstances, he could not have taught his motherless son what he himself did not know.

"It's not what you think. Let me rephrase. It's a gift *for* us. Both of us. Two *kadas* to celebrate our two years together."

They were sitting under a shady tree on campus between classes.

She was in the process of untying the ribbon when Joshikaka passed by. He winked at Ram, then said to Shalini, "I promise I didn't read a word of what I engraved on those things."

Two identical metal bracelets, *kadas*, emerged from the box, each with fine lettering engraved, by Ram's faithful assistant, Joshikaka. She blushed.

"This is for both of us to remember when we disagree and fight over who's right or wrong," Ram explained.

Ram slid one bracelet onto her wrist, and when she shivered, couldn't help wondering if it was because of the cold metal or his touch.

●●●●

Oh, why hadn't I just climbed into the attic and got that out of the box?

The sound of the bubbling overheated water brought Shalini back to the kitchen. Reducing the flame, she added tea leaves, milk and grated ginger to the water.

How should she greet him? Would it be too presumptuous to hug him? Not a cursory pat but a real hug...her head buried in his neck and her hands around him, their bodies making full contact? Or maybe, she should just let him take the lead. But she didn't want to do that, she wanted to be spontaneous.

Stop it, she told herself, *spontaneous for you might mean stripping him right there in the lobby and making love to him. You are married. Thinking these thoughts is bad enough, acting on them might guarantee disaster.*

The tea had boiled over. Hurriedly, she turned off the burner, grabbed a kitchen towel and performed first aid on the kitchen counter.

Then she strained the remaining tea into a cup and piled the utensils into the sink.

Maybe she could start by extending her hand, as if to shake his. Ram would certainly extend his, and as soon as he touched her, he would pull her into a hug and say, "C'mon, Shalini, we don't need to get formal with each other." At which point she would willingly melt in his embrace, "Oh, Ram…"

God, Shalini, you're getting totally filmy, stop it.

Finishing her tea in three long gulps, she headed to the bathroom, turned on the shower and stood under the water, the temperature perfect. The water emerged without much force, dripping like rain, the pitter-patter taking Shalini back once again.

●●●●

It was past midnight. Even with calm waters, the boat rocked every now and then. Shalini and Ram lay huddled on an old *gaddi*, or a mattress, under the sheltered part of the fishing boat. Strangely, even though the approach to where the boats stood anchored was odorous, on the boat itself, the air was fresh. There were occasional whiffs every time a breeze blew, but for the most part, it was a still night. The evening had not gone as planned.

"What are we going to do?" Shalini asked when Ram tried to kick start his motorcycle and it refused to start.

"Don't worry. Hopefully, the last bus hasn't left."

He glanced at his wristwatch, the light from a street lamp glinting off his bracelet.

"Isn't it way late for that?"

The hawkers had closed shop and packed up for the day. There was no sign of mankind anywhere at this end of Marvé, a small fishing village bound by mangroves in the northern outskirts of Bombay. Joshikaka, born into a fisherman's family, was one of the first to venture out into the city for a better paying job. His brothers were still fishermen and they owned a couple of fishing boats. It was Joshikaka who had offered one of his boats so that the couple could watch the sun set over the Arabian Sea, assuring them of a memorably romantic evening together.

"Too late for buses," Ram agreed, parking his bike under the streetlamp and taking her hand. "Let's go back to the boat."

"Why? We should be heading back. Ammijaan and Marzia will get worried."

For the first time, Shalini was afraid.

"You're right. There should be a call box not too far. Let's call." Ram began walking with purpose, and Shalini had to take quick steps to keep up with him.

"What will we tell them?"

They kept walking.

"That we're working at my house on an assignment and I'll drop you as soon as we're done. Hopefully they'll fall asleep and not realize that you haven't come back until morning. The first bus comes at 4:00 a.m."

"Clever Ram." But her relief was short-lived.

From out of the darkness, stray dogs appeared, furiously barking as they protected their territories, making Shalini jump out of her skin. The added sounds of crickets rubbing their wings and owls hooting from trees composed a perfect soundtrack for a horror movie. She clung to Ram as they scurried along the only major road in Marvé for twenty minutes before finding a call box. Ram dropped in the coins and, after two unsuccessful attempts, finally got through to Marzia. Then they retraced their steps back to the bike, weariness overcoming their tense bodies.

"Let's go back to the boat. It has a mattress, should be more comfortable than sitting here on the sidewalk." Ram suggested.

"I don't think we have much choice." Shalini stood up, pointing to the menacing dogs baring their teeth and growling, as they increased in numbers and began to circle them.

His steps firm on a plank that unsteadily connected shore to boat, Ram helped Shalini balance in the dark. Jumping in first, he carried her over the water that had now leaked into the sides of the boat. The mattress lay atop a built-in cabinet, a rickety box, painted green, that was padlocked to protect the fishing nets and accessories. The good news was that over this green makeshift bed spread a canopy, a piece of black plastic tarp tied with string to bamboo poles, then arranged and secured to the boat. When the rain paid them a surprise visit that night, Ram and Shalini lay somewhat protected.

Shalini shivered even as he held her close. She wore a sleeveless blouse over linen pants, not enough clothing for a night on a boat.

"Here, put this on. It should help." Ram unbuttoned his shirt, midnight blue that looked pitch black in the dark, and adjusted it around her shoulder.

"You'll freeze," she said, burrowing under the additional layer.

"There are other ways to stay warm," he murmured as he nuzzled his face into her chest.

Shalini laughed as she pulled him even closer and held on to him tightly.

They kissed, long passionate kisses, in no hurry. The heat rose in their bodies as they embraced and rolled over and on top of each other, the boat rocking with their movements, adding a beat to the dance they had not planned. It was the first time they had made love, and it couldn't have been more perfect, more right.

When she stared at Ram's tranquil face while he lay lightly snoring on her naked breast, Shalini was left with no doubt in her mind, of her undying, unapologetic love for this gentle man. In that moment, she knew that she was bound to him forever.

"Marvel," Ram muttered in his sleep. What was he dreaming about?

It was indeed a marvelous night. Even without stars. That was her last thought before she fell asleep to the steady pitter-patter of rain on the tarp.

••••

Shalini had called Raghunath Patil's office each of the last five days. And each time she reached a staid assistant who answered in the same monotone as if he were a robot, "Yes, ma'am. I will forward your message to Mr. Patil. Thank you. *Jai Hind.*"

Sure, patriotic inefficient son of a gun, she thought.

When she called back and insisted she had left five unreturned messages already and that she was getting ready to leave the country, she finally heard a hint of emotion in his voice, "I am sorry, ma'am. But I hope you understand Mr. Patil is a very busy man and he gets at least a hundred such messages from so-called 'friends' every day. Have a good day. *Jai Hind.*"

By the twenty-sixth, she was furious and frustrated with the bureaucracy surrounding Raghunath Patil. At this rate, how was she expected to make any progress? She realized that she couldn't manage this on her own. She felt emotionally drained. Overcome with skepticism and hopelessness, she was too depleted, in every sense, to lose anything more. From her heart, no more than a burnt pot, she scraped the charred remains of strength and grudgingly gave in to her last resort.

She would beg, plead, implore, pray — just about anything — to Ram when she met him that night. Rushi was his son too, after all. She had nowhere else to turn.

••••

$\mathcal{A}$arush

Eleven

"Where are we going? Who are we meeting?" Aarush asked Nana, his hand in his pocket rubbing the cold metal bracelet that he had uncovered minutes earlier.

"Bombay," Nana answered, only partly answering the question, Aarush couldn't help noticing, a completely different train of thought now distracting him.

"Do we have a magnifying glass?"

"I know there's one lying somewhere around the house. In one of those drawers." Nana pointed to his desk and continued. "Why don't you look for it while I have Hosgé fill up the car with petrol?"

Aarush, preoccupied and in a daze, absentmindedly started going through the drawers. After mechanically opening and shutting a stack of drawers, he stopped himself.

Wait a minute, what am I looking for?

He had lost that train of thought as well.

••••

Hosgé at the wheel, Aarush and Nana drove to Bombay, on Saturday night, soon after they had gone through Shalini's eclectic memorabilia, which had left Nana looking crushed. Nana instructed Hosgé to take the Eastern Express Highway to Powai, located in the suburbs of Bombay, northwest of the Chhatrapati Shivaji International Airport.

It was obvious to Aarush that his grandfather was struggling to find the right words to tell his story, a story that seemed to be shrouded in secrecy. He sensed that it was best to let Nana reveal it at his own pace. To that end, Aarush maintained a deferential silence most of the way from Pune until they crossed the Vashi Bridge, each lost in his own thoughts. After two and half hours of exercising extreme control, Aarush wasn't able to keep quiet any longer.

"Where are we going? Who are we going to meet?"

"I want you to meet Rushi, my other grandson. Also Shalini's son. Shalini and Ram's son. Your older brother," Nana replied as if he had been waiting all along for Aarush to ask.

"What did you say?" Had he heard wrong? Was he dreaming?

Nana took Aarush's hand in his, turned his face away and gazed out the window.

"Yes, *beta.* You have a brother, Rushi. He is in his second year at IIT

Powai. If I didn't think you had the maturity to handle the story, I wouldn't be doing this. Rushi has no idea, either. So this is going to be as much a shock for him as it is for you."

"Did Mom know all along? What happened?"

"Shalini had no idea that I was so intimately involved with Rushi. That, in fact, both Shanti and I were part of his life. I couldn't have done it without her help."

"So, Mom's marriage to Dad was her second marriage? Why didn't she take Rushi with her?" Aarush's mind was racing along, a train of random thoughts.

"No, *beta*. Both you and Rushi came to us from the Seva Gram. That's why Nani dedicated the later years of her life to volunteering there. She'd be so proud to know that you are continuing her work."

Nana patted Aarush's back as he spoke. Aarush still couldn't believe what he was hearing.

"But what do you mean, both of us came from the Seva Gram?"

"Shalini had Ram's baby out of wedlock at the Seva Gram..."

"But I don't understand..." Stumped and speechless, he didn't know which of a hundred questions to ask. His pulse quickened, suddenly doubtful whether he even wanted to know any more.

"I wish I had helped Shalini when she begged me to help her locate Rushi. She wouldn't have tried to use Ram's help to contact Raghunath Patil. She would have taken her flight back to the U.S. as planned on the twenty-fifth and would be alive today. It's all my fault."

Nana was clearly distraught, barely breathing before continuing,

"But I really believed it was in everybody's best interests. Rushi is a fine young man and has been raised without a mom, but by a great dad and doting grandparents. I wasn't sure if Shalini's marriage to Amit would survive the discovery of a child from Shalini's heartrending past. It didn't seem like there was any good that could come out of Shalini reconnecting with Rushi. I also worried how you, Aarush, might react. I am so sorry. Everything looks so easy and clear in retrospect..."

Nana's whole body was convulsing. Concern for him helped Aarush regain his composure just a little. "Nana...Nana...slow down. It's okay. Nothing is anybody's fault."

Aarush waited for Nana's shaking to subside before asking more. "Does my dad know about Rushi?"

"I talked to Amit earlier this evening. Before we left. I wanted to make sure he was okay with my plan to introduce you two. He's as much my son as he's your father, Aarush."

"How did he take it?" Aarush asked, worried for his father as he pictured him receiving this shocking news, all by himself in his office, and over the phone.

"He was awfully quiet. At least he was with David and Kathy having breakfast. I felt better that he wasn't alone."

"What did he say? He did say something, right?"

"Yes, he did. That he was totally fine with me introducing the two of you. That he would love to meet Rushi. Graceful and magnanimous, as always."

"I need time to take in all this information. Let's go back to the beginning. Tell me what happened in chronological order. This is too confusing."

"Just as soon as Rushi's here," Nana said.

The car came to a halt. Aarush peered out and read the sign, INDIAN INSTITUTE OF TECHNOLOGY in large letters, both in English and Marathi, on a concrete boundary wall next to a manned gate. He could make out the outline of palm trees and other foliage but not much else. The night had descended and the light from the street lamps was not enough.

"Hello?"

Nana asked Hosgé to pull over and park along the side of the road as he placed a call.

"Yes, Rushi, it's me. I'm here. At the main gate. The usual place, yes."

"He knew we were coming?" Aarush asked, surprised.

"I called just before we left Pune. To give him a heads-up. He has to get permission before leaving the hostel for an overnight. It also gave him time to complete his assignments. He's a night owl."

Aarush was nervous. And curious. "So he knows I'm with you?"

"I told him exactly what I told you. That I was bringing my grandson Aarush to meet him."

"And he didn't ask you for any explanation?" The whole situation to him seemed preposterous.

"Of course, he had a million questions. I asked him to be patient and that I wanted to talk to both of you. Together." Nana was a fair man. He would keep them both on an even field.

The pedestrian gate opened and out walked a lean but muscular, floppy-haired young man, about the same height as Aarush, but with longer legs. Aarush had been trying to picture him all the way since the instant Nana had revealed Rushi's existence. Though he had no idea what to expect, it still came as a surprise, not an unpleasant one, when Rushi opened the front passenger door, scooted in next to Hosgé and greeted him, "*Kay mhantay*, Hosgé?"

So Hosgé knew Rushi…

"I'm so glad you got me out of here. They're serving the most godawful dinner in the hostel cafeteria tonight. I could really do with some good food," Rushi announced.

Everybody laughed.

He twisted around. "Hi Nana. Hi, I'm Rushi. Aarush, right?"

Talkative, and not shy at all, Aarush noted.

"We tease Rushi that he gets his garrulous nature from his mother," Nana remarked.

Suddenly envious, Aarush felt their familiarity with each other unsettling.

*Though Rushi did have something about his mother…*he couldn't quite tell what. He felt suddenly alone. He missed his mom. He wished Lara were with him. Nana must have sensed his feelings because he took his hand in his and gave it a squeeze.

"Just like we tease you, Aarush, for getting your mother's absentminded genius that results in such fantastic art." Even field again. *Thanks, Nana.*

"So Nana," began Rushi, "when you said on the phone that Aarush was my brother, you meant cousin, right? I thought my mother was your only daughter. How come neither you nor Nani told me anything about Aarush all these years?" And then he added, "Or is there something Nani didn't know?" Rushi smiled and winked at Aarush.

Aarush had a feeling it was going to be a tough evening — for all of them.

••••

"How did I get to be with Baba," Rushi asked Nana, "when um... Shalini...um, is it weird if I call her Mom?" He had turned toward Aarush.

"No, not at all. She is...was Mom to both of us." Aarush was still in a daze...so much information.

Aarush and Rushi had readily agreed to their grandfather's suggestion to have dinner in the Peshwa Pavilion at the Grand Maratha, Nana's preferred hotel, close to the International Airport. Sitting around a quiet corner table, they were waiting for their order to be served.

"Shalini nursed you for one week before she signed papers releasing you for adoption. She must have brought this back with her as her only proof of your existence."

Nana showed Rushi the Ziploc bag that they had discovered amongst the other treasured items. Rushi had to take a closer look at the bag before it dawned on him that what he was seeing were locks of his baby hair and nail clippings.

"So I had at least one week with her," Rushi said softly, nervously twirling his fork.

"I wish I had been more supportive of Shalini and less worried about the world. When she decided not to abort, much against your Baba's wishes, she did it knowing she risked losing Ram forever. I think where she miscalculated was in her expectation of support from me to help raise her child out of wedlock. I took the practical stance that it was the best thing for you, Rushi, as well as Shalini. I let your mother down when she begged not to give you up for adoption. She was emotionally exhausted without support from the two most important men in her life, your Baba and me."

"Then what happened?" Aarush asked.

"Not wanting to burden anybody, she swallowed her grief and pretty much did whatever I asked of her. She blindly signed documents, never questioning, once she realized that this was what I was convinced was best for everybody. Everybody except her, of course."

"It still doesn't explain how I came to be with Baba?" Rushi asked again, bending down to retrieve the fork he had dropped on the floor, nervousness making him fidgety.

Aarush offered Rushi his fork. "That's true. How did that happen?"

"Once Shalini got married and moved to the U.S., I visited the Seva Gram regularly. As a helpless grandfather, ridden with guilt, I vowed to redeem myself for my lack of courage, by helping place Rushi in a good, known family."

"What did you do?" Aarush urged, worried that every time Nana paused, that he might want to call it a night.

"A second cousin's daughter and son-in-law who lived in Australia were eager to adopt because they were unable to conceive. I used my connections with a member on the Seva Gram's board to ensure that Rushi was referred to her."

"Then how come I didn't end up in Australia?"

Aarush could feel Rushi jiggling his legs anxiously under the table.

"All thanks to your mother."

"Mom? How was that?" Aarush asked.

"When Rushi was born at Sassoon, they recorded Shalini as the birth mother on the birth certificate. What none of us realized was that Shalini also had them record Ram as the birth father."

"How did that make a difference to anybody?" Rushi asked.

"Well, it didn't, until the judge in family court pointed out that there were no release documents from the father of the child. You see, only Shalini had signed the release documents when she left the Seva Gram. Your Baba didn't even know you had been born."

Aarush glanced at Rushi, who still looked baffled, at a complete loss. "Wow...then what did you do?"

"I tracked down Ram, of course. He came down to Pune to sign the papers."

"But he didn't, did he?" Rushi asked, though it sounded like a statement, not a question.

"No, he didn't." Nana nodded.

"But why? He didn't want me to be born in the first place, right? What made him change his mind?" Rushi looked as if he was ready to explode.

"To be completely honest, he approached me right after Shalini's wedding, looking for her. He was devastated when I told him that she belonged to another man and that he was to promise never to try and contact her ever again. I have to confess it wasn't my proudest moment." Nana stared at his plate, his voice catching on the emotion.

"That's okay, Nana. You were mad at Baba. I would have been too."

"When Ram came down to sign your release papers, he had just lost his own father less than a month before. He was a broken man. In less than a year, he had lost the only two people who had loved him unconditionally."

"Poor Baba," Rushi whispered.

In those few moments, with his innocuous words of empathy for Nana and Ram, Aarush witnessed Rushi absolve them, without any formality or drama, letting his pain gather itself up and leave quietly unannounced and without any fanfare.

"Then what happened?" Aarush pressed.

"Ram stared at the papers for a long time and finally broke down. He said he couldn't do it. He felt the Universe was offering him one more chance at love. He begged me for the opportunity to embrace his son. He promised me he would be the best father he could. That he wouldn't marry anybody else. So that you, Rushi, wouldn't have a stepmother."

Nana stopped, took off his glasses and rubbed his eyes. Aarush offered him a glass of water.

All three of them needed a few moments to let the story with its painful facts sink in. Aarush wished he could have met Ram, the man his mother had loved so much. The man who had eventually given her exactly what she had yearned for — and she never knew it.

"I agreed to help Ram. Secretly, I couldn't have been happier. It just pained me that Shalini had to be kept in the dark. I wasn't one to keep secrets from her, and definitely not such a big one. Of course, I had to work even harder to find another child for my niece from Australia, quickly, so as not to draw too much attention."

"The family from Australia got another baby, and Ram got Rushi. Perfect." Aarush said. At least that chapter of the story had a happy ending.

"I wish I had met Mom." Rushi looked at Aarush.

"You didn't? I thought you were with Ram at the Taj that night?" That they must have met was a fact Aarush had taken for granted.

"I was at the Taj. Baba said he was going to meet a close friend that evening and wanted to introduce me to her, but later after dinner. He said he had some important work-related stuff to discuss with her. So we were to meet up in our suite, maybe have dessert together," Rushi explained.

"Where were you all evening then?" Nana asked.

"I watched TV in the room for a while and then went down to the pool. I showered in the men's room and then went into the lobby. I wanted to ask the concierge about bike routes in and around Colaba and if I could rent a bike the next day."

"You bike too?" Aarush asked.

"Yeah. You do too?"

"Yup. Sorry I interrupted. You were saying something about the lobby."

"Yeah, so I spotted Baba and a lady in an off-white long summer dress, sitting side by side on one of those lobby couches. I had never seen Baba sit so intimately with a lady friend, and I was embarrassed and curious. Any other time I would have walked up to them and introduced myself. But something held me back that day."

"My poor Shalini. All she wanted was to know you were fine. If only I had told her, at least hinted to her, that you were more than okay." A tear rolled down Nana's cheek as he tortured himself, over and over, about how he could have or should have done things differently.

"I watched them from a distance. Baba and the lady, um…Mom, were turned toward each other. He didn't break physical contact with her even for a moment during all the time that I surreptitiously watched them. They seemed to be in an intense conversation. Her face was flushed. Baba looked very solemn. Either she had been crying or she was angry. I couldn't tell from where I was. She definitely had a lot to say. Baba kept stroking her cheek and kissing her hands. All I could think was why in the world was Baba making a spectacle of himself. And in a public place like the Taj lobby. I wish I had paid more attention to Mom instead of worrying about how all this was causing me embarrassment." Rushi looked disconsolate.

"Don't we all wish, looking back…?" Nana whispered under his breath.

Aarush put one hand over Nana's on the table, and another over Rushi's. Then Rushi lay his free hand over Aarush's, like a sandwich, and they all sat in silence. Just then, Aarush noticed a *kada* glinting around Rushi's wrist.

"You won't believe what I have to show you," Aarush cried as he hurriedly searched his pockets.

"Look what Nana and I found today. It was in Mom's box."

Aarush set the metal bracelet he had earlier claimed on the table.

Rushi stroked the *kada* on his wrist. "Mine is Baba's. He wore it all the time. It was among the few items that I retrieved from our suite before I was rescued by an NSG (National Security Guard) commando."

Rushi's expression had changed. Anxiously he drummed his fingers on the tabletop, looking agitated, the memory of that horrific night bringing back a chaos of emotions.

"Where were you when the terrorists attacked? Your account of the story supports what we thought, that Ram and Shalini were in the lobby, because isn't that where they first opened fire?"

.   Nana, just like Amit and Aaarush, had read every piece of news reporting on what came to be known as the 26/11 bombings, the almost simultaneous attacks at the Taj Mahal Hotel, the Oberoi Trident, The Chhatrapati Shivaji Terminus (CST) train station, the Cama Hospital, Café Leopold and the Chabad Lubavitch Jewish Center, also called Nariman House, in Colaba — all locations in South Bombay. There had even been a couple of explosions in taxis. The Pakistani group Lashkar-e-Taiba (LeT) and the Students Islamic Movement of India (SIMI) ended up taking responsibility for the attacks, which claimed the lives of several hundred innocent people.

"At one point, as I stared from a distance at Baba and er...Mom... shit, I find it hard to say that." Rushi had to pause and breathe.

"So, like I was saying, at one point," he inhaled.

Aarush offered an encouraging look.

"Mom looked so excited and emotional, Baba got up and pulled her up too. They walked to the main entrance and outside toward the Gateway. At that point I took the elevator to our suite on the sixth floor of the heritage section of the Taj. We had the view of the Gateway, and I knew I'd be able to see them from our room window. I had never seen Baba in this state, ever. It was like I was uncovering a whole new side to him that I didn't know existed. By this time it was amusing to me. I remember thinking how much they reminded me of long lost lovers from a Bollywood movie. If only I'd realized then how far from amused I'd be once I found out how close to the truth I'd been..."

"If they went out for a walk, they should have been fine. The attacks happened inside the hotel, correct?" Aarush persisted. It wasn't adding up. The terrorists had opened fire in the lobby. That was where everybody assumed Ram and his mother had been. Caught unaware.

"Yes, they did. It was still daylight. Baba called me an hour or so later to let me know he would be back to the room a little late. He must have called me from the lobby. Because he left his cell phone in the room. In fact, he forgot the *kada* and his wallet there too. It seemed like he had left the room in a rush, probably to greet Mom in the lobby, with plans of coming back up before dinner. I don't know. It was around 8:30 p.m. when he called. I remember he asked if I had eaten dinner. I told him I would order room service and that I was fine."

"Why didn't they find the bodies, I wonder?" Aarush said to nobody in particular.

"They could have been anywhere, not necessarily in the lobby. There were six separate explosions at the Taj and huge fires. Baba was friends with the general manager and may have taken Mom to introduce her to the GM's wife. The GM lost his family that night. After the lobby, I think the terrorists targeted the Golden Dragon restaurant. They could have been there having dinner. Baba loved sushi. He may have even taken Mom to Wasabi, the Japanese restaurant on the first floor that was completely gutted. Or they may have been held hostage and killed later. There are so many possibilities."

Rushi had obviously thought through the events even longer and harder than all of them.

"That explains how you called me," Nana said. "You had Ram's phone with you."

"Yeah. When I heard the first explosion, I unlocked our suite door and looked out. Several other guests were at their doors too, all wondering what just happened. There was a lot of smoke. I heard screaming in the distance. A bellboy ran down our corridor and shouted, 'Attack, attack, go back into your rooms!' And I did just that. I was extremely frightened. That night and the next morning I had the TV on all the time. I figured out what was going on by watching the news. I prayed that Baba would come soon. At some point — and I had lost all time sense by then — the TV stopped working. My only contact to the outside world was gone."

Nana, taking a quick sip of water, explained: "Initially, CNN reported that all hostages were freed by the twenty-seventh itself. However, reports soon emerged that the terrorists were receiving television broadcasts and holding more hostages. That's when the security forces blocked all feeds to the hotel rooms. I lost contact with you after that and was sick to my stomach until I heard from you on the twenty-ninth once you had

215

been rescued."

"So that's why you rushed to Bombay instead of staying back in Pune for the last rites…" Things started, somewhat, to make sense for Aarush.

This cannot not be easy to recover from, Aarush thought. *Rushi was actually there.*

He had been barricaded in his room for more than fifty hours before being freed. What a nightmare. And at the end of it, he lost the most essential person in his life.

For the first time since his mother's death, Aarush did not feel alone in his loss. As much as everybody understood and sympathized with him, Rushi and he shared that one thing — the loss of a parent and the excruciating pain accompanying it.

But Rushi had it even worse. He had no parent left and Aarush had his father.

Aarush and Rushi had begun life at the very same place, Sassoon Hospital in Pune, and under the same circumstances — born to unwed mothers and given up for adoption. From that point on, their lives were anything but similar. Their paths had diverged over the next two decades, only to converge and bring them together, again, because of a common loss.

*The irony…*Aarush thought.

They sat without conversation for a while.

"I'll go up to the room and rest. I need to take my blood-pressure medicine," Nana announced.

"You don't need to turn in. It's only 11:30 p.m. Too early for young ones like you."

He gave a weak smile as he got up from his chair, exhaustion lining his face, an older man than he had been that morning.

After Nana left, Aarush and Rushi sat in awkward silence for a few minutes. All Aarush could think of was that he was sitting across from his mother's son. This made him his brother. *My brother*, he thought, having trouble digesting the idea, the reality of it.

Rushi broke the spell. "You like biking, you said."

"My girlfriend and I biked a lot in California."

"You have a girlfriend?" Rushi grinned.

"Her name's Lara. We've known each other for two years now. Because of Mom." Then Aarush told him the story of how his mother's blood type brought Lara and him together.

"Mom called me Rushi all the time…" Aarush had been wanting to tell him that since the moment Rushi introduced himself in the car.

It explained Shalini's choice of name for him. Fifteen minutes earlier, Aarush would have resented this fact; to think that every time his mother addressed him, she was thinking of her firstborn. That Aarush was a replacement, a consolation for whom she really wanted to raise as her son.

When he found that he suffered none of these feelings, Aarush felt inexplicably liberated. Also, it occurred to him that, had it not been for Rushi, his mother would never have requested an older child for adoption. In which case, his prospects of being adopted at all would have dwindled to nothing, with his severe vision problem. His life would have been no different from little Hari's.

"She called you Rushi? Tell me more about her. Do you mind?" he asked intently, eagerness shining in his eyes.

And so Aarush told his brother about their mother, the fun times, and it helped them break the ice. Rushi, in turn, related stories about Shalini as told to him by Ram.

"Wow, your dad told you so much," Aarush said.

"You mean you and Mom visited Singapore in 2004? I was in Singapore then, too. To think we may have crossed paths and would never have even known…"

Rushi's excitement was hard not to love. It was mind-boggling that he was conversing with Rushi as much as he was when they had just met. Barely four hours…

217

Whoa, Mom! he thought, *you'd be proud of me, your shy child.*

"Mom was really funny about certain foods. Like mushrooms. She wouldn't eat them because she thought they tasted like meat. 'How would you know, if you haven't ever eaten meat?' I'd tease her all the time," Aarush chuckled.

"You know what? I don't like mushrooms, either. And Baba always teased me about that."

"It's funny, isn't it? I don't share any of Mom's genes, but I am told by everyone who knew her, even Nana-Nani, that I couldn't be more like her. Not in looks but in my personality. And especially in my love for painting."

"And I have been told that I look exactly like her, but beyond the mushroom dislike that I just learned, I am nothing like her. It *is* funny." Rushi nodded and added with unconcealed pride, "I am just like Baba."

"Where did you think Mom was all these years? What did Ram and Nana-Nani tell you?"

"You know, now that I think about it, I don't remember them really saying anything. I grew up knowing she wasn't part of our life. I know this will sound strange, but I just assumed she was dead. They all sort of went along with it. Nana-Nani very rarely mentioned her. When I was younger, I remember asking Nani once, and it made her cry. I decided never to bring it up with her again. Baba talked a lot about Mom and kept her really alive through our conversations, but he never put up any pictures. I asked him about that, and he said that it was hard for him. He offered to put one up, get one from Nana-Nani, if I really wanted, but honestly, I didn't care. Especially once I realized that Baba wasn't inclined, anyway. I liked that I could imagine her any way I wanted in my head."

"But Nana-Nani's house has a ton of pictures. Of Mom, Dad and me. Didn't you ever ask them?"

"You know what? I have never been to their house. They always visited us, never the other way around. And I never thought to ask why. I guess I just didn't know any better."

Aarush ran out of questions for the moment. He was lost in his thoughts.

After a while, Rushi asked, "Are you up for a bike ride tomorrow? I can borrow two bikes from a friend who lives close by, in Juhu. I'd love to show you a place Baba took me to many times. He said it was Mom's favorite too."

"I'd love to," Aarush said. He could hardly sleep that night.

••••

Aarush felt his legs stiffen and become heavy even as he tried to pedal faster. It was almost impossible to maintain balance on the bicycle, the ear-piercing barks of the stray dogs making him jump out of his skin. He was afraid it was only a matter of time before he felt their angry jaws grabbing his ankle, their bristling teeth sinking into his flesh.

It was 5:30 a.m. Hosgé had dropped them off in Juhu, where Rushi's friend had arranged for bikes. After adjusting seats and handles, with helmets on their heads and cold water bottles in cages, they were off. Aarush followed Rushi who knew the roads well and had made the ride many times before. As they rode through the dark, there was a long stretch of the main road lit by fluorescent streetlamps every fifty meters that was home to a multitude of stray dogs. A pack of them raced after Rushi and Aarush as they violated their "established" territories.

"Stay calm. Don't make any eye contact and keep riding," Rushi told him.

"I'm glad you know that. My instinct would have been to stop," Aarush said, his heart pounding.

Within a mile or so they had safely crossed the canine zone.

"Phew. That was scary," said Aarush.

Rushi laughed at the look on Aarush's face. "The first time we rode through here, I got the same instructions from Baba."

"You did this a lot? Riding together?" Aarush asked.

"Yes. Especially once I moved to Powai for college."

"How often did he visit you?"

"Every month. And Nana visits at least twice a month. Now, more often. Almost every weekend unless I am busy with something. Nani would have moved here if she were alive. Watch, Aarush…" Rushi cautioned, as they approached insidious looking speed bumps.

"Whoa…" Aarush exclaimed as he lifted his bottom from the seat just in time, shifting his weight to the pedals and handle and saving himself from the impact.

"When did you move to Singapore?" Aarush asked, catching up with Rushi once again.

"When I went into first grade. I think I was about six."

"That must have been right around the time I met Mom." Aarush said, counting back.

"Stay to the left. We have to take that left at the fork after that big junction."

Aarush scanned the crossroad in all directions. The traffic lights were out. He had learnt from having ridden with the Pedal Pushers, that even with traffic lights functioning, one never took chances with traffic in Bombay.

"Where did you live before moving to Singapore? Bombay?"

"No, Pune actually. That was the only way Baba could go to work. Nani came every weekday morning. Nana hadn't yet sold his factory and was very busy himself."

The sky was lit with the first light of dawn, though there was no sign of the sun yet. They had crossed the wide main roads and now entered a web of *galis*, narrow lanes. Little stores lined one side of each lane. Even that early in the morning, there was the smell of frying as little chai stalls offered *batata vadas* and samosas for breakfast. It seemed strange to Aarush that suddenly out of nowhere, rickshaws bearing passengers and a crowd of two-wheelers joined them, headed in the same direction.

"Why is there so much traffic in our direction?" he asked Rushi.

"They're all heading to the ferry. People who work on Madh Island take it to cross over without having to take the longer circuitous route from Malad."

"Are we taking the ferry?" Aarush was excited to try something new.

"Yes, we are."

The boarding dock was comprised of just a plank to load and unload passengers and vehicles. It connected the edge of the shore to the stern section of the ferry and was wide enough to accommodate two-wheelers onto the ferry. There was a person assigned to physically place and remove the makeshift walkway each time a ferry arrived or prepared to depart. The distance from the end of the road to the waiting ferry was not more than fifty yards, but Aarush and Rushi had to dodge a rush of passengers who were either unaware, or chose to turn a blind eye to the courtesy of forming a line.

"Here, can you hold onto my bike? I'll go get tickets," Rushi said as he hurried off to the ticket counter.

Holding the two bicycles, Aarush waited for him on the side, feeling self-conscious as people stared at him. He must have looked like an alien — dressed in padded bicycling shorts, helmet, gloves, while the rest of the passengers were people heading to work, wearing regular clothes, some on scooters or bicycles with entire families hanging off the vehicles, no protective gear, not even for children or wives.

There was trash everywhere and the stench along the approach to the ferry was unbearable. Within minutes Aarush was breathing through his mouth, the odor turning his stomach. At last Rushi returned, immediately registering the look of discomfort on Aarush's face. "It's just till we get onto the ferry, bro. That odor won't travel far."

Aarush smiled. Rushi's subtle display of affection had not been lost on him. In fact, so much was said in that quick, three-letter word that Aarush beamed at him, unable to explain even to himself his heart swelling with pride and joy.

They were the last to board the ferry, resting their bicycles against the metal rails as the ferry blew its horn announcing departure.

"Nana said your Baba was an architect?" Aarush asked, once they were moving smoothly.

"In Pune. He worked for a construction firm." He leaned on the side rail, looking into the distance as he spoke. "Nana arranged for the job, is what I understood. Baba wasn't excited about it at all. I don't think he was ever happy in Pune, either. Too conservative and claustrophobic for him. He had an offer from a firm in Singapore for a few years. But he waited for me to get old enough." He paused before adding, "He was an amazing father," his voice wavering ever so slightly.

The sun was just beginning to lift above the horizon.

"It seems to me like my first year at IIT, away from Baba, was in preparation for me to learn to live without him. Until then I don't remember being away from Baba longer than a weekend."

Aarush leaned on the rails as well, gazing at the rising sun. "What else did you guys do together? Apart from biking, I mean?"

"Cricket. Watching even more than playing. Baba took me to the West Indies for the 2007 World Cup. It was our most memorable vacation together before I left home."

"Mom loved cricket too. She usually followed it online through cricinfo.com."

Rushi swung around toward Aarush, his attention suddenly keen.

"Baba was the opening batsman for the Mumbai Cricket Team and even played in the Ranji Trophy when he was in college. He said Mom came to watch him every single match he played. She'd bunk classes but never miss a game."

"That explains where she got her passion for cricket. Dad loves baseball." Aarush smiled at him.

The ferry sounded its horn. They had arrived at Madh Island.

"I'd love for you to meet my Dad one day. He's been an amazing father too. In spite of all his travel and work commitments. I've realized it more so, since Mom died," Aarush said.

Most of last night he had spent speculating on how his father would react to this story — Shalini's story — the parts his father had not been privy to. *It just seems so...so brutal. Cruel almost*, he thought.

"I would like that," Rushi was saying, "maybe the next time he visits?"

Aarush nodded.

They waited for the hurried rush of passengers to subside before they hauled their bikes onto the plank and rolled them down to shore. Aarush noticed that this end of the ferry's route was significantly trash-free — and odor-free.

They mounted and took off once again, the road now fairly straightforward, the only main thoroughfare on the island. It wound its way over and across a few gentle inclines and traversed a landscape that was unlike anything Aarush had seen anywhere in and around the concrete jungle of Bombay. He was intrigued by the sheep bleating and grazing in open expanses of grass while shepherds and their young boys-in-training rested under the scattered shades of banyan and *peepal* trees.

It was then that he registered the sun's ascent into the sky, quick and bright, and uncomfortably warm. It was not even 7:00 a.m.

For the next ten miles they kept biking, Aarush following Rushi without any conversation, as they concentrated on staying out of the way of the red BEST buses plowing down the narrow road that had been designed as a single lane but that was accommodating, God knew how, two-way traffic.

The sky could not have been clearer, and yet, every now and then, they were cast into the shadow of dense clouds of crows that came in waves, soaring in unison from one area, landing in another open patch, their *caw-cawing* so loud and piercing that it drowned out the sound of honking vehicles. Finally, they reached the end of the main road, having crossed several resorts, many big bungalows, small fishing villages, dense mangroves and dozens of coconut trees. The expanse of the Arabian Sea lay before them, a welcome surprise, as the dense foliage had been hiding the water from them for the last twenty minutes. They leaned their bikes against a light post, and Aarush quickly trailed Rushi as he headed toward a chai stall.

"Would you like some tea?" he asked when Aarush caught up with him.

"Sure."

"*Do chai. Aur ek Parle-G.*" Rushi handed a twenty-rupee note to the boy working the counter of the little shack of a stall.

"That's it?" Aarush asked. Twenty rupees translated to about half a dollar. He was still not over the habit of converting everything into U.S. currency.

Rushi chuckled as the boy gave back five rupees change.

"Have you ever wondered about your birth mother?" Rushi asked.

The question caught Aarush by surprise.

"Umm…to be honest, the thought has crossed my mind only a few times. Only since Mom died. But I concluded nobody could ever be my mother other than Mom." Aarush paused, then asked, "How about you? Did you think about it a lot?"

"Baba was both mother and father to me, and that was all I knew. I never really missed having a mother. But I have to confess I wondered, sometimes fantasized, how it would be to have one. Because all my friends had moms, of course. And also because Baba kept her alive between us with all the stories…"

They hiked over to a small rocky beach, not far from the stall, where several multicolored boats lay dispersed and anchored around the banks.

"This place looks very familiar to me," Aarush said as he scanned the view, a pagoda emerging through the fog in the distance.

"I wonder why I feel like I've been here before," Aarush persisted.

"This was Baba's all-time favorite spot. He said it was Mom's too. That's why I wanted to bring you here," Rushi explained.

"Oh-my-gosh, Rushi." Suddenly it all clicked.

"What?"

"You have to visit me at JJ, and I'll show you something. Something marvelous."

That was all the explanation Aarush would offer him for now. Rushi would have to see *Marve'l* in person. Aarush soaked in the view, wishing he had brought his camera. It would have been fun to compare, painting and photograph…

"You know, I could never make sense of what's written on Baba's *kada*. What's on yours?" Rushi asked, sliding it off his wrist.

"Neither Nana or I have good enough eyesight to read it. The lettering has dulled and there is a lot squeezed into a small space. We've been meaning to get a magnifying glass," Aarush laughed, gesturing to his thick glasses and handing Rushi his *kada*.

"Mine simply says, '*I'll meet you there — Rumi.*' I have wondered if that was how Mom addressed Baba or some code between them. It just seemed too strange to be engraved..." Rushi said as he peered at the inner side of Aarush's.

"What does mine say?"

"'*Out beyond ideas of wrongdoing and rightdoing, there is a field.*'"

He read aloud each word slowly as he carefully deciphered the fine, faint engraving.

"Aarush. Look, look at this!" From his pocket Rushi hurriedly fished out his cell phone. "This used to be Baba's phone. My gosh, the two *kada*s together make sense! Look at their last text exchange...I just couldn't get myself to delete it...Thank goodness..."

"Marzia will drop me at the Taj around 5pm," Shalini texted.
"Where do you want to meet? In the lobby?" Baba texted back.
"Out beyond ideas of wrongdoing and rightdoing, remember our field?" Shalini texted back.
And Baba had texted back. "I'll meet you there."

They stared at each other. Rushi returned his bracelet and they slid them back around their respective wrists in silence.

"I hope Baba got a chance to tell Mom about me before they..." Rushi's voice trailed off.

They sat looking out over the sea long after they had finished drinking their tea and eating the pack of Parle-G biscuits.

••••

"We plan to come during Thanksgiving, my One Good, bug!" Lara was practically shrieking with excitement.

It was the Monday following the weekend of revelations spent with Rushi and Nana, the bike ride to Marvé, all of it. It had been a test of his patience, waiting to talk with Lara. She had been out camping with friends and had had no cell phone coverage all weekend.

"That's awesome. How come?" Aarush was pleasantly surprised. Nana had called Aunty Amy Jo, as promised, and actually invited them. He had just expected that by default it would be over the Winter Holidays.

"Soph's idea."

"Whoa, whoa, whoa…Soph, Aunt Kathy and Uncle David joining you guys too?" Aarush asked.

"Not Uncle David. He'll visit his parents. Your mom talked so much about Aunt Kathy to your granddad that he asked my mom to extend the invitation to her as well. In fact, he insisted that hosting the people his daughter loved so much would be the best gift anybody could give him. He is such a sweetheart, Aar."

"This is going to be awesome. Murtaza and Tulsi will help me plan it all. Marziamaasi is going to be ecstatic when she hears this."

"I know. We'll all have faces to match names. Finally."

"What made you guys decide on Thanksgiving?"

Thanksgiving was such an American tradition, a family event. It was unheard of, especially for Aunt Kathy and Uncle David, to spend that day apart without stuffed turkeys and all.

"It will be one year this November…Aunt Kathy really wanted to be there."

"Oh…" Now he understood.

"Soph accidentally found a saved text trail on Aunt Kathy's cell phone."

Aarush chuckled. "They texted each other like a hundred texts a day. I always teased Mom they were worse than teenagers."

"Aar, Aunt Kathy knew everything. In some ways even more than Marziamaasi. About Ram. And the baby she gave up. Soph said she called her baby by a name that had part of your name in it...I can't remember it exactly..."

"Rushi."

"Yes, Rushi. That's it. You knew? How come you didn't tell me?"

"Bug, I just found out myself. I'll tell you all about it. Why don't you finish first?"

"It appears your mom and Aunt Kathy ran into Ram, very briefly, in Singapore. Aunt Kathy feels responsible for supporting your mom in her quest to locate Rushi. And meet Ram," Lara continued, but her voice had lost some of its steam.

"She must have known how tormented Mom was...any good friend would have done that." Aarush couldn't help wondering what else Aunt Kathy knew.

"Bugaboo, tell me what happened over the weekend. I've been rattling away, but I get a feeling something big happened. How did you find out about Rushi?" She asked, suddenly impatient.

Aarush took a deep breath, unsure where to begin.

"Aar, tell me..."

"Bug, I discovered over the weekend, like you did, and Dad did, that for eighteen years I had no idea I had a brother — my One Bad..." Then he quickly added, "My One Good, too," wishing Lara could see his face. "I have him for the rest of my life."

•••••

227

Shalini

Twelve

Shalini wore a white, shin-teasing, sleeveless dress, an appropriate choice for the hot and humid Bombay afternoon. She had embroidered the dress herself. Ram had told her he'd be at the Taj after 4:00 p.m. She had told him she couldn't be there before 5:00 p.m. — why she couldn't imagine. Time seemed to have come to a standstill — or at best was moving at a snail's pace.

Marzia had awakened from her afternoon siesta at her usual time, 3:30. Seeing Shalini already dressed and ready, she asked, "Are you leaving already?"

"Uh, no. Not yet. I have to be at the Taj at 5:00."

"I want to pick up some scarves for gifts from that store at the Courtyard. I can give you a ride. It's only a few blocks from the Taj."

"Terrific."

Marzia must have sensed Shalini's anxiousness around about the rendezvous, because she added, "Give me ten minutes. I'll get dressed. We can leave right away. Maybe you can help me pick scarves? You have great taste, and I can never seem to decide. Takes me forever."

Shalini hugged Marzia. Marzia didn't need her help with anything, certainly not choosing scarves. "Why am I so nervous, Mars?"

"I'm sure he is too. Don't worry." Marzia squeezed her reassuringly.

"Thanks," Shalini muttered, "for everything."

"You do what you have to, okay? We only have one life to live. *Inshallah*, God willing, He will figure everything out," Marzia said softly, not letting go of her friend.

As they approached the Appolo Bunder area where Bombay's two quintessential landmarks stood in all their majesty — the Taj Hotel, with its legendary façade complementing the striking Tower Wing, and the Gateway of India — Shalini was overcome with nostalgia. Sights and sounds along the way had transported her back to their JJ days.

"Remember how we sneaked out of class to see a matinee show of *QSQT*?" Marzia asked as the car passed the Regal Cinema Circle. *QSQT* became a popular acronym for the 1988 Bollywood blockbuster hit *Quyamat Se Quyamat Tak*, starring the then-teenage heartthrob Amir Khan.

"It was our first time bunking classes. Little did we know then that that was just the beginning," Shalini laughed.

"And the thrill of shopping at these street markets."

"That too, on such scant budgets. We became great bargainers, didn't we?"

Picking out the scarves took no more than twenty minutes, and it was still only 4:45 p.m. when their car pulled up in front of the Taj lobby main entrance.

Matching the majestic look of this old-world building from the early 1900s, a turbaned doorman, dressed in all the grandeur of the royal guard, held open the car door for her.

"Do you want me to pick you up?"

"I don't think that will be necessary. I'll call you if I need a ride. You know Ram."

"If he is anything like I remember, he will bring you right to my doorstep. Give him a hug from me," Marzia winked.

"Mars…" Shalini blushed.

Marzia reached out and gave Shalini one last reassuring hug.

●●●●

The revolving door leading into the sumptuous lobby smoothly transferred Shalini from the sultry and stifling world outdoors to the cool, air-conditioned indoors, a clear and not entirely unexpected contrast for any five-star hotel in western India. She pulled out her cell phone to let Ram know she was early. There were no bars on her cell phone screen, indicating poor service. She headed to the concierge desk.

"Could you please put in a call to Mr. Ram Rugge? He just checked in and I don't know his room number."

"Sure, ma'am. Who can I say is here for Mr. Rugge?"

"Shalini."

After looking up the room number, the concierge called Ram's room and handed her the phone.

"Hello," Ram said, casually.

"It's me. I'm a little early."

"You're here? Sorry I was…um…I'll be down in a minute."

"No, no. Don't worry. You don't need to rush. I'll wait."

Shalini hung up and found a quiet corner. Her heart was furiously palpitating in nervous anticipation. She tried to distract herself by looking around and admiring the elegant onyx pillars, the luminous alabaster ceilings, the pietra-dura floor panels and hand-woven silk carpets adorning the lobby floor. She had hardly sat down when Ram appeared at the far end of the room.

That was fast, she thought as her heart skipped a few more beats.

Waving to catch his attention, she waited nervously as he crossed the lobby and approached her.

For days she had wondered how this moment would play out. Would it be awkward? How should she greet him? After all, how do you say hello to somebody you are meeting after decades, somebody who in that previous lifetime not only shared love and promises, but also a child? (She had long written Singapore off as a fluke.)

"Hey..." he said softly, reaching for her right arm without missing a beat, pulling her toward him and giving her a long tight bear hug, almost lifting her off her feet. She could hear and feel his heart racing through the crumpled white linen shirt he had donned over a pair of jeans. He kissed her once on her right cheek, before burying her face in the crook of his neck, holding her close for a long moment.

So she needn't have worried. Her heart leapt with joy, still racing, every inch of their torsos in contact, their bodies communicating what words could not.

They sat down beside each other on the red soft couch Shalini had claimed. Ram held her hand, never once letting go throughout the ensuing conversation. His thumbs caressed the space between her thumb and index finger, putting her at ease immediately.

They sat for a long time. Emotions kept overwhelming Shalini, and she found herself alternately laughing and crying, sobbing and smiling, exactly where they had left off in 1991. Very soon, she reported the story of her life after they had parted ways — Amit, her choices and decisions that had resulted in so much regret, Aarush and the meaning he gave to her flawed life, her struggle with depression and resulting turmoil, and finally her inability to continue with the way it was any longer.

"I'm so sorry, Ram. You shouldn't be at the receiving end of my mess. I didn't ask to meet you for this." Shalini sniffed as she wiped her eyes with the back of her hand.

Ram looked around for tissues. Not finding any, he simply pulled Shalini into an embrace, her face pressed into his shoulder. "Feel free to use my shirt…you haven't forgotten your favorite spot, have you?" he said, stroking the nape of her neck.

Shalini smiled weakly through her tears and she gently pushed herself out of his embrace, her nose watering, suddenly embarrassed as she became aware of the curious eyes of onlookers. Ram sensed her need for fresh air and pulled her to her feet. "Let's take a walk."

The simple act of stepping out helped to change the mood of their conversation.

"I've said enough about myself. Tell me, what have you been up to?"

"Well…I live in Singapore. I've been there for more than a decade. I have my own architectural firm. But I am thinking of moving back to Bombay."

"What made you move to Singapore?" What she really wanted to know was whom he was married to, what was she like…like her, or different?

"I got a great job offer, one I couldn't refuse."

"But what made you settle down there?"

"One thing led to another. Singapore was close to Bombay without being Bombay. Besides, the schools were great."

"You went back to school?" Shalini asked, surprised.

"No, not me. I meant schools for kids."

She felt stupid. "Oh, of course. And now you want to move back to Bombay because…?"

"To be closer to my son. He got into IIT, Bombay."

So that was his son in the picture she had seen at his apartment in Singapore.

"He's your only child?"

"Yes."

Shalini hoped that Ram would throw some light on his family life, especially on his wife, but he didn't offer much explanation.

I could ask him directly...

Though she was not sure she wanted to know, she had a feeling he was happily married. That was it.

He was being sensitive, and polite. So that I won't feel worse than I already do. What else could you expect after having just recounted your entire sorry tale?

They were silent for a while, watching, hand in hand, hundreds of pigeons staging a choreographed, synchronized performance, as if exclusively for them.

The sun set and the breeze cooled ever so slightly. Shalini propped herself and scooted onto the low concrete wall lining the sidewalk along the harbor, her face toward the road, away from the sea. Ram leaned on the same wall looking in the opposite direction, toward the sea, absentmindedly stroking Shalini's bare arm. Her skin, like the ocean water, was pebbled with the gooseflesh of anticipation and chilled by gusts of uncertainty.

"Ram..." she whispered, his touch making her tremble.

"What?" he asked, oblivious to the feelings he was eliciting.

"I can't think..." she said leaning forward, her lips gravitating toward his.

"Then don't."

Their eyes locked, their lips within a hair's breadth, the intensity palpable between them.

"Look at those love birds," somebody whistled and called out.

"Go get a room, auntie," another voice taunted.

There were catcalls and lewd gestures accompanied by condescending laughter from a group of young bawdy Eve-teasers hanging out not far away.

We should know better, Shalini thought as her face went crimson with embarrassment.

Ram abruptly straightened, took Shalini by her elbow and said, "Let's get out of here."

Offering no resistance, she made note of the fact that Ram had not succumbed to an altercation with the hooligans, as he would have twenty years earlier.

They walked back to the Taj and through the main entrance re-entered the lobby. Shalini excused herself to find the restroom. Her make-up needed some repair. She had been so emotional all evening, she was certain she looked awful. Ram had made dinner reservations in one of the fancier restaurants of the Taj, and looking pathetic was not an option.

Now, as she stared in the ladies' room mirror, touching up her face and nose, outlining her lips with fresh lipstick, the evening flashed through her mind.

So far, it had been both intense and overwhelming. It had also gone contrary to expectations. In matters of their personal chemistry, where she had prepared herself to face heartbreak and internal struggle, it had actually been surreal, almost dreamlike. Their connection had been instantaneous; any lingering doubts about their picking up from where they'd left off were solidly put to rest.

But Ram's unwillingness to contact Raghunath Patil and the resistance she sensed from him in helping track down Rushi was bewildering. It felt like a rejection. In the mix of emotions that the evening was conjuring, she was having difficulty processing his reactions, one way or the other.

On the one hand, she wanted to get angry with him. How could he refuse? It wasn't such a big favor. It wouldn't be that much of a favor for Ram himself to ask Raghunath. It wasn't as though what they wanted would in any way take from anybody else?

On the other hand, she was enjoying their magical evening so much that for selfish reasons she didn't want to spoil it by pushing him too hard on the issue. Also, to be completely fair, Ram hadn't exactly refused. He had only hesitated.

"I haven't met Raghunath in over a decade. I don't feel comfortable asking him for favors," was what he had said. "But I'll see what I can do. Maybe, we can find some other way of tracking Rushi down," he had also added.

She was suddenly irritated. It was but a polite refusal. "There is no other way," she snapped. "Pappa won't help, though I know he knows more than he thinks I know. Has he ever said anything suspicious to you in your conversations with him? You two *have* been in touch, haven't you? About what? Tell me Ram, please."

They had been standing right in the middle of the opening of the Gateway, under its magnificent arch. Ram, in his characteristic but frustrating way, did not answer her question and offered no explanation. He had simply pulled Shalini in to him, his arm around her shoulder and murmured, "Shhhh, Shalini, shhhh."

She splashed her face with cold water, trying to reset her expression. She was so happy when she was with him. She felt things that she had never felt with Amit. Or anybody else. And she had an uncontrollable desire to touch him, taste him, disrobe him, and probe him. In the mirror's reflection she watched her neck and face turn crimson. Lowering her eyes, she tried to maneuver her thoughts in another direction.

But did he feel the same? He seemed eager and responsive. He had demonstrated that he still cared. He was thoughtful, affectionate. Did he want her the way she wanted him? Where reason ceased and passion ruled.

Shalini made one last effort to shake herself out of her passionate stupor.

It doesn't matter, she thought. *I am almost certain Ram won't do anything about it. Even in the remote possibility that he feels the same strong feelings. He was resistant about meeting in the first place. He probably risked a lot when he succumbed to that weak moment in Singapore. He has obviously given it a lot of thought since then. He does have existing commitments. And he is a gentle soul. He would never desert his family. I wouldn't want him to, either. No, I wouldn't, would I? And Amit? What about Amit? Oh God, what about Amit?*

Tears started flowing freely down her cheeks like the tap water she'd been running to wash her face, her effort at fixing her makeup literally going down the drain. She hurried into a stall for privacy as another hotel guest entered the ladies' room. Dabbing her face dry with toilet paper, she returned to the sink and made one final attempt to touch up her face, along with a resolve to hold herself together for the rest of the evening.

Be in the moment, be in the moment...don't spoil today thinking about tomorrow, she kept repeating.

It had taken her much longer than planned in the restroom. And now Ram was missing. She scanned the vast busy space and, after a few moments of alarm, spotted him talking on one of the lobby phones. She hoped her face didn't betray her turmoil, as she approached him with a deliberately bright and chirpy look.

Just before she walked within hearing distance, he hung up.

"Are you all right?" He almost reached out but closed his fists and exercised restraint.

"I'm sorry I took long. The restroom was busy. Must be a wedding or something."

For the first time since they met earlier that evening there was an awkwardness between them.

Maybe he was having second thoughts. About their meeting. About them and whatever it was they still had. He must have been thinking about what just almost happened. And he was heaving a sigh of relief that nothing had. And that thank goodness they were on the street where nothing could have. It was all her fault. She was taking advantage of him. In a moment of weakness.

"I'm sorry about what happened," she said, gathering her courage.

He looked surprised, as if he had no idea what she was saying.

"I mean about what happened outside. I didn't mean to put you in an embarrassing situation. I'm not like that. I don't know what came over me..."

"Shalini."

"I promise I'll behave myself. From this moment. You won't have to worry..."

"Shalini. Stop."

She looked at him, tears threatening to spill over.

He was right. They were playing with fire. Why was he right? And why was it that what she wanted seemed always at odds with what was right?

"Let's go to the poolside. I made reservations for us at Wasabi. But we have another hour. We can order drinks. What do you think?"

He took her hand in his. Firmly.

"Okay," she said, relieved.

They walked from the lobby toward the elevators to the beautiful open courtyard poolside. Along the way Ram greeted and smiled at a couple of staff members.

"Why does everyone know you?" Shalini asked, bouncing back to her curious playful self, her hand still safely ensconced in Ram's. "Have you become a famous someone that I don't know about?"

"If only. It's because my father and the Taj GM are childhood buddies. Should that be 'were buddies,' now that my father's no more, I wonder?"

"Then, isn't it a little awkward for us to be holding hands?" Shalini felt instantly worried. "What will they think? Or is this something you do regularly?"

Ram's expression changed, the lightness vanishing.

Shalini bit her lip and gave his hand an apologetic squeeze. "I'm sorry. I was only kidding." *Still as sensitive*, she thought.

Ram held open the glass door that led guests from the air-conditioned hotel interior out to the open-air pool, and they found an unoccupied table. Ram pulled out a chair for Shalini, then he took a seat across from her.

They sat quietly for a while. Shalini's thoughts wandered to Amit. She felt that dark shadow of guilt envelope her. What was she doing here with Ram? This was not just about Rushi? Or Raghunath Patil? She couldn't fool herself into believing that.

She squeezed her palms together, resisting the urge to reach out and touch him. It was becoming clear to her, in spite of herself, that what she really wanted was Ram. She wasn't sure the clarity was doing either of them any good. It would only complicate an already complicated situation.

Besides, wasn't it entirely possible that she was romanticizing her feelings for Ram because things were not that great with Amit?

And things had been crumbling for a while now. Amit had never elicited the passionate, wild and explosive feelings that Ram had. Neither had Amit ever been able to engage with Shalini or share interests the way Ram had.

With time, though, they had built a life together, and Shalini had indeed come to love him in an affectionate, caring sort of a way. Wasn't that what real life was all about? Shalini entered Amit's world to find the place where they could connect. She listened to him share with her his deepest thoughts — about his research topics, his teaching experiences, his desire to set up a charitable foundation to serve deserving underprivileged children in developing countries like India, and so on. She became his rock as she supported him in his endeavors and provided all the administrative and logistical help that Amit wasn't capable of doing himself.

Over their sixteen years of marriage, they had been blessed with a modest fortune, what with Amit's students having started successful start-ups with the research they had done under his guidance. Along with raising Aarush, it had all seemed fulfilling enough.

In the last couple of years, however, Shalini had begun to feel an intense and burning need to return to the world she had closed doors to so long ago. With help from her therapist, Shalini concluded that the only solution was to tackle her inner demons and the recurring panic attacks, to stop running away from her past by burying herself in work that left no time to think. The scary part was, the more she faced her problems head on and the more she addressed her core issues, the more obvious it became to her how disconnected she had become from Amit. She had to wonder if they had ever been connected.

It was true she couldn't completely blame Amit. From the

beginning of their marriage, Shalini had set the stage. She encouraged Amit's dependency on her so that she became his crutch. In trying to make up for her feelings of guilt over her inability to give Amit access to her emotional landscape, she overindulged him. Without the foresight to predict the consequences of her overcompensation, Shalini inadvertently unbalanced their relationship, eventually rendering it unsustainable.

In the beginning Amit was happy as a lark. He had a devoted wife who had taken the load of mundane activities from his shoulders, freeing his mind to pursue what he loved most — pushing the frontiers of pure and applied mathematics through research. A simple human being by nature, he approached every situation with his characteristic earnest straightforwardness. Ironically, the contradiction in Amit's personality that battled with Shalini was the inconsistency between his professional and personal beliefs. Where Amit routinely questioned and challenged established mathematical assumptions and beliefs, keeping an open mind to new scientific evidence and allowing his mind to be flexible and grow in his professional world, he stubbornly stuck to conventional social thinking, strictly adhering to patronizing customs, unquestioning belief in traditional philosophies belonging to a bygone era with an antiquated assumptions about the role of his wife. To Shalini this presented itself as an obdurate resistance to growth and change, to raising awareness and evolving consciousness, an adamant rejection of new ways to look at old ideas — in short, stunting the growth of their relationship.

Unable or, perhaps, unwilling to consider any of his wife's desires or passions as anything more than a mere pastime, Amit, time and again, frustrated Shalini with his disinclination to engage with her at any level beyond Aarush and his education.

Against all logic, Shalini had played along over the years, making Amit, and later Aarush, her life's mission, her only purpose, as if somehow this would help her escape her past.

Unfortunately, it was only a matter of time before she began to stumble and break under the strain of her self-generated pandemonium.

With constructive tips from her counseling sessions, Shalini first freed herself from a lifetime of self-repudiation, self-rejection and self-blame. She made sincere efforts to take steps to repair the growing separation between them. She tried hard to engage Amit in her interests, invite him into her universe.

"Amit, next weekend is Open Studio at Hunters Point Shipyard."

Shalini had reminded Amit about her upcoming exhibition, her debut, in San Francisco, at least a dozen times. She had worked hard over several years to rediscover her inspiration and resurrect her creative spirit, and finally felt confident enough to register at the popular Spring Art Festival.

"I'm not here next weekend. I forgot to mention, it's the annual scientists' retreat weekend in Bodega Bay."

"Amit, you can't be serious. I put the dates in your calendar four months ago when I registered."

"It's no big deal, Shalini."

"What do you mean, it's no big deal? It is a big deal. It's my first appearance as an exhibiting artist. I've worked really hard and I could use some moral support. You've gone there every year since we got married. And didn't you say all you guys do is golf and fish? Can't you skip it one year?"

"This is my annual chance to network with research scientists from other universities. Even more importantly, this is an informal but crucial opportunity to raise funds from the industry representatives who also spend the weekend with us. So I can hire research assistants to keep my department running. Surely you understand the importance of my job, my career? After all, it pays the bills."

She was appalled by his condescension. "Network? Is that male-euphemism for gossip?"

"Shalini!" Amit's face was red with anger. "How dare you talk to me like that?"

"I am allowed to feel disappointed, upset, angry — whatever — and express it too. I am your wife."

"What is wrong with you? What happened to the patient, understanding, supportive Shalini? When did you stop appreciating the importance of my work?"

"When I realized that you never even began to appreciate mine," Shalini replied.

"I can't believe we're having this conversation."

"Neither can I. You know what, Amit, I've made excuses for you far too long. I wanted to believe that you'd try to understand and appreciate my world just as I learned to appreciate yours."

"Are you suggesting that I don't? All your art-vart needs money. Where do you think it comes from? I'll earn more from the interactions that'll happen over the weekend with my colleagues than..." Amit stopped short, his face purple.

"Say it...than I will at Hunters Point. Why don't you complete what you started to say? That it's all about the return on investment. Of your time. I've been present for every event or milestone while you've pursued your passion. I ask you to show support by attending one event, my very first event, and what do you do? Trivialize it. Reduce it to a comparable dollar amount."

"Shalini, stop making a mountain out of a molehill. I have shown you more support and given you more freedom than most husbands give their wives. Look around you. You don't appreciate how lucky you are."

His words made her cringe. And Amit actually believed the words in all sincerity, didn't think there was anything wrong with them. He was the "giver of freedom," which by simply having said so reflected the inequality in their relationship. And, by being "better" than other husbands, he justified his position and provided sufficient proof to cinch his argument that it was Shalini who was being not only unreasonable but, even worse, ungrateful.

*What an arrogant, conceited, self-righteous, unconscious, unawakened son of a gun...*Shalini, exercising immense self-restraint, and knowing that she could not take words back, let her mind vent its fury in silence.

"I have an idea," Amit said, softening his tone. "Why don't Kathy and you make it a girls' weekend? I'll treat you ladies to an overnight at the Fairmont?"

*How generous....*Shalini bit her tongue and kept her thought to herself.

"You don't get it, Amit," she said instead, and shrugged as much in disbelief as resignation, "and you never will."

That had been the end of that. Amit headed to his retreat without blinking an eye. Shalini sucked it up and with Aarush, Lara, Sam and Kathy managed transporting and installing canvases of different shapes and sizes, mingling and socializing with visiting art lovers, the final dismantling and cleanup followed by a celebratory dinner at Chipotle (the joy of selling three of nineteen pieces!) late Sunday night — all without her husband.

His inability or absence of desire to enter her world, however much she tried to initiate and welcome him, and the subsequent resentment that kept building up in her, further aggravated their situation.

The chasm between them widened, eventually reaching a point where crossing over began to seem impossible. She accepted failure in her attempts to reset their relationship as equal partners. It became very clear to Shalini that it was beyond Amit's understanding that spouses with unspoken but assumed ranks wasn't something Shalini could live with.

The frustrating part was that Amit couldn't even see what she saw. He hoped naïvely that this was just a phase, that his wife would outgrow it sooner or later. Unfortunately for both of them, it had gone on too long to qualify as merely a "passing phase." The only thing that had kept them together was Aarush. Shalini could no longer turn a blind eye to the now completely lost connection between them. What had once been weak was now severed.

So it was entirely possible that she was romanticizing her feelings about Ram because things were not good with Amit.

But what about all the years? People change. Ram may no longer be the man she thought he was. *Though change didn't always mean for the worse.*

There was nothing that evening, or in any interaction they had

242

had so far, that suggested even a hint of detrimental change in Ram. In fact, there was something almost therapeutic about his energy, his presence. Everything felt right. When had long silences felt so comfortable?

But one evening doesn't a life make, Shalini thought. *And besides, I have no idea what's on* his *mind.*

Clearly he had shown affection and tenderness. They had a lot of history — why wouldn't he? There was no doubt that they still shared a physical chemistry...no surprise there. But could that in any way warrant that his feelings corresponded to hers? In exactly the same way with as much intensity?

Why did it feel as though her world had just been rocked? Seeing him in person, meeting him, has made her fall head over heels in love, again. It felt cruel.

At thirty-six, did love and passion have any meaning at all? Any point or purpose? Did everything always need to have meaning and relevance?

"Life is not just about love and fresh air." Her mother's words of caution echoed down the years.

But life for Shalini was nothing without love and fresh air.

And what about him? What did he want?

She couldn't be so presumptuous as to expect him to be available now that she had figured out her true desire. He had made a life without her, just as she had without him. And unlike the state of her affairs, there was no reason to believe that his life was in any state of disorder. *Leave him be,* she thought. *Don't mess with him. You don't want to be a homebreaker.*

He's a kind and gentle man. You had a chance with him. You let him go when you could have held on. It's too late now. Don't read more into today than the fact that he is simply accommodating you. Being a really good friend.

Her heart twisted in pain, filled with regret over lost opportunities.

Oh, just for once, why couldn't she be brutally honest even if it revealed her selfishness? Acknowledge a wish even if requital was not rightfully hers? Why couldn't she be just this one time, a bitch?

In spite of the emotionally overwrought evening, and no sign of help forthcoming from Ram, Shalini felt at peace, even as she felt awash in chaos. There was a clear shift inside her, toward a state of tranquility, a feeling conspicuous by its absence so long.

Yet how fleeting the feeling was, serving only to tease, perhaps a reminder of how she *should* be feeling…

"Shalini…"

Shalini snapped out of her trance. "Yes…sorry…"

"I have been thinking and…I have something I want to tell you."

Her heart began to pound.

"Oh, I know, I know. Don't worry. I understand."

"Shalini…"

Don't spell it out, please. A girl can be allowed some hope, can't she?

"I don't expect anything of you…I mean from you…no, I mean, nothing other than a phone call to Raghunath…you know what I mean?"

"No, I don't think you understand. There is no way you'd understand."

There was a surprising firmness in his voice.

"Sir, would you like to order your drinks?" a waiter interrupted them.

They had just placed their drinks order when sounds of a commotion inside the building erupted, people were screaming and shouting, rushing and panicking as gunshots peppered the air.

Two gunmen, shockingly young, clean-cut and well-dressed boys in their early twenties, rifles strapped to their chests, backpacks of supplies over their shoulders, with pistols and guns in their hands, opened fire, cold-bloodedly killing any one in sight. Within minutes, they were joined by two, similar-looking perpetrators. Pandemonium. Panic.

Everything happened so fast that nobody, neither Shalini nor Ram, or even one of the stunned hotel guests, had any time to think or respond, the drama like a movie, surreal and bizarre. In spite of that, looking back, Shalini could replay the entire production in her head with the clarity of a video in slow motion, the smallest movement permanently etched.

Ram jumped up and shoved Shalini behind him, shielding her. One of the gunmen shot a merciless round of bullets, victims of the shots dropping like flies. The murderers calmly continued striding toward them, heartlessly stepping over the dead and dying. Ram became a target of one of the random bullets. Blood spewed from his shoulder as Shalini screamed. Ram winced in pain, but continued to block Shalini from harm's way.

"I'm fine. I'm fine," Ram gasped as he touched his shoulder.

On his white linen shirt a red stain the size of a penny kept expanding until, within seconds, it was like a color-dye job gone terribly wrong.

"The bullet has only grazed my shoulder. Stay calm. Stay with me," his voice hoarse through the pain.

Two of the gunmen kept firing while another two grabbed Ram and Shalini, twisting their arms behind their backs and taking them hostage, using them to ward off hotel security as they headed upstairs toward the guest rooms of the Tower Wing.

When Shalini let out a cry for help, her abductor rammed the pistol into her temple, "*Chup raho*, shut your mouth, lady, or you will end up like the rest of them."

"Just listen to them," Ram said as Shalini whimpered in pain.

As the gunmen made the short trip from the first floor to the rooms, they chose to use the elevator instead of the dramatic staircase. It became obvious to Shalini from the mesmerized look on the faces of the young terrorists that none of them had ever seen such opulent surroundings. Clearly dazzled, they were definitely distracted from their mission.

They dragged Ram and Shalini and shoved them into one room, guns still pointed at their heads.

Dear God, what makes them choose this path? They're only kids. They couldn't be much older than Aarush, Shalini thought.

The lack of emotion on their faces was appalling as they locked the door behind them to regroup and strategize with help from their masters in Pakistan. First, the gunmen bound and gagged them. Shalini's abductor then pulled out a cell phone and made a call.

A voice crackled through a cell phone on speaker. "Do you have the hostages?"

"*Haan*, we do."

"Now, pile up the carpets and mattresses from the room you've opened. Douse them with alcohol and set them alight," the same voice instructed, cold and businesslike, adding, "Get a couple of floors burning."

"*Theek hai*, okay," replied Shalini's abductor.

"And when we ring, make sure you answer." Then the caller hung up.

Fear had paralyzed Shalini by now. Ram's shoulder continued to bleed and more than once she saw him grimace in pain.

The four gunmen spoke in low voices to each other, discussing and planning the next steps. Once again the phone rang.

"*Salaamalekum*. Peace be with you," Ram's abductor answered this time.

"*Waalekumasalaam*. How are you getting along? Have you started any fires yet?"

"No, we haven't started it yet."

"You must start the fire now. Nothing's going to happen until you start the fire. When people see the flames, they will begin to be afraid."

"Umm, okay," the gunman said, his tone unconvincing.

"And throw some grenades, my brother. There's no harm in throwing a few grenades."

Shalini winced at the choice of words.

How could "no harm" and "grenades" go together?

"How hard can it be to throw a grenade? Just pull the pin and throw it," the caller persisted, recognizing the hesitation in these young martyrs-to-be.

"There are big, big computers here with thirty-inch screens."

"So what? Haven't you set fire to them?" The caller was clearly frustrated.

"We're just about to. You'll see the fire in a sec," the third gunman answered for the rest of them, sensing the urgency in their senior's orders.

After a minute the voice asked, "We can't see anything unless there are fires. Where are they?"

"It's amazing! The windows are huge. This room has two kitchens, a bath and a little shop. We are trying," Shalini's abductor explained.

"Start a proper fire, that's the important thing," the master insisted.

The gunmen left Shalini and Ram in the suite briefly while they went to neighboring rooms to start fires as instructed. Before leaving, as they pulled out hand grenades from their unzipped backpacks, Shalini noted that the bags were packed with hundreds of bullets, fruit and nuts, water bottles, enough ammunition and nutrition to last them several days if required.

Cold-blooded monsters. No fear. No remorse, she shuddered.

Raising his eyebrows, Ram looked at Shalini, gagged and unable to talk, and she blinked back to reassure him that she was okay even as her face had lost all color.

In the corridors, smoke was building up, and they could hear in the distance chilling cries pleading for help. There were loud thuds as the terrorists kicked on doors, hunting for guests to kill, followed by the distinctive sound of bullets spraying.

Eventually, the gunmen returned to the room where they had left Ram and Shalini. From subsequent phone conversations, Shalini understood that it had been more challenging for the captors, and had taken them longer than anticipated, breaking down the heavy double doors of the guest rooms. They had managed to set three or four of the rooms facing the sea on fire. To the delight of the terrorist controllers in Pakistan, who instructed them to turn on the TV in their room, news reports confirmed with pictures and live coverage, that the Taj was indeed in flames. It was an image they knew would travel in minutes around the world.

"My brothers, the media is covering your target, the Taj Hotel, more than any other," the caller praised the four men.

Shalini kept her eyes on Ram, afraid even to blink, using her eyes to stay connected and communicate, and the only way to remain reasonably sane and alert.

When the gunmen described to their controllers how they had broken down doors of several guest rooms and killed their inhabitants before setting them on fire, Ram's expression changed. His eyes widened with fresh fear as if somehow that information made their situation even worse. He started thrashing his bound feet against the bedpost and strained at the gag, as if he needed to say something to the gunmen. Shalini, already full of dread, began hyperventilating, unable to understand what exactly had set off Ram's frenzy, panic striking her already shaken body.

Their sudden agitation drew the attention of the gunmen.

"What do we do with the hostages?" one of them asked his senior.

"The taxi should be waiting for you. Put them in the trunk and then head back to complete your mission."

One of them kicked Ram in his groin. Shalini flinched, squeezing shut her eyes, but only for a moment. When she opened them, Ram was curling with pain. They were then hauled to their feet and dragged through a smoke-filled corridor toward the service staircase.

Ram, subdued after the resistance he had just put up minutes earlier, seemed to be looking for something, his head twisting sideways, peering through the smoke at the room doors, and alternately looking back at Shalini, his eyes trying to communicate something to her, without success, as her abductor pulled her along, a few steps behind. She gathered some strength — at least they were still together.

Meanwhile, the voice on the cell phone kept talking to the gunmen. "You mustn't let them arrest you."

"*Inshallah, inshallah,* God willing."

"*Himmat karna, ghabraana naheen.* Be brave, don't panic. For your mission to end successfully, you must be killed. God is waiting for you in heaven."

"*Jeen haan. Inshallah.*"

"Fight bravely, put the phone in your pocket but leave it on."

"We already did."

Each time she heard their senseless propaganda, she winced… promises of salvation and a ticket to heaven…in exchange for murder, all in the name of defending their religion.

What God would want this? Don't you see they are taking advantage of you? she screamed silently at the young men.

Shalini kept her eyes focused on Ram, desperate to communicate with him, frantically trying to comprehend what it was he was trying to say or do.

There was blood everywhere, on the floor, walls, carpets, railings, even on the ceilings. She felt nauseous and dizzy, a fresh wave of horror suffocating her.

Her foot slipped in a sticky red pool as she tried to step over the body of a woman blocking their path. The gunman leading Ram ruthlessly kicked the body aside.

Do you think this is a video game? she asked silently, horrified by the inhumanity, by the faces empty of emotion. *No fear, no sensitivity. Who are you? What makes you so…so evil?*

The calm, business-like voices over cell phones walking the perpetrators matter-of-factly through a detailed, step-by-step process, offering both logistical as well as psychological guidance, shed light on the remarkably organized brutality and meticulous execution of the attack.

In a quiet back alleyway behind the Taj near its service entrance, stood a taxi, its engine running. Their escorts bundled them into the trunk, still bound and gagged but now also blindfolded.

First Ram, and following his lead, Shalini, started creating a ruckus as they kicked the body of the car from the inside. The impatient *jihadis* reopened the trunk and somebody stabbed each of their upper arms with a syringe.

Within moments darkness descended on Shalini, but not before Ram's reassuring finger interlocked with one of hers. It was the last thing she remembered.

She had no idea how much time and distance had passed when consciousness returned, her eyes fluttering as she tried to adjust to the dark, dingy space in which she lay, still bound and gagged. She became aware of her blindfold, still present, but having slipped off partially, allowing her limited vision. Overcome with panic, she searched the space around her, and her first thought was of Ram. Where was he?

Let this be a nightmare, she prayed, waiting with a pounding heart for that moment when she would awaken.

••••

Aarush

Thirteen

"Can you turn your face, Marziamaasi?" Aarush asked, pointing toward the balcony.

"Okay, *jaan*. But you better hurry. I'm going to need a bathroom break pretty soon."

"No, not that much, just slightly so the light makes the right shadows on your face."

It was a hot Saturday evening in mid-October. Normally, Aarush would have been in Pune, but he was on break from his English tutoring at the Mahila Seva Gram as the kids were on an annual camping trip organized by the orphanage.

He was using Marzia as his live model for a charcoal portrait assignment, his last one before the Diwali holidays. Across the room, Rushi was multitasking, simultaneously watching a cricket match on TV and completing his engineering drawing submission, with all the supporting paraphernalia spread out across the dining table. Uncle Saleem had combined work with a visit to his sister's house in Ahmedabad, and was gone for a week. Murtaza had made excuses to run an errand, and Aarush was betting that Tulsi was the errand.

Since their bike ride to Marvé almost three months ago, Aarush and Rushi had settled into a comfortable routine. Rushi accompanied Aarush to Pune every weekend and they spent it together with Nana. Rushi eagerly accepted Aarush's offer to show him around the Seva Gram. Rushi had asked the matron in charge if there was any way he could help. One thing led to another, and soon Rushi began tutoring math. They biked together in Pune every Sunday morning. It couldn't have been more perfect.

One Saturday, as was inevitable, they even had an emotional meeting with Shakutai.

"You can imagine that I have seen hundreds of kids over the years adopted by wonderful families. But yours is a special story, my dear boys, and you will always be very close to my heart. Your mother would have been so proud."

"Were we ever here together?" Rushi asked.

"You were born about a year and a half apart. In the same hospital. But you had left the Seva Gram before Aarush was born."

She looked from one to the other. "Life is full of twists. And this is a good one. Treasure each other."

Shakutai had brought them little amulets on a black thread that she then tied around each of their necks. "These amulets have Lord Ganesha inscribed on them. He will take care of both of you."

"Woohoo!" Rushi pumped his fists. Somebody had been bowled out of the match.

"I really need a break, Aarush," Marzia said.

"Okay, Marziamaasi. If you must. Let's continue tomorrow."

Aarush began to gather his pencils and organize them in his toolbox when the phone rang. It was the ring of a cell phone. Amit had bought Aarush a cell phone when he last visited in August. Instinctively, Aarush looked at his phone and Rushi looked at his, both with the same signature Nokia ringtone. It wasn't the first time for the confusion, and they both laughed.

"Sorry, bro, I still haven't changed mine. It's my phone." Rushi answered his phone. "Hello."

"Sorry, can you repeat what you said? I can't hear you."

Rushi used the remote to lower the volume of the TV.

"What?" His expression was indecipherable.

"Baba? *Baba!* Where are you? Where have you been? Baba. Is that you? I hope this is not a joke. Baba..."

Rushi's voice had modulated from a whisper to a shriek and back to a whisper.

"Yes, yes. I am totally fine...

"No, they didn't break down our door...

"No Baba. I wasn't injured...

"Fifty hours...

"The commandoes...

"Baba, where *are* you?...

Marzia had rushed out of the bathroom, having heard Rushi's cries.

"Who is it? Rushi, tell me. Who *Baba?* What are you blabbering?"

Marzia took the phone from Rushi as he stood there, a string of incoherent words pouring out of his mouth.

*Baba? Is it possible? That Ram's alive? And does that mean...*Aarush thought wildly.

"Hello, this is Marzia. Who is this?"

A voice crackled into the phone.

"*Hai Allah!* Ram. I can't believe this. Is Shalini with you? Where are you? Can we come get you? What should I do?"

The voice said something. Marzia brought herself back under control.

"Okay. I'll do that. So you have no idea where you are?...

"Okay...

"Who's phone are you calling from?...

"I see...

"*Inshallah*, please be careful. I'll contact the police station only after I hear back from you. No, no. Don't worry. I promise to say nothing to anybody. Neither will the boys...

"And Ram...

"Nothing. Never mind. God be with you."

She hung up the phone and saved the number immediately. She sat down on the couch, holding her head in her hands.

Aarush and Rushi stared expectantly at her.

"Shalini and he were taken hostage that night and transferred to a place he has no idea about. He managed to convince them into releasing him and Shalini. But he hasn't seen her since the night of the 26th last year. He has cautioned us not to raise our expectations. He used a drunk trucker's cell phone to call his own phone number, the only one he had memorized. Thank God, Rushi, you kept Ram's phone. He said he would tell us everything soon. He is still trying to figure out exactly where he is. Apparently, the truck driver is so drunk, he is barely cognizant of his surroundings and far from coherent. Ram doesn't want us to say a word to anybody. He plans on contacting the police once Shalini is released. They told him they would drop her off in the same neighborhood but didn't give him any time estimate. Oh. My. God."

Aarush looked from Marzia's face to Rushi's. Color had returned to his cheeks, the shock of the unexpected call giving way to the joy of being granted an impossible wish.

"Baba will bring back your mom...our mom. I just know it," he reassured Aarush.

Aarush's eyes suddenly came into focus, and he found himself staring at that day's newspaper, with his astrology forecast staring conveniently back at him.

"...good things are waiting to happen, dear Gemini. Saturn continues to move through your fourth house right now, giving positive energy, meaning less stress than in the last year. There will be delays and some frustration..."

Aarush's heart was thudding in his chest. He stood frozen to the ground, petrified, afraid to think, to hope. And afraid of more pain and disappointment.

••••

"Amit, are you done reading the newspaper?" Aarush could hear his mother's voice holler from the kitchen.

"Not yet," Amit mumbled over shuffling pages.

"Can you pass me the page with the Sudoku puzzle, please?"

"Since when are you into number puzzles?" Amit teased.

"Oh, Amit, just pass that one page. You take forever to read."

"Are you sure you want the Sudoku or..." Amit looked tickled.

"Dad. Just give her the page she wants. You don't care about it, anyway," Aarush said, coming to his mother's rescue. He retrieved the right sheet of newsprint and handed it to her. Shalini lay the knife she was using to chop onions on the kitchen counter, wiped her hands on her apron and hastily took the paper.

"So what is the prediction for the day?" Amit continued to pester her.

"Dad! Let her be." Aarush looked over his mother's shoulder as she read her day's forecast.

"Okay, okay. I will. But I can't seem to convince your mother that the stars have more important agendas than to be preoccupied with mundane human matters."

Amit had always been a fan of astronomy and he had found a willing partner in his son. Over the years, they had dabbled in amateur astronomy and even spent a summer building a crude but effective "Newtonian" telescope together. Staring at the stars had become their thing.

"Just like you can enjoy music without ever learning to play a single note on an instrument, you can read and rejoice in science without having to perform a single laboratory experiment," Amit liked to say.

Aarush had been instinctively skeptical about all things religion-based, especially beliefs founded on superstition and mysticism. His life's journey — from his start in the orphanage, his adoption that had felt like a super lottery, his surgeries to "repair" the "damaged goods" he saw himself as, and his consequent struggle with a sense of worthiness, and finally to the tragic loss of his mother — had imparted Aarush with more than his share of and understanding of loss, pain and profound disappointment. If anything, the sum of his life's experiences had answered fewer, and raised more questions in his mind about God's design abilities and even His "existence probabilities," as his father would have said.

If there really was a God, he would have to by definition be omniscient, omnipotent and omnipresent. If the state of affairs in the world was any evidence, the three couldn't possibly exist together, he had often reasoned.

Since Aarush's move to Bombay, his father had introduced him to the writer Richard Dawkins, whose work had opened up the world to Aarush. Unlike most of Dawkins's critics, who insisted that Darwin's evolution theory produced more anguish in their minds than anything useful, *The Selfish Gene*, *Unweaving the Rainbow*, *The Blind Watchmaker* and *The God Delusion* addressed many of Aarush's doubts, and provided him with invaluable comfort and even a sense of liberation. Liberation provided by scientific evidence and mathematical theory that proved the probability of the existence of a creator to such a small number that it all but eliminated a "punishing" God. Or even a "loving" God. How else could one explain the devastation caused by the injustice of poverty, natural calamities, disease and the like? There *had* to be an explanation beyond or besides a divine creator. And Aarush had found convincing answers through evolution theory.

"Once you appreciate astronomy for what it is worth in all its wonder and magnificence, doesn't astrology look like a joke?" Aarush said to his father during his last visit.

"It does. And what makes me really upset is that even the educated get sucked into it. I would have hoped that by the end of the most scientifically successful of all centuries science would have been better incorporated into our culture. Do you know that even today, in this new millennium, astrology books outsell astronomy books?"

"No way."

"Astrology, superstition, blind faith — all of these are for the gullible....Credulity is a child's strength but a man's weakness....I think Charles Lamb said that, and I couldn't agree more."

Aarush read the newspaper again.

"...good things are waiting to happen, dear Gemini."

Even though he knew in his heart that there was nothing more to the words than false power to influence a gullible soul, for just this one time, how he longed to take comfort in mere words.

••••

It had been three hours since Ram's call. Murtaza had returned from his errand and had been filled in. They swore each other to secrecy.

"Not a word, anybody," Marzia warned. "Not even to Tulsi," she added.

Murtaza scowled.

"Or Lara." She winked at Aarush, trying to dispel some of the tension that filled up the room.

"In fact, I'm not even going to risk calling Saleem or Amit. Narsi Uncle is driving up tomorrow. We'll tell him in person. The fewer people in the know the better. Until Shalini is released. If word leaks out to the abductors, who knows, they might change their mind. We can't take any chances."

All three boys nodded.

257

"Let's pray while we wait," Marzia suggested.

It seemed an eternity before Rushi's phone rang again. It was already dark, almost 10:00. The caller ID showed a different number.

Marzia answered directly this time. "Hello."

Rushi and Murtaza flanked Aarush on either side, solid in their support. They couldn't hear a word on the other end, just a crackling voice, as they waited patiently for Marzia to finish the conversation before getting an update.

This time most of the talking came from the other end. Except for a few requests like "Pardon? I missed what you said," Marzia didn't say much. She listened carefully with total concentration.

Only toward the end did she say anything at all. "How long before we hear from you again?…

"Okay…

"No, please. Don't worry about us sleeping. I don't think any of us is going to anyway. Just call. Please…

"Ram…

"I wish we were talking under different circumstances…

"I'm sorry I didn't stay in touch…

"Thank you. You know each one of us here appreciates what you are doing for Shalini…

"Yes, even him." She looked at Rushi when she said that.

"Narsi Uncle…

"Yes…

"Uh-huh…

"I'll fill them in…

"No, I haven't. But Narsi Uncle is driving up tomorrow, anyway…

"Call soon. God bless you…

"What did you say?…

"Of course. Wait a second…

"Here…" Marzia made the few steps and hurriedly handed the phone to Rushi.

"Baba…

"Yes, Baba...

"I'm fine. Especially now...

"Yes...

"He loves to bike. I took him to Marvé." Rushi looked around and held Aarush's gaze.

"It's okay, Baba. I have a lot to tell you too...

"Don't be sorry. You are alive and that's all that matters...

"I love you too. Baba...

"Keep calling. Come soon," and after a brief pause, "with Mom."

Marzia looked drained. They were all quiet after Rushi hung up, a terrible mix of feelings enveloping them. Reason to rejoice, reason for dread.

●●●●

Aarush broke the silence. "Any news about Mom?"

"No, *jaan*, not yet. Ram has found a rest area where truck drivers routinely stop. Every once in a while a friendly driver gives him a cell phone to make a call."

"What did he say about Mom?"

"This is what he told me. He bartered a release with his guard-slash-caretaker, Ali is his name, after much convincing and negotiating over the last few months.

"Apparently Shalini and Ram were a case of mistaken identity. Ali is only a fifteen years old. His older brother, Fahadullah, was one of the ten *jihadis* enlisted and trained by Lashkar-e-Taiba (LeT) in Pakistan. Fahadullah was recruited after his father died. They tried to recruit Ali too, but he was too young and didn't demonstrate the mental fortitude required of suicide bombers. Instead, they paid him and his mother to guard hostages. Bribed is more like it, especially since their father, the only breadwinner, was dead.

"Ali's mother is guarding Shalini but in a separate location not too far away. Ram has promised to help Ali on the condition he gets Shalini released as well. Ram is reasonably confident that this Ali fellow is speaking the truth and is dependable."

"What help does Ali need?" Murtaza asked.

"Ali wants an out from the situation he's in. He wants a chance to lead an honest life. He wants to study. He's worried about his mother who is sick and needs medical attention. He's the only surviving male member of the family. Apparently the money that was coming from the LeT dried up in the last month or so. That has put Ali and his mother in a desperate situation. They barely have anything to go by, let alone feed two more mouths. This actually turned out to be a good thing for Ram. He used it as leverage to negotiate a release."

"So what is Baba waiting for?" Rushi asked.

"For Shalini to be dropped off where he was. That's what Ali promised he would do."

"Why is that taking so long?" Aarush asked.

"Good question. I don't know. We'll ask Ram when he calls next."

"What else did he say?" Murtaza asked his mother.

"On the night that he and Shalini were taken hostages, they were drugged before being transported to wherever they are. When Ram came back to his senses, he was alone. There was no Shalini. Ali, using a mask to present himself as an older man and guns to intimidate, stood guard over Ram. Ram was kept bound and gagged in a dark, smelly room, with no opening even for daylight to enter. In the basement of a larger building.

"Ram lost sense of day and night in the initial period when he remained incarcerated. Once Ram won over Ali's confidence, Ali removed his mask and started interacting with Ram. He started taking Ram outside, blindfolded, to go to the bathroom.

"At that point I lost part of the conversation because there was a sudden disturbance and Ram's voice cut in and out.

"When the line was clear again, Ram asked about you, Rushi. You heard my end of the conversation when I told him that Narsi Uncle had introduced you and Aarush, and that you guys know everything. He sounded happy about that."

"Anything else? About Mom?" Aarush was feeling dejected.

"He said he would call soon. It's a waiting game. I wish it were otherwise."

Marzia nudged Murtaza aside so that she could sit beside Aarush, pulling him into a hug and rocking him against her chest.

"I really hope we hear good news soon. It's going to be a hard night."

"This brings back memories of the night I waited terrified, in our Taj room. I can still hear the screams for help, loud pounding on doors, the smell of smoke. I had wished only for Baba to stay alive." Rushi shuddered, his entire body beginning to convulse.

And so Marzia pulled Rushi into her embrace as well. Murtaza kneeled in front of them, and with Rushi and Aarush on either side of Marzia, they remained like that, each giving the other the strength to last through the night as they waited for Ram to call again.

●●●●

It was 3:00 a.m. before the lilting Nokia ringtone shook each of them into alertness. Rushi and Murtaza were staring at cricket highlights on the TV, which was on mute. Marzia dozed in and out of a disturbed sleep, asking urgently, each time she awakened, "Was that the phone I heard?"

This time it was.

Rushi answered. "Hello?…

"Tried to…

"Okay." He handed the phone to Marzia.

"Anything new?…

"I see…

"I understand…

"Don't worry. Call whenever you can…

"Just one question, Ram?…

261

"That night when you met, did you tell Shalini? About Rushi?"

They spoke for a bit longer, then hung up.

"I guess there's no news about Mom, right?" Aarush asked.

"No, *jaan*. Ram doesn't think he'll hear from anybody until daylight. They won't take chances transporting a lady in the middle of the night. They would risk drawing attention."

"Then why did he call?" Aarush's irritated tone surprised everybody.

"Because, apart from Ali, he hasn't talked to a soul in almost a year. He's grabbing any opportunity he gets to stay in contact. Not all truck drivers have phones. And of those that do, not all have a trusting heart," Marzia explained gently.

"I'm sorry. I didn't mean it that way." Aarush buried his face in his hands and sank into the armchair.

"Every time the phone rings, I have the same hope as you. I want all of us to be happy. I want *you* to get Mom. And I want Baba to come home," Rushi blurted.

Aarush raised his face from his palms, his eyes bloodshot from stress and waiting and lack of sleep.

"It's okay. I'll be fine." Looking at Marzia, he asked, "Did he tell Mom about Rushi?"

"No. He was torn between the promise he'd made to Narsi Uncle and the extreme distress he saw Shalini in that night. After much wavering, he finally decided not only to tell her but he even planned to take her up to their suite so she could meet Rushi in person…"

"They were attacked before he could tell her," Rushi said matter-of-factly.

"So if she's dead, she didn't even die in peace…" Aarush's voice trembled.

"Shake out of it, guys. Think good thoughts, for heaven's sake!" Murtaza bellowed, suddenly making his presence felt.

"I agree. If Ram is alive, there's no reason they'd harm Shalini." Marzia said.

"Unless she got sick or something…" Aarush said despondently.

262

"We can't be much help to Ram if we lose hope so easily. Besides, there's no reason to. We haven't even given Ali a chance. Let's put strong positive intentions out there," Marzia declared.

●●●●

"Why do you think Ali will follow through with his promise? Why not call the police?" Marzia asked Ram the next time he called.

It was 8:30 a.m. Everybody had grabbed some sleep, at best fitful.

"What if his mother doesn't agree?…

"No, no. I trust your intuition, Ram. It's not like that…

"Okay…

"*Haanji*…

"I see…

"Hm."

A long pause while Ram spoke at length on the other end.

"I understand…

"Okay. We'll wait some more time. But Ram, we will have to make a call. At *some* point…

"*Inshallah*."

Marzia set the phone down on the coffee table.

"What was he saying? Why should we wait to call the police?" Rushi asked.

"He says he finally has some idea where he is located. He hopes to hitch a ride on a truck and get dropped off closer to Bombay. But only once they release Shalini.

"He promised Ali he would not draw attention to their village. If he calls the police they are sure to raid it, and that would result in serious repercussions. It would destroy Ali and his mother. That was one of the conditions of release."

"What makes him so confident that Ali will drop Mom like he promised?"

"Ram said that, as hard as it may be for all of us here to understand, over the last year, Ram and Ali developed a very strong bond. Ram saw Ali through the eyes of a father, and Ali looked up to Ram as a role model. As his hope to a brighter future.

"Apparently, during the July monsoons, their village experienced flash floods. The basement where Ram was being held was so badly flooded, and so fast, that Ram almost drowned. Ali managed to get down and unlock the door just in time to save him. After that flood, Ram used his civil engineering and architectural background to help Ali design and dig trenches around the building to direct water away from the structures. Ali said his mother's house had the same problem. Ram asked him to sketch the layout of his mother's home and came up with a drainage plan. Between the two of them, they spent the rest of July, August and September implementing this new drainage plan. Ram noticed that Ali had great drafting skills. Without any training, he had been able to detail the layout of his mother's house and showed an inherent knack for understanding construction fundamentals.

"That's when it dawned on Ram that this could be Ali's ticket to a normal life. He hatched a plan."

Murtaza brows met in the center of his forehead. "And what was that?"

"Ram pointed out several things to Ali.

"For one, the only reason Ali and his mother were continuing to guard them, the hostages, was because they feared for Fahadullah's life. Very soon, Ali had found out that his brother had died that night, the 26th. So, Ram pointed out to him, there was no real reason to continue something that he was being forced to do, anyway.

"Secondly, the LeT had stopped sending money. Nobody had visited them in many months. For all they knew, the hostages could have become victims of the flash floods. So why not report that to the LeT? That way Ali and his mother would be totally off the radar screen of the Pakistani bosses.

"Thirdly, Ram promised Ali a job as a draftsman, at his own firm, which would help him earn an honest living and support his ailing mother.

"Ram also promised Ali that, even though he would have to report Shalini and himself to the police as having been released, he wouldn't give any information whatsoever about Ali or his mother. They would have to lie low for a few months, but Ram would totally take care of them."

Hope lit Aarush's eyes for the first time that morning. "Brilliant. So did Ali do what Ram told him to do?"

"Yes he did. The LeT told Ali to bugger off. That he was done with his part in the mission. That Allah would take care of him. Only further proving to Ali how little these LeT bosses really cared about them."

"So now what?" Rushi asked.

"As soon as Shalini is released, Ram will get them to a place farther away from the village and then call us. I told him we were ready to leave as soon as he called. Narsi Uncle should be here soon too."

"We still don't know *when* Mom will be released, though?"

"Let's keep praying. It shouldn't be long. I feel it in my bones." Marzia said. And she looked genuinely encouraged.

●●●●

$\int$halini

Fourteen

$\int$halini heard a voice whisper furiously. "*...kuch khaaya?...achcha hai... abhi bhi behosh hai?...maregi to naheen?...abhi koi samaachar aaya naheen...sunte heen aaunga.*"

Shalini's eyelids felt glued shut, impossible to open. As much as she tried, it seemed there was nothing she could do to remove the veil of darkness surrounding her. Wild thoughts were jumping like monkeys in her head.

Am I blind? Paralyzed?

Her lips were dry and her mouth parched. The veins in her temples throbbed in pain. She tried to move her limbs and was relieved to find that her toes and fingers still wiggled. Her wrists and ankles were still bound, but her instinct to snap the cord only resulted in excruciating pain, a soreness that reminded her of the futile attempts she had made in the trunk of the taxi.

Ram. What about Ram? Where was he?

She tried to call out to him, but no words emerged through the rag in her mouth. She was so thirsty...

"...theek dhyaan rakhna. Kuch gadbad mat hone dena. Khuda haaf-is ammi."

The whispering ended and suddenly there was utter silence. Then she heard the sound of fading footsteps, the thud of a door shutting, followed by the click of a latch. Metal against metal as someone slid a chain down a groove, a second-level security lock.

Don't go! Don't leave me alone, she screamed in her head.

Within minutes, Shalini came to the realization that she was neither blind nor paralyzed, but captive in a dark confined place. It was unclear to her how large or small the enclosure was. A room? A box!

Claustrophobia overwhelmed her like an avalanche. Fear rose from the pit of her stomach, up to her throat, suffocating her. Terrified beyond control, she broke into a sweat. Her body started shuddering violently. Her chest burned with the lack of oxygen as she hyperventilated. In the midst of her terror, Shalini heard her own inner voice calmly reason with her, as if consciousness had separated from body, taking charge.

You will kill yourself like this. Think, Shalini, think. Take a deep breath.

Incapable of moving, all she could do was depend upon her imagination. The air was stale. Her joints ached from lack of circulation and movement. She strained her ears, seeking a hint, some clue that might throw light on her situation, help her regain orientation and gather some semblance of control.

For the longest time, her breathing was the only sound in that quiet space. She focused on each inhalation, each exhalation, using every bit of concentration she could muster to prevent herself from falling to pieces.

If only I knew how long this was going to last. I could at least count down, she thought.

In and out of consciousness she drifted. She would nod off to sleep, overwrought with exhaustion, sleep her only escape and means of accelerating time. Soon she lost all concept of time. After what seemed like hours — or was it days? — Shalini finally heard a light swishing of fabric and soft footsteps that indicated an approaching presence, somebody in her vicinity.

There was the distinct sound of creaking wood, as if the weight of someone or something was stressing it beyond capacity.

Was somebody trying to climb onto an old desk? Maybe it was a ladder? But why?

Suddenly there was a crashing sound, something metallic dropping to the floor, along with someone groaning in pain.

After a few moments of silence, there was a flurry of activity. More thuds and bangs, like pieces of furniture being arranged and rearranged in a room. Once again, the creaking sound of planks or furniture in distress. This was followed by a long pause, some heaving breaths and then a sudden sharp burst of light into Shalini's space.

She squeezed her eyes shut, momentarily blinded. Gradually, she fluttered her eyes open, blinking rapidly, as they adjusted to the piercing sensation of sunshine, the rays illuminating every dust particle, the vision simultaneously joyous and terrifying.

There was joy in being able to see, but what she saw horrified her. She was in some sort of an attic, no more than a five-by-five-foot area, with the roof at best six feet high.

So she hadn't been far from the truth! She was in a box.

She scanned the room once more. *A largish box*, she conceded.

From the window-size opening, a burqa-clad woman heaved herself into the enclosure. Shalini's eyes, having adjusted to the light, were able to see past the black bundle attempting to climb inside, only to realize that she was scaling a rickety ladder, a stainless steel *lota*, or pitcher, in one hand, the other holding onto the ladder for dear life. She must've taken a fall with her first attempt.

With the veiled figure backlit as it approached Shalini, the features and details merged into a menacing shadow to Shalini's already surprised eyes. The approaching shadow, now completely in the room, stood up and hobbled toward the corner where Shalini lay, gagged and bound. She looked for all the world like Darth Vader, only instead of a lightsaber, this one was brandishing a shiny pitcher.

Shalini was faintly amused by her ability to find some humor in her wretchedness. *This is what makes humans resilient,* she thought.

Shalini lay motionless, her eyes wide open. The shadow kneeled and touched her forehead and felt the pulse at her temple. It was a cold and unsteady touch, as if the person, obviously Shalini's guard, was also nervous. As the shadow extended her hands over Shalini's body to reach behind her head and untie the rag around her mouth, Shalini experienced her first sense of relief. The relief of imminent freedom, of being able to talk again. She knew not to risk losing that freedom by shouting or screaming, even while it would be her instinct.

The gag loosened, and fell to the floor. She ran her tongue over her parched lips, aware again of her pounding head. Then her vision narrowed and darkness spread before her eyes. She struggled not to pass out.

I need water, she thought. *"Pani..."* Shalini whispered hoarsely.

The burqa-clad woman raised Shalini's head from the floor and helped her take a few sips from the glinting pitcher.

After Shalini had swallowed the last drop of water, the woman put the empty pitcher on the floor and lowered Shalini's head. With much difficulty she untied the cord, releasing her sore ankles. Now optimistic, Shalini waited for the woman to untie her wrists bound and cramped behind her back, but the woman shuffled around Shalini, tugged at the cord, and then did nothing! She straightened as if, for no obvious reason, she had changed her mind.

Without a word, the woman collected the pitcher and carefully lowered herself onto the ladder, and climbed down, leaving the small door to Shalini's room unlatched and cracked open, so it wasn't pitch dark any longer.

Shalini's heart sank.

The woman had said nothing. Shalini had not been able to see her face. For all it was worth, she might not have even been a "she." She might be a man wearing a burqa as a disguise. A shiver of dread traveled down her spine as thoughts of violent and torturous treatment wreaked havoc in her mind.

Calm down, she told herself. *If they had wanted to, they would have killed you by now. At least you can move your feet. You can even talk if you want to.*

She rolled her ankles, wincing in pain, her body having forgotten the movement. There were sounds of doors and drawers being opened, followed by the clatter of rummaging and thuds as they were shut again. Footsteps provided some idea of her guard's movements around the house below. Soon, she heard the creaking of the ladder again, each rung groaning beneath the weight of her guard, threatening to give way.

Once more Darth Vader appeared before Shalini, but this time she was wielding a knife.

She's going to kill me. Make it quick, God. I don't want to suffer!

"Please…" Shalini whimpered as the veiled shadow hobbled once more toward her. Her body trembled uncontrollably. Fright paralyzed her vocal chords and she could hardly emit a single sound from her throat. Shalini thrashed her legs, an instinctive attempt to protect herself with the only body part that was free. Panic brought on an adrenaline rush that charged her with energy impossible otherwise.

The woman was now behind Shalini. She tried to restrain Shalini with her free hand but without success. Shalini's rapid random leg movements, only resulted in her rotating in circles, her arms still behind her back. The woman, frustrated with her inability to calm her captive down, slapped her hard across the face.

Already having expended more energy than her weakened body held in store, Shalini was stunned into stillness, her cheek stinging and black and white spots dancing before her eyes. The woman sat down behind Shalini, and wiped the sweat from Shalini's forehead with the fabric of her burqa. She stroked her forehead a few times. Little by little Shalini calmed down.

Behind her back the cold blade of the knife pressed into the skin of her arms.

Win over my trust with kind gestures and then slaughter me when I least suspect an attack? Isn't this how Aarush had once explained what Shock and Awe meant in military vocabulary — show dominant display of force, paralyze my perception of the battlefield and then destroy my will to fight. Is this how you kill? Who are *you?*

She screamed in anguish and kicked her legs again, in the process knocking over the woman. The knife went flying to the other side of the room.

Again, the woman slapped Shalini. This time, more than once. She picked up the rag and with her knee holding Shalini to the ground, gagged her. There was not enough light for Shalini to see the woman's face. No way to make eye contact and reach out to her as a fellow human being.

The woman hobbled to the corner of the room, retrieved the knife, then walked back toward Shalini.

I give up, God. I give up. I can't do anymore...

Shalini had run out, run down. She closed her eyes and offered no further resistance. Clenching her teeth through the gag, she readied herself for whatever was in store for her. She felt the cold blade of the knife against her arm, the excruciating pain as the blade pressed into her flesh. She imagined her blood coursing out, and within moments, lost consciousness.

●●●●

"*...utho...arre baba...utho...*" Shalini heard a male voice shaking her into consciousness.

With some difficulty she opened her eyes and squinted toward the voice, into the face of a boy.

"*Ammi...ammi,*" he beckoned urgently. The woman in the burqa appeared at the edge of Shalini's frame of vision.

"Zinda hai...behosh padi thi."

The knife-wielding incident flashed across Shalini's mind. Suddenly she realized that she was neither bound nor gagged. Her arms were free and so was her mouth. She made an attempt to sit up, but lacked strength and almost collapsed back down had it not been for the boy who caught her.

"Ammi can't talk, *bole naheen sakhti*," he explained. "She was only trying to cut the cord around your wrists, not kill you. I'll visit once in a while. Just don't trouble her and you'll be fine," he warned.

"Now follow me down the ladder. You are being moved to a room. This is too hard for Ammi to climb up and down."

First the woman climbed down.

"Now you go. I'll come after. Be careful. The ladder isn't stable."

Shalini stood up with help from the boy. She felt light-headed and dizzy. Her head spun and she dropped to the floor. When she woke up, the boy was gone.

She was still in the attic, its door wide open. And now there was also a bulb, though of lowest wattage, that lit the room.

Night time, thought Shalini.

Outside the attic door, darkness. The only sounds that Shalini could hear beyond her own breathing were those of crickets. A moth circled the bulb.

Next to her, she noticed a plate, a dented aluminum dish, with one *roti* and a mound of unidentifiable curried food next to it. There was the same *lota* filled with water. The sight of food made her realize how hungry she was.

She raised herself into a sitting position, reached out and took a sip of water from the *lota*. This time she realized how different the water tasted. She devoured the food, not caring what it was. It could be meat, for all she cared.

She stretched her limbs and cracked her joints. Everything ached. Dark, angry bruises surrounded her wrists and ankles, and mosquito bites stippled her body. She was wearing the same white dress she'd worn on that last night. *Ram. I hope you are safe.*

Now that her physical strength had a chance to return, and her life didn't seem to be in immediate danger, her mind made room for the turmoil she had set aside. She thought of all her loved ones and wondered what they thought had happened to her. Were they looking for her? Did they have any clue about her whereabouts? What happened that night? Why were they being held hostage? Were there ransom demands? What were they?

She leaned out the attic door to determine whether or not she could climb down. Weakness had caused her to faint the last time the young boy instructed her to go down. There was no ladder now, but she finally got a view of the house below.

It was a traditional courtyard house, separate small structures arranged around a central open space. To Shalini's left was a large main door, bolted shut. It was impossible for anybody to jump from where she stood down to the stone floor of the open courtyard without serious injury. She looked around for signs of life. A fan whirred in a corner room, and she imagined the burqa woman sleeping there. Shalini went to the back corner of the attic and sat down, her back pressed against the wall.

Aarush, Pappa, Amit…everybody must be sick to their stomach by now. I wonder how long it has been since the 26th?

The image of Aarush brought tears to her eyes. She let herself feel sorry for her pathetic fate and cried freely.

Think happy thoughts, she finally told herself. *Think of what you will do once you are free.*

Will I ever be free?

It was a struggle to banish negative thoughts from her mind, but for the first time she felt hope. She had concluded that both the woman and her son were not capable of evil deeds. In that respect, at least, she was safe. This would be an ultimate test of patience and endurance.

She started chanting the Gayatri Mantra in her head, over and over. *Om bhoor bhoovah svah…*Before long, she dozed off.

●●●●

"Can you show me how you do the French knot? That pattern on your new kaftan is beautiful. I'm tired of cross-stitch. Can you teach me a new stitch, please?"

Shalini was sitting on her upgraded *khaat*, or cot, a rickety structure of four bamboo poles supporting a jute net, a luxury compared to her previous bed on the attic's hard, cold floor. She had been brought down and settled into one of the rooms on the ground floor, now under constant lock and key. The room had a tiny window that opened onto the courtyard. Daylight entered through the window. The ceiling was higher and the room was spacious, almost too spacious for her meager belongings, which included the cot, a torn white bedsheet to cover it, and a single change of clothes, a *salwar kameez* the boy had brought for her.

The boy had visited a few days after her fainting episode. Gradual food and water intake over those days had helped Shalini regain her strength. This time she climbed down the ladder without losing her balance or passing out.

She was cared for by Zarin, her guard.

"If I am going to live here with this person for any significant period of time, I have to know her name," Shalini had said to the boy, then added, "If you don't want to tell me her real name, to protect her identity, give me any name. Just so I can address her, for heaven's sake."

"Then take your pick," he suggested adamantly.

"Zarin. I'll call her Zarin," Shalini said arbitrarily.

The boy simply shrugged and left.

Most days there were no visitors. The boy came with supplies every week, but there was no exact pattern to his comings and goings. Shalini wondered how the mother and son communicated because there were no phones in the house. The mother was clearly mute. She also seemed hard of hearing. In person, the boy used sign language, which worked well for them since Shalini was clueless.

Twice since she had been brought down from the attic and held captive in the downstairs room, she heard a group congregate in the courtyard, all male voices, for what appeared to be meetings. Both times, in anticipation of their arrival and to prevent any trouble, Shalini had been gagged and bound. The boy had explained to her that they needed to do this as a precautionary step. The window to her room and the door had been shut and locked from the outside. The visitors spoke in a dialect that sounded mostly alien. She could understand a word here or there, but nothing much made sense. The voices always sounded very excited and as if they disagreed a lot. But both times, the men had left after prayers and exchanging many *Inshallahs*. Both times, as soon as they left, Zarin unlocked her door and window, and the boy removed the gag and untied her before departing.

But most days there was no excitement.

Zarin sat on a chair in the courtyard in the mornings until the sun became unbearably hot, after which she moved into her room. She embroidered endlessly, mostly kaftans that she labored over, making delicate detailed patterns in various stitches with different colors of thread, usually white, red and green. Sometimes she embroidered several identical kaftans. In all probability, Zarin was part of a group that earned extra money from home by offering their needlework talent to designers catering to the world of fashion.

Shalini watched her through the window. Zarin kept a laminated sheet of paper tabulating the different types of stitches for reference. Every time he visited, the boy, acting as the courier, brought her new items with pattern instructions, taking away the completed work when he left.

Haunting and beautiful, almond-shaped, hazel eyes, was all that Shalini ever saw of Zarin. She towered over Shalini, her slender and elegant gait under the yards of material offering only hints of her curves, adding to the mystery of this elusive woman. The hobble that she'd first demonstrated had now disappeared. Shalini surmised that it must have come from the fall Zarin had taken the first time she tried to climb the ladder to bring Shalini water.

It seemed to Shalini that Zarin was as trapped in that house guarding her as Shalini was hostage. Zarin watched Shalini twenty-four hours a day, never once leaving the house.

What a life. At least she would either die or be freed. But what about Zarin? She would be stuck in this world forever.

Every time the boy visited, Shalini pleaded with him to share any information he may have about Ram's whereabouts, begging to see him. Since their trip in the trunk of the taxi that had transported her out of the only world she knew, Shalini had no idea what happened to Ram.

"I don't know what you're talking about," he replied every time, not making eye contact, and only fueling further doubt and distress in Shalini's heart.

Even though Shalini felt lucky not to have experienced any brutality beyond shoving and pushing, gagging and blindfolding, tying and restraining, she had to get used to the indignities of being taken blindfolded to answer nature's call, defecating while being watched, at the same time fumbling, unable to see for herself.

Despite the constant vigilance and confinement, within a few weeks Shalini completed an emotional arc that had begun with intense fear, followed by overpowering panic, then seething anger, and finally deep sadness, resignation — every emotion infused with self-pity and, underlying that, persistent anxiety that refused to go away.

One day in an unexpected moment of kindness, Zarin offered a needle and colored thread to Shalini. Without exchanging a single word, she demonstrated the technique with a few lines of cross-stitch embroidery.

Quick to learn, Shalini understood from Zarin's gesture that this was going to be a long confinement. She held herself together as best she could, even as panic and fear threatened to break her.

The mechanical work of creating larger patterns from crossed pixels stimulated the creativity in Shalini, not only helping her pass time, but more importantly, maintaining her sanity as she decorated the only canvas available to her — her torn bedsheet. Very soon, the manual exercise of fine needlework became a form of meditation, leading her, with Zarin as her accidental guide, toward the discovery of an inner life within her confinement, harsh and tedious, yet rich in creativity and spiritual development.

To address her immediate need to keep track of nights and days, Shalini came up with an ingenious plan to devise a calendar. She decided to assume, for lack of any source to corroborate otherwise, that the day she started keeping count was a Monday, December 1, with no idea how long it had been since her night at the Taj.

To record the passing days, she sewed a single cross-stitch in black thread, her only marking implement, on the inner lining of her *kameez* every evening, with the last day of every month cross-stitched in red. She was careful not to draw the attention of her captors, primarily Zarin.

In this manner, she survived by adopting an anthropological perspective toward her own captivity. To stay alive by taking it one day at a time, as if she were driving a car at night and only able to see as far as the headlights would allow.

"Can you please teach me that?" Shalini repeated her question, this time adding hand gestures and finger pointing to communicate her desire to learn a new embroidery stitch.

Zarin had neither heard nor understood what Shalini had said the first time. But this time around Zarin smiled and nodded.

It's February 14, 2009, today, by my calendar. Valentine's Day. I hope Aarush and Lara are coping. I wonder where they think I am? Probably dead.

••••

By June Shalini had become an expert at French knots. After all, she had made hundreds, perhaps thousands of French knots by then, dotting the centers of a field of blood-red poppies. Placing the needle at the back of the black thread, she wound it twice, twisting the needle to the back and to the right from the place where her needle had initially emerged. With her left hand she held the thread taut, tightening the loops around the needle. Then she pushed the needle down through the fabric, releasing surface thread as she went along. This, she repeated, knot after knot, dot after dot.

Her bed sheet had gradually evolved from a torn and dirty piece of cloth to a tapestry depicting a California landscape only Shalini recognized.

Under Zarin's guidance, she had begun by mending a tear in her sheet. Using a fine needle and white thread, she made tiny stitches back and forth along the tear. To prevent the raw seams of her sheet from unraveling, Shalini then learned a basic blanket stitch. She folded the edge of her sheet, turned it once, and used the basic looped stitch to even out the edges.

At first, she simply lay on the mended sheet and stared at the wall. She couldn't get inspired to do any further embroidery. She noticed her tears only when the dampness made her shiver. Over and over she replayed the night at the Taj.

Ram's bleeding shoulder was still so vivid, it produced a physical pain in her own shoulder. She imagined his wound festering with infection, the agony he must have experienced. She replayed his attempt at protecting her that night and wondered how much torture he might have had to endure since then.

One of her lowest points during captivity was a day in April — April 17, 2009, according to her private inner-lining calendar. She finally mustered enough courage to ask the question, the answer to which she had avoided until then.

"Zarin…" Shalini said tentatively as she tapped Zarin's shoulder. Zarin looked up.

"Tell me Ram's okay." Shalini begged, gesturing furiously.

"Ram, Ram…" she repeated, her mouth exaggerating his name.

Zarin dropped her gaze avoiding eye contact.

"Please. Just nod yes once and I'll never ask you this question again." Shalini's heart tightened with fear.

No nod, Shalini thought, *no nod*. "Do you understand what I'm asking?"

Zarin persisted with her needle and thread.

"They killed him, didn't they?" Shalini screamed in fear.

Zarin looked up at her, her eyes emotionless, eyebrows quivering ever so slightly.

Shalini's insides seemed to curdle. She felt the room close in on her as her vision narrowed, darkness rushing in from all sides. She steadied herself, holding on to the sides of her bed, a physical pain tearing her heart as if it were being pried out of her chest with a dull knife. Before she knew it, her head was spinning and she was throwing up uncontrollably.

Zarin rushed to her but within minutes Shalini had passed out.

••••

For a long while she stared blankly at the dirty white canvas the bed sheet presented to her. She had never had much difficulty finding a source of inspiration, sad or happy, for any of her art before. The numbness that she created inside in order to protect herself from the pain of separation from the life she had been forced to leave behind brought with it a form of death. Even though Zarin had left different needles and colors of thread wound on spools to experiment with, Shalini's mind drew a blank

Several days later, Zarin came to Shalini's room to drop off a large cone of red thread, excess from a previous order. The color of the thread shocked Shalini out of her stupor. To her it was Ram's blood.

With the needle as brush and the red thread as paint, Shalini attacked her bed sheet like a woman possessed. She started with tiny cross-stitches that circled around each other, forming a small, penny-sized red dot, reminiscent of the bloodstain on Ram's white linen shirt that had erupted the instant he was shot. She did so painstakingly for days until the red embroidery gradually increased in size, not unlike the bloodstain that had spread across Ram's shirt that night.

Tears dropped and the cross-stitches blurred.

Ram, you must heal. You must! I will help you the only way I can.

In that moment she knew, she understood that she couldn't remain helpless anymore. She would channel positive energy to Ram, wherever he was. There was nothing to lose and everything to gain. Until she had proof that he was dead, she would not entertain another negative thought. *What would be the point?*

•••

Was it sleep or death that poppies represented? Or both? Something to do with the opium extracted from them and their blood-red color... why can't I remember? Shalini's head hurt as she rummaged through her memory for a conversation from long ago.

*A children's novel...*The Wonderful Wizard of Oz...*a magical poppy field threatening to make the characters sleep forever? How many times did I read that story to Aarush!* Shalini smiled as it came back to her.

"Ma, do you know why we wear 'Buddy Poppies' made up of paper or plastic in the weeks before Memorial Day? And why they are red in color even though the state flower of California is the golden one?"

Aarush was thirteen years old.

"Why?" Shalini remembered asking mechanically, her mind preoccupied, as she absent-mindedly folded laundry.

"Because red is the color of the blood of fallen soldiers. Just exactly the color of that T-shirt."

Shalini had looked up, startled. "Oh."

For some reason the coincidence of the red color of that last shirt she had been folding and Aarush's analogy to it had awakened her to the conversation, one that otherwise would have passed like water through a sieve.

"Ma, did you also know that in classical mythology there's a second interpretation of poppies?" Aarush had persisted in his typical way, brimming with newfound knowledge.

"What?" Shalini asked, now completely engaged.

"That the bright scarlet color signifies a promise of resurrection after death."

"Oh, Rushi, how do you know all this?" It had been more a statement than a question, because Aarush always knew the darnedest things.

••••

With fresh determination, Shalini's imagination took over. She became a vessel to the Muse — to goddess of flowers, Flora, or goddess of growth, Maia? Perhaps both.

Because soon, her cross-stitched bloodstains became blood red poppies that grew and grew until they covered the entire bed sheet.

That was what it was. The blood, which the original stitches represented, didn't just represent Ram's blood, but hers as well, as she had died not once but twice — first when she left Ram and then when she gave up their baby. The poppies reflected her will to restore and rebuild. To resurrect.

••••

With Zarin's help she learned every stitch on the laminated piece of paper — satin, plaited, chain, bullion, velvet, roman, and stem stitch.

Learning each stitch was a journey in itself. Often frustrating, every mistake required undoing and fixing. It was a labor of love that didn't always end up as she intended. Sometimes it surprised her pleasantly, and other times it disappointed terribly. But she never stopped. She persevered.

"No, Zarin, don't shake your head like that. I did it wrong again, didn't I? Why can't I get it to look like yours?"

Shalini tried to hide the distress in her voice. She had been hard at work trying the plaited stitch in laid work to make leaves on her bedsheet. Even as she had made the first few leaves, she sensed that she was somehow not getting it quite right.

That morning Zarin had demonstrated on one of her kaftans a three-step pattern that on paper looked simple enough. It required that she first fill in each leaf surface using the stab method, coloring the leaf by leaving a space between each stitch for a single strand, and filling this space on the return journey. The second step called for the use of a tapestry needle to create a basket-weave effect by pulling the same colored thread under four threads, and over four threads, at times perpendicular to the laid-ground threads from step one. Finally, each leaf was outlined with a herringbone stitch, giving it an exquisite finished look.

But that was Zarin's leaf. None of Shalini's leaves looked quite like that.

Zarin went to her room and brought back her sample kaftan, turning it inside out and pointing to the needle's path on the back.

Shalini looked, appalled. "Oh, no. Not the very first step! The back of my work looks nothing like yours. A neat running stitch."

Zarin nodded in agreement.

"Is there an easy way to fix this?"

Zarin shook her head sympathetically.

"You mean I have to undo all of this?"

Zarin nodded.

"That's impossible. It will be so much work. There has to be a shortcut."

Exhaustion and frustration brought Shalini to the verge of tears.

Zarin, in a gesture of commiseration, took Shalini's work, folded it neatly and put it under her cot, gently signaling to her to go to bed and start afresh the following day.

Offering no resistance, Shalini collapsed into a weary slumber.

The next morning, she woke with renewed determination. As she scrupulously unstitched the previous day's work, it occurred to her more than once that if she could only start over, on a fresh sheet; it would be so much easier.

It was during this process of painstaking and repetitive effort, that it dawned on her, as clear as day, that this experience with embroidery art was nothing but a metaphor for her life.

If she ever got out of this place alive, she would have to undo the mistakes she had made during her lifetime that had produced, in effect, undesirable results.

She would have to come to a decision about Amit. As painful as it would be. As inconvenient as it might end up for everybody concerned.

What had changed her love for him? The reason she could never convincingly answer the question was that the question itself was flawed. The right question would have been — was it ever love?

She knew for a fact that she was not in love with him in that moment. But had she ever been? She fooled herself into believing that she was, when what she felt in all likelihood was admiration and awe. Maybe even tenderness and affection — but not love as she knew love.

This was her only bedsheet, her only canvas. And this was her only life.

The thought summoned an old memory, Ram was reading to her, Emily Dickinson on one of their Friday rendezvous at Duke's Nose...

That it will never come again
Is what makes life so sweet.

She couldn't go back in time and ask for a fresh start, but she could undo what was wrong and change the course of her life from now on.

She had been taken hostage that night at the Taj, but she had been hostage for a very long time — to her own choices.

Like the effort and patience it took to unravel a sequence of finely stitched patterns, leaving minimal marks on the canvas, life was not very different. There was no way to avoid leaving scars.

Her decision to continue with Amit, with their destiny together, was clearly independent of Ram and his availability. Whatever she might improvise now did not depend upon previous unsuccessful endeavors.

The clarity that came to Shalini every day, with needle, thread and sheet as her tools, vivified her will to continue to live her life meaningfully, with an identity that was authentic. In that quest she committed herself to this new art form.

Even when she fell ill with a stomach virus, and almost died of dehydration, delirium accompanying severe bouts of diarrhea and vomiting, her mind would not let go of the metaphor. Her will to overcome her emotional and physical struggles only grew stronger.

This time in isolation is my gift. My chance to look into my heart's deepest concerns. To understand my underlying honest desires.

Zarin, using needle and thread to compensate for her inability to communicate through words, along with *ayurvedic* medication, patiently nursed Shalini back to health.

●●●●

Hours became days, and days blended into months. July brought the monsoons and with the monsoons, floods. The courtyard house wasn't prepared for the deluge, its open space a swimming pool in no time. But equally obvious was the fact that none of this was a surprise to Zarin and her boy.

It must happen every year, Shalini thought. *How sad that they have no way to fix the problem.*

The water threatened to flood their rooms, and the boy, on one of his visits, marked one of the walls with a chalk, instructing Zarin to move into the attic if the water reached the chalk mark. Before leaving, he carried up two rolled mattresses and deposited them in the attic, as if it were only a matter of when and not if they would need to move upstairs.

Within twenty-four hours both women climbed the ladder, carrying food supplies and water, and moved into Shalini's first room of introduction, this time not as intimidating or even as claustrophobic.

Over the months, the boy's demeanor had transformed to one of bashful reverence toward Shalini. He seemed appreciative of the companionship Shalini provided his mother. But beyond that, Shalini's attempts to connect with him on any level only met with failure.

One day the boy explained that he would need to lock both Zarin and Shalini in the attic. "I have a worker who is going to help me dig trenches and fix this flooding problem once and for all. But I can't risk him seeing either of you. It's only for two days."

Shalini could hear the sound of digging and heaving, muttering and whispering, and eventually what sounded like a celebration at the swooshing sound of water finding its way out of the enclosed courtyard.

●●●●

She couldn't believe that sunshine could be so excruciating. The sudden brightness hurt her eyes, and instantly she squeezed them shut, the harshness of the afternoon rays like searing tongs scooping out her eyes and forcing her into blindness. *What was the time…?*

She couldn't remember when she had looked at a watch, a clock or a calendar, but she knew it had been a great while. More than nine months and seventeen days, her cross-stitched calendar evidence of that much.

Since she had been "taken captive," "taken hostage" — did it matter? The human brain was an amazing and strange organ.

Hadn't it proven to her its capacity to imagine, create, continually adapt and rewire, and finally help her to survive her ordeal? And yet it seemed to wander every now and then into mundane and frivolous territories, as if looking for respite from the tense drudgery of continually creating, imagining, adapting and rewiring.

*Even the brain needed some R&R…*she smiled, her eyes closed.

285

Shalini was sitting on a sidewalk, or something like a sidewalk.

Surely, once upon a time it had been a sidewalk? Or, as these ruffians call it, a footpath.

She heard the sounds of children shouting and screaming. Joyful sounds. Playful. She decided to keep her eyes shut.

I am actually enjoying this, she thought.

"*Kabaddi, kabaddi, kabaddi...*" chanted one voice, not pausing to take a breath.

In her mind, Aarush's face appeared.

"Mom, try this one. World Sports. This is the national game of Bangladesh."

He gave her another moment to think.

"Hint, you played it as a child."

Aarush had qualified as a finalist on the *Jeopardy* show and was preparing for the upcoming round.

"What is Badminton?" Shalini asked uncertainly.

"No, Mom. Another try?"

"What is *Kho-Kho*?"

"Good guess...but no...the answer is, What is *Kabaddi*?"

"*Kabaddi*? Never heard of it," Amit had remarked, lifting his eyes from the latest copy of *Forbes* magazine that always seemed to occupy his attention.

"It's quite popular in India as well. In fact, it is the state sport for Punjab, Tamil Nadu and Andhra Pradesh. Two teams occupy opposite halves of a field and take turns sending a 'raider' into the other half, in order to win points by tagging or wrestling members of the opposing team; the raider then tries to return to his own half, holding his breath and chanting, '*Kabaddi, kabaddi, kabaddi.*' The name — always chanted during a game — derives from a Tamil word meaning 'holding of hand,' which is indeed the crucial aspect of play," Aarush explained in a single long breath himself, as if to make a point.

How that had made Shalini laugh.

Was she really free?

She pinched herself as she forced her eyes to open into narrow slits, enough to capture the movement of the game unfolding before her.

The dust rose as the players, barefoot and barely clothed, entertained a crowd of casual spectators. A bout of coughing overcame her, and her eyes watered profusely. She lowered her head to the ground to protect herself from the relentless glare, and found herself staring at the trash surrounding her — rotting banana peels, plastic bags stuffed with garbage, nasty smelling unidentifiable waste and even a — "Good God!" She closed her eyes once again and cringed. It was the decomposing remains of a dog.

But she *was* free. It was all and everything she had prayed for, but why was she not ecstatic?

There was at least one reason: she had no idea where she was. Disoriented…

They had released her from captivity with slightly more dignity than they had taken her captive, transported in an old taxi, blindfolded as she and Ram had been on that night at the Taj, only this time they didn't gag and bind her. She had long since quit putting up any resistance.

And just like that, they dumped her back into her old world, without warning, without any intimation. But what else might a captive expect from her captor?

I should be grateful I'm free. I am free! she screamed in her head.

She kept trying to make sense of her emotions but failed. She felt unsettled, frightened, at a complete loss.

What is wrong with me? This is what I have been praying for all these months.

Is anybody really free unless they know what they want to do with that freedom? And can you really do anything with your freedom unless you can plan for it, prepare for it? Without permission or intimation, planning or tools, she sensed the freedom but felt abandonment.

The thought brought her up short, cutting through her consciousness, painfully reaffirming lessons from the past — that the essentiality of desire was nothing more than the knowledge of what one wanted, and in knowing that, to recognize one's freedom for what it was — a path into the world of that wish, a path that could not guarantee requital.

Jeers, from mostly men hanging out in the streets, broke Shalini's trance, returning her to her present situation.

She felt like a zoo animal let loose in the jungle. How could she make a call? She had no money. Whom could she trust?

As frightened as she had been when they were first taken hostage, at least she hadn't been alone. Ram had been with her.

Once separated, the small dark room in which her captors had confined her had, incredibly, become her home.

Human resilience. That was what it was. And now she needed it again.

With the bedsheet as her canvas, the needle her paintbrush and yarn spools her palette, embroidery had become creative outlet, sanity and lifesaver. If nothing else, it had allowed her the luxury of time, to piece together her life, stitch by stitch, bringing some semblance of order to her emotional chaos as she wandered life's labyrinth, making sense of choices made along the way.

Zarin, despite her inability to speak, or more likely *because* of it, became Shalini's alter ego. She provided her with the opportunity to clear the cobwebs of her mind, forcing Shalini down to another, deeper level of inquiry into the nature of human life and human resourcefulness. She was the listener who could not judge, did not judge, making no comments, offering no opinions. And because of the burqa, no visible body language.

Now, Shalini realized, she found herself at the mercy of the elements surrounding her. More susceptible to capricious designs, ill-equipped to fight, and lacking any natural instinct to survive.

She needed to think logically. She looked around for a better place to wait while she planned a course of action. There were no trees, no shade whatsoever, unless she were to enter one of the many houses, if they could be called that. Arranged in an untidy line, little shacks side by side, with corrugated aluminum for walls and blue plastic tarps for roofs. If she didn't know better, she would have thought it was a refugee camp.

But she had seen enough slums in her lifetime to recognize this place. But which slum? In which town or city? She scanned the area, searching for some clue, any clue.

She was wearing one of Zarin's burqas over her worn-out *salwar kameez.* In her lap she clutched a plastic bag containing her white dress and her embroidered bed sheet, which she had begged to keep. Removing her head-veil, she ran her hand over her bald head, an indignity she had had had to suffer as Zarin shaved her head to relieve her from the torture of lice.

How many times had she prayed for this very freedom? Now it terrified her. Freedom hadn't brought instant gratification, as she had imagined. It had given her a path into the world she craved, but she had to maneuver her way, genuinely, honestly. Why was it so hard?

Her heart felt leaden as she looked around. She knew her life with Amit was over. She had enough time to reflect on that part of her life. She had given herself sufficient time to grieve. The lines from the "Autumn Song" by Sarojini Naidu played in her head —

> *Like a joy on the heart of a sorrow*
> *The sunset hangs on a cloud;*
> *A golden storm of glittering sheaves,*
> *Of fair and frail and fluttering leaves,*
> *The wild wind blows in a cloud.*
>
> *Hark to a voice that is calling*
> *To my heart in the voice of the wind:*
> *My heart is weary and sad and alone,*
> *For its dreams like the fluttering leaves*
> *And why should I stay behind?*

Inevitably, this was followed by the one thought she had success-fully avoided — until then.

Why hadn't they killed me as well? Oh, Ram!

••••

A tender pat on her shoulder made her jump. She hadn't been touched in so long; a gentle, kind and innocuous touch, one she had missed so dearly; one that she had taken for granted in the past, because it had been so readily available; her father tapping her five-year-old shoulder, a treat hidden in one hand behind his back; her mother patting with an urgency as she tried to pry Shalini's teenage attention from a TV show; Rushi's two-day-old fingers against her naked breast as she nursed him; Aarush's chubby five-year-old hand on her cheek, his only way to get her attention as she yakked with Kathy.

She looked up from where she sat in the filth, her eyes following the leaning figure as it straightened…a drawn, bearded face with a traditional *kufi* prayer cap on his head gazing down at her, a *salwar kameez* hanging on his tall, wasted body.

"Shalini…"

Her heart jumped. It took only a moment for her to recognize his eyes, the only familiar part of his body.

"Ram?"

He offered his hand.

She reached out to him, afraid she might wake up to find that she was dreaming.

He pulled her to her feet.

She concentrated on finding her balance.

He traced the outline of her face with his fingers.

She waited, certain that this was an illusion.

He leaned forward and kissed her bald head.

She could not speak.

He pulled her skeletal body into an embrace.

Her body stiffened, preparing for the rude shock of reality.

He squeezed her tight, so tight, it hurt.

It hurt so much that it *had* to be real.

Not a dream. Not an illusion.

A wonder. A miracle.

No, a marvel.

She shuddered violently as she caved into his arms.

●●●●

Acknowledgments

Heritageshoppe.com — embroidery details
Dispatches: Terror in Mumbai — documentary directed by Dan Reed

Akhil, Divya, Kapil, Rashmi, Sapna, Anisha, Rupal, Gauri, Monica, Shital, Sawita, Jenny, Arun, Rushiraj, Satyen, Nikhil, Lynn, Rouhaan, Sakina, Simran, Nitasha, Navan, Dhrupal, Mona, Shriti, Meghna, Shishir, Suchita, Bhupendra, Dada, Erica, Lola, Ariana, Suzy, Jing, Surinder, Jerri, Nickhil

Sudnya Shroff is an artist and writer. *Unraveling* is Sudnya's first novel. She lives in Northern California.

Throughout her wide-ranging career in the fine arts, Sudnya Shroff has reached out and connected with her audience by sharing her life experiences and reflections through her two favorite vehicles of expression — color and words.

Having received recognition in New York and California for her sensuous explorations of emotions through color, Sudnya, in her debut novel *Unraveling*, uses the written word to paint a riveting and deeply moving portrait, taking the readers with her to culturally disparate and geographically distant places spanning California, Singapore and India.

www.sudnyashroff.com